SECRETS IN
ZARAHEMLA

a novel

SARIAH S. WILSON

Covenant Communications, Inc.

Cover illustration by Justin Taylor ©
Thanks to Michael and Lluvia Campbell of ROC (Remembering Our Culture) for helping provide the models. www.ROCthePLANET.com

Cover design copyrighted 2007 by Covenant Communications, Inc.

Published by Covenant Communications, Inc.
American Fork, Utah

Printed in Canada
First Printing: February 2007

12 11 10 09 08 07   10 9 8 7 6 5 4 3 2 1

ISBN 978-1-59811-119-1

For Kaleb and Kameron, who laughed and loved.
For Mom and Dad, who cheered and believed.
And especially for Kevin, who did all those things, and who knew.

ACKNOWLEDGMENTS

I'd like to thank my family for their love, support, and belief that I could write and publish a book. Special thanks to my mother, Melody Salisbury, for helpful suggestions.

I would also like to thank my publisher and especially my editor, Kirk Shaw, for all of his hard work on my behalf, and for showing me how to make my story even better. (Although I still think "For Frodo" would have worked.) Thanks also to Julie Coulter Bellon for her advice and support, and to Robison Wells for answering my questions.

I am indebted to the great Book of Mormon scholarship that has been done by people like Drs. John L. Sorenson and Joseph L. Allen, Stephen D. Ricks, William J. Hamblin, and all the brilliant minds at the Foundation for Ancient Research and Mormon Studies (FARMS) and the Foundation for Apologetic Information and Research (FAIR).

Last, but certainly not least, I want to thank my wonderful husband, Kevin, and my sons for their patience, encouragement, and love. You're my everything.

ONE

Kiah hung upside down in the snare, the rope cutting and burning her ankle. She thought that this must be her punishment for wandering so far away from Zarahemla despite her father's warnings. She knew she was not supposed to cross the River Sidon while the Nephites and Lamanites were at war. Now her disobedience had her dangling from a high branch of an ancient heartwood tree. Kiah could only blink at the rich, red-brown bark in surprise as she bobbed up and down, too stunned to move.

If nothing else, at least her shock had stopped her crying. The tears that had blinded her, allowing her to walk right into a hunter's trap, had finally dried up.

Kiah felt as helpless now as she had earlier that day when she had tried to learn how to . . . Kiah shook her head and refused to think of it. She had to get down.

Blood rushed to her head as Kiah observed the area around her. She had stumbled into a small clearing, encircled by jungle on three sides, that abutted a tributary pool of clear water that fed off the Sidon. Kiah looked up and saw that her short swords had fallen to the ground. Only one other way to cut herself down.

Her pale yellow tunic, heavily encrusted with cornmeal, hung down toward her head. Kiah tucked the front half in between her calves and tried to reach behind her to grab the edge where she kept a light obsidian blade sewn into the hem. Kiah comforted herself with the thought that at least she could sew.

You'll never get married. No man would want a woman like you.

The words were so clear in her mind that Kiah thought for a moment that her sister-in-law, Shabana, had followed her in order to torment her further.

Kiah closed her eyes and tried to get Shabana's abrasive cries out of her mind. No matter how hard Kiah tried, she couldn't cook. Today's attempt had been yet another disastrous endeavor that ended with Kiah causing the cornmeal to explode all over everything. It didn't matter to Shabana how well Kiah could throw a knife or shoot an arrow. As she constantly reminded Kiah, a woman's worth was measured not on a battlefield but in the home.

She choked back a sob that threatened to break free from her throat. She was tougher than this. Having a husband, children . . . that was not important to her like it was to other women. Kiah repeated her usual mantra, but today she couldn't fool herself. Kiah knew the truth was that no one wanted to marry her, regardless of who her father was. No man wanted a woman that couldn't care for a home.

Kiah pushed the thoughts away and reached again for the hem of her tunic. She stopped when she heard the sound of something coming through the undergrowth toward her. It was large and wasn't trying to disguise the sound of its approach. A predator.

A red brocket deer broke clear of the jungle. Kiah heard the whoosh of a spear and saw the weapon pin the animal to the base of the heartwood tree.

Before she had a chance to speculate at who had used the spear, a Lamanite stepped into the clearing. In a rush of thought, Kiah knew she was going to die. Her insides turned to silvery liquid, and her lungs pumped so rapidly that she couldn't catch her breath.

"Interesting. I've never caught a girl before."

She didn't know what to be more shocked about—that he spoke her language so flawlessly or that it sounded like he was teasing her, like he planned on playing with her before the kill. Kiah resolved he would soon find out that she wasn't so easy to defeat.

Kiah reached behind her, trying to get at her blade. At the same time, she pushed the bottom of her tunic against her backside to cover herself.

Although he faced her front, a look of embarrassment crossed the Lamanite's face, and he fumbled over an apology. He turned his back and went to the tree where the other end of the trap had been tied off.

She expected him to cut the line and braced herself for the impact of hitting the ground. Instead, the Lamanite untied the rope and began to carefully lower her down.

"I'm sorry you got caught in the trap. I didn't realize that anyone came out this far. It's fortunate I happened to be hunting in this area already. Otherwise you might have been stuck up there for a while."

Kiah wondered if he was trying to lull her into complacency by talking to her. She ignored his words and used her palms to ease herself onto the ground. Then she grabbed at the rope to release it from her ankle while she watched the Lamanite. He kept his back to her.

She inched toward her knives, waiting for him to turn and attack. She tasted warm, bitter bile in her mouth; her limbs shook. Kiah's heart pounded so hard in her chest that she was afraid it would punch through. It was one thing to practice on a field with her brother or father. It was quite another to be facing a real enemy who intended to harm her. The paralyzing fear almost overwhelmed her. Kiah tried to swallow it. She had to regain her control.

For one fleeting moment, Kiah was sorely tempted to throw one of her knives into his back, but she refrained. It would be murder to kill an unarmed man.

Holding the obsidian short swords tightly, she got into a defensive position, her knees slightly bent, her swords at the ready.

The Lamanite finally turned to face Kiah. He stared at her, and Kiah noticed that his eyes were a startling, sky blue. Kiah had admittedly seen very few Lamanites in her life, but never had she seen one with blue eyes.

One corner of his mouth pulled up in what looked like amusement. "What do you plan on doing with those?"

His voice was rich and deep and tinged with laughter. Kiah did not find her current predicament amusing. Her grip on the knives tightened, and she held them up higher. At the expression on her face, the laughter faded from his eyes, and the Lamanite turned to wrench his spear free from the tree.

"I have no wish to fight you," he said.

"And I have no wish to find out what will happen to me if I don't fight," Kiah retorted, thrusting at him with her right hand. His spear came up, barely blocking her blow. He lightly pushed her to the side so that she had to come at him from behind. She again lunged toward him, turning in a half-circle to try and surprise him.

But he wasn't caught off guard. His spear moved quickly from one side to the other, easily parrying each of Kiah's thrusts. She kicked at him, hoping to knock him back. He stepped aside as though he had already read her mind and knew what she would do. She resorted to coming at him with her swords, and he moved as if dancing with her, as if it were nothing to anticipate her next advance.

The Lamanite pushed the side of his spear toward her to create some distance between them. Kiah crossed her swords to absorb the blow and jumped back. With breathing room, Kiah began to circle the Lamanite as he moved opposite her. She felt great beads of sweat pouring down her back from the smothering heat and her exertion. Kiah considered her chances at outrunning him and ruled the idea out. His spear would catch her before she reached the jungle.

Kiah engaged the Lamanite, her weapons flashing back and forth as she came at him. Over and over Kiah feinted, looking for an opening in his defense. He had none. Every strike she made was met with immediate deflection.

She was going to lose, she suddenly realized. It didn't matter how many men she had bested in the past. This Lamanite was better. Kiah was going to die out here in this clearing, away from the city walls of Zarahemla. Her father might never even know what had happened to her. With a renewed vigor, she sliced and swiped at him with her short swords. If she was going to die, she would do her best to take him with her.

Her breathing sounded overly harsh in her ears, and she could hear that the man's breaths were as short and fast as her own. The sound of her obsidian swords hitting his silver-plated spear echoed through the surrounding jungle.

Kiah became conscious of how he hadn't tried to attack her offensively. He was only blocking her moves. Why wasn't he trying to stab at her with his spear? In letting her mind wander for that brief moment, Kiah gave her opponent an edge. He kicked at the back of her feet, causing her to flail through the air until she landed flat on her back.

The wind was knocked from her as she hit the ground hard, and Kiah couldn't catch her breath. It didn't help when a moment later the Lamanite had pinned her upper arms to the ground with his spear. He locked her legs down with one of his own. "Enough," he ground out. "Stop."

Kiah glared at him defiantly and struggled to move. The Lamanite pushed down harder. "Stop," he commanded again. Kiah relaxed. Maybe if it seemed like she was obeying, he would let her up, and she could gain the advantage.

After a couple of moments, the Lamanite got up, walking backward and away from her. She quickly rolled and stood, pushing her unbound, waist-length hair behind her shoulder.

He tossed his spear to one side. She watched in confusion as he removed some other small weapons from his person, throwing them next to the spear. He held his hands up to show that he was defenseless. "I have no reason to fight you."

Kiah was in a quandary. What if he had a hidden weapon? Did he want her to let her guard down so that he could attack again?

"How do I know this isn't a trick?" she finally asked.

"I give you my word that it isn't," the man said, studying her carefully. Something about him seemed intimidating to her. Kiah remembered when she was little and her father had taken her to see a caged jaguar. This man reminded her of that cat. There was power and strength behind his tightly leashed façade. She would have to be careful.

But she knew she couldn't attack a man without weapons, a man who said he did not want to fight. It was the first thing her father taught all his soldiers. They fought only to protect themselves. Kiah nodded and put her weapons back in their sheaths. Before Kiah had arrived at her decision, the Lamanite seemed to know he had nothing to fear. The young man acted oblivious to her presence as he collected the deer he had killed.

Kiah watched him out of the corner of her eye. Now that she wasn't anticipating her own premature death, she could better appreciate what she saw. He wore the clothing of the highland Lamanites, a short tunic bottom and vest over bare chest. He pushed his fingers through his short, spiky black hair. Kiah followed the movement of his hand from his hair to his face, where he wiped dirt off of high cheekbones that looked as if they had been cut from stone. He was tall, even taller than she was. The only men Kiah knew that were taller than her were her family members. With a strange tingling in her stomach, Kiah realized that he was, quite possibly, the most handsome man she had ever seen.

Feeling a different kind of fear, Kiah desperately wished that she had given in and let Aunt Linoah do her hair that morning. She looked around for the hair tie she had lost in the fight but didn't see it. She thought enviously for a moment of Shabana's always perfectly coifed hair and decided there was nothing she could do.

"Hungry?"

"What?" Kiah responded, not sure she'd heard him correctly. For a moment she thought he was offering to eat with her. Kiah had never actually eaten with a man before—her father and brother always took their meals first and in a different room. This stranger was treating her as if it didn't matter that she was a woman, as if she were his equal.

The man grinned at her with a dazzling smile. "Are you hungry? Fighting makes me famished."

Kiah saw that the man was skinning the deer with one of his discarded knives. Much as she hated to admit it, she was hungry. She had run out of the house so upset that morning that she hadn't had a chance to eat. Blowing up the kitchen had put a damper on her whole day.

Her stomach rumbled loudly in response, and the man laughed. "That sounds like a yes. Did you want to . . ." he asked, motioning toward the deer with his eyes. Kiah realized that he was asking if she wanted to cook it. Of course, he would assume that she would want to take over.

"You seem to know what you're doing." Kiah shrugged, trying to appear casual. She began picking up pieces of wood so that she could start a fire. Since she couldn't cook the deer, she could at least provide the means of doing so.

Kiah continued walking along the tree line, gathering wood and dried fronds for kindling.

"You fight well," the man offered over his shoulder.

"So do you," Kiah said. She walked back to where he was and stacked the wood she had found, sticking the kindling in the gaps that had formed.

The man took the brocket deer he'd skinned and placed it on a stick over Kiah's fire. "I'm Jeran."

"Kiah," she returned. The entire experience started to seem completely unreal. She was about to have a meal that a Lamanite had prepared for her in the wilderness. Her father would kill her for being so reckless. Kiah considered that Jeran could have poisoned the deer when she had her back turned. She reminded herself that he could have killed her in their fight at any point and that he had promised he wouldn't hurt her.

They sat in strained silence as the cooking fire crackled and popped. It wasn't long before the air was filled with the sweet smell of the cooked meat. Jeran took one of his knives, cutting off some of the outer meat and handing it to Kiah first.

She blew on the meat, trying to cool it down enough to put it in her mouth. "Good," she said after taking the first bite.

"I'm glad you like it," he replied, swatting a fly away from the rest of the meat. He cut off a large piece for himself.

Jeran cleared his throat. "I know it isn't my concern, but when I found you dangling from my snare, you looked like you were crying. Are you all right?"

Kiah carefully avoided his gaze. "I don't want to talk about it."

"Are you certain?"

"Do you want to tell me what you're doing in Nephite country?" Kiah challenged.

She was rewarded with Jeran's beautiful smile. "Not particularly."

"You aren't a spy, are you?" she gasped. The thought hadn't occurred to her earlier. What would she do if he were a spy, sent here to gather information for his people?

"I'm not a spy."

Something in his tone told her that Jeran was telling the truth. But if he wasn't a spy and didn't want to fight . . . Kiah wondered what he was doing so close to Zarahemla.

Once she had her fill, Kiah turned her body away from Jeran in order to quietly pray and give thanks for the food. She opened her eyes to see if Jeran had noticed, but he was focused on his meat.

Kiah had to will herself not to stare at Jeran. Her gaze wandered and stopped on Jeran's weapons. She stared with longing at the spear. Her father hadn't allowed her to train with a spear because he thought the spear a waste since it had only a one-time use in battle. Arrows at least could be restocked. Swords were his main choice of weapon—used from the beginning of a fight to the end. He told her spears expended needless energy and effort.

Without speaking, Jeran picked up the spear and handed it to her. Kiah raised one eyebrow at him in question. Jeran nodded to indicate that Kiah could take the spear.

Kiah hefted the weapon in her palms. It was made of a smooth, polished shaft of wood, overlaid with intricately engraved silver metalworking. It looked costly.

"It's beautiful," Kiah breathed, running her fingers lightly along the edge.

"It was my father's," Jeran said. "Do you know how to use one?"

Kiah told him she didn't.

"I could teach you," Jeran said.

Kiah's eyes widened in surprise. "Now?"

"Not now. It will be dark soon." Jeran laughed and took his spear back. "Another time. Tomorrow, perhaps."

A strong inner struggle took over. She wanted to learn how to use the spear. And, truth be told, some traitorous part of her wanted to see Jeran again. The fact that he wasn't repulsed by her ability to use weapons was enough to make her want to come back. She knew she should say no. She should go home and forget this afternoon ever happened. Kiah looked into Jeran's eyes and found herself nodding and echoing, "Tomorrow. But how do I know you won't come back tomorrow with an army of Lamanites to kidnap me?"

"How do I know you won't come back tomorrow with an army of Nephites to kidnap me?" Jeran challenged back. Kiah could again see the playfulness in his eyes, and she couldn't help but relax.

"I won't," she said with a shy smile.

"Neither will I."

"Well, then. I should, um, leave," Kiah said, surprised that she didn't really want to go. Jeran stood and offered Kiah his hand to help her up. His grasp was firm and warm. She nearly gasped when a shock of something like lightning seemed to pass between them in that simple contact. Kiah stood and pulled her hand back as if she'd been scalded. She wondered if he had felt it too.

"Until tomorrow."

"Tomorrow." She nodded and headed in the direction of the Sidon. Kiah stopped at the jungle's edge to sneak a look back at Jeran and felt embarrassed when she saw that he was watching her. She raised her hand in farewell and faded into the thick underbrush.

* * *

Jeran lay on top of a hill, looking down into the valley of
Zarahemla. He felt overwhelmed by the number of Nephites that
scurried like ants all over the valley floor. They were not nearly as
numerous as the Lamanites, but there were more than he had
expected. How would he find one man among so many?

The sun had begun to set, and its dying rays cast a soft pink
glow across the large, white temple in the center of the city. It
made Jeran feel homesick. He missed his mother all over again. He
remembered how badly she had longed to return to her home in
Zarahemla.

He knew he should be coming up with a plan to find Captain
Moroni. Without Moroni's help, he feared he would always be an
outcast, never belonging anywhere. Jeran saw that he had severely
underestimated the size of the army that would be traveling with
the mighty chief captain. And it looked like they were preparing
to return to battle. Jeran didn't know how he would find Captain
Moroni before they departed. If he just walked up to the city
walls, or to the departing army, they might kill him first and ask
questions later.

Jeran turned over on his back and looked up at the darkening
sky. He tried to focus on finding Moroni, but he found that his
thoughts kept returning to the girl he had met that day. Never had
he met a woman so skilled with weapons. He thought of all the
girls from his own village, simpering and trying to showcase what
kind of wives and mothers they would be. Jeran could honestly
and thankfully say he didn't know anyone quite like Kiah. He
conjured the image of her long, dark brown hair. It reminded him
of his mother's favorite chocolate drink—swirling and moving as if
it had a life of its own.

But it was her eyes that had held him captive, eyes that had
nearly gotten him killed when he almost hadn't blocked one of her
attacks in time. Jeran tried to decide on the right color to call them
and could think only of a stone that his father had brought home

many years ago from his travels. It had been a dark, yellowish brown jewel, one that glittered intensely. *Like golden honey,* he thought.

A slow smile crept across his face. She had seemed completely unaware of her own beauty, something that intrigued him as much as her athletic prowess. She hadn't tried to flirt or play coy with him. He tried to discern what had prompted him to make his impulsive offer to teach her to use the spear, and as shocked as he was by his unintended suggestion, he was even more shocked that she had accepted.

Jeran had to wonder what kind of family allowed their daughter to roam the wilderness alone. She was lucky he had been the one to find her. He smiled. No. He felt like the lucky one.

Until that moment, Jeran hadn't realized just how overwhelmingly lonely he was. He had wandered the wilderness for the last four years, hunted by both Lamanites and Nephites. He couldn't remember the last conversation he'd had with another person.

He wondered if it was his loneliness that had prompted him to ask Kiah to return. He smiled again, because Jeran knew that even if he were living at home with his own people, he would have wanted to see more of Kiah.

Jeran stood and watched as the city was eaten up by the darkness, like a snake swallowing its prey whole. When he could no longer make out the city walls, he turned to go back into the jungle. He was anxious to go to sleep, eager for morning to arrive so that he could see Kiah again.

He stopped to make sure that the band of cloth tied to his right upper arm was still securely in place. Jeran couldn't afford for Kiah, or anyone for that matter, to see what lay beneath it.

TWO

Kiah blended in seamlessly with the farmers that were returning from the fields into the city proper. The guards in the towers that overlooked the outer wall's earthen fortifications paid her no attention.

She was wrapped up in her own thoughts as she moved through one of the emptying smaller markets where the goods were of a lesser quality and therefore less expensive. The merchants and tradesmen were closing down for the night, locking fabrics, jewelry, weapons, tools, and all sorts of foods into containers. Kiah ignored them as she headed for her home near the center of the city.

The closer she moved to the center, the more beautiful and sturdy the buildings became. She passed by the homes made of bound poles with thatched roofs and could see families through open doorframes as they ate their evening meal by firelight. Some huts were daubed with mud and plaster; others were left open to permit ventilation. Each had a high-pitched roof made of palm thatch that sloped so that rains would run off quickly.

As she came into her family's section of the city, the noise of the livestock that people kept in fences by their homes suddenly seemed leagues away. The limestone buildings surrounding her blocked out the noise. The homes here were clean, large, and, in some cases, ornate. The smell from citrus trees in private gardens filled the air. The stars shone brightly over it all, like a blanket of sparkling dewdrops.

Kiah laughed at her own sudden desire to be poetic. She ran up the steps that lined the platform her home was built upon and saw her father in the front room where he knelt in prayer. His advisors and captains surrounded him as he led them in supplication to their God, asking Him for protection as they fought for their homes, their wives, their children, and their liberty.

It was such a usual sight that Kiah hardly noticed him. Her father praying was as typical as Shabana screaming at someone. It was a more-than-daily occurrence in the home of her family.

Kiah sat on the floor in the front gallery outside of the room her father was in. She listened as he prayed for the safety of the loved ones they would leave behind. Her father ended the prayer, and she heard the busyness of the men returning to their feet and talking in low tones to one another.

Helaman the Younger walked out of the room clutching a letter. "Kiah!" he exclaimed as he dropped his bags to the floor.

She smiled up at him and stood. "Helaman, I'm glad to see you." Kiah had a hard time remembering when they had last crossed paths. Helaman had been a close childhood friend, and Kiah knew that her father had hoped Helaman might make an offer of marriage. However, he had recently become betrothed to a young girl from a family that held positions of authority within the Church of Christ, like his own.

He had changed so much in the last few years. Their childhood friendship had been forged by the mischievous streak Helaman had inherited from his mother, but recently he had grown into his father's humility and piety. Helaman had started to settle into the man he would become.

"Look at this." He grinned, rolling out the parchment. "It's an epistle from my father—a report from their battles. They have taken the cities of Antiparah, Cumeni, and Manti, and not one of his two thousand stripling warriors was killed. Not one! Isn't that wonderful?"

"It's a miracle," Kiah said as Helaman handed her the epistle. It was hard to believe that none of the children of the people of Ammon had fallen in battle. So many Nephites and Lamanites had died that it was miraculous to hear of one band that suffered no casualties.

"That's what happens when the righteous keep God's commandments. We are blessed and preserved." Helaman took the parchment back from Kiah. "I should be there with him."

"You know your father needs you here to help lead the Church in his absence."

"I know. But I dislike feeling that I am useless," Helaman said. His expression changed from wistful to determined. "I need to take my leave of you. Your father has asked me to oversee the letters being sent throughout the land telling our people of the victory. There will be great celebrations in Jershon." With that, Helaman swept through the front entrance along with several other departing men.

Kiah noticed that Helaman had left his bags behind. She picked them up, and one of them sloshed. From the smell, it could only be the maguey wine that the priests used in ordinances. Kiah went outside and called Helaman's name, but he had already disappeared. She decided to put his things in the kitchen and return them to him tomorrow.

Kiah thought over Helaman's words and knew all too well the feeling of uselessness. She knew she could fight better than many of the men that her father had conscripted for battle. But it was absolutely out of the question; she was not allowed to go. She had argued with her father about it, and he had made it very clear that he would never put her life in that kind of danger. The discussion had been completely closed.

Once the last man had left, Kiah entered her father's room. He was collecting the maps spread all over the low tables. "Trouble in the east?" she asked as she glanced at them.

"Several Nephite cities have fallen. We have to retake them. If the Lamanites are allowed to stay there, they will have us bottled in on all sides." Kiah's father, Captain Moroni, sighed deeply, and Kiah studied the man who had passed his features along to her—he had the same dark brown hair, proud chin, and yellow-brown eyes. She noted with some surprise the gray at his temples and the lines of worry that had started to mar his face, deepened by the dim candlelight in the room. In her mind her father was perpetually young—the strongest, the biggest, the best warrior that had ever lived. The man in front of her seemed bogged down with a pain and sadness she couldn't begin to comprehend.

"I thought that men had been sent to Nephihah. I thought they would be able to maintain it." Moroni said the words more to himself than to Kiah. Kiah noticed that the scar running from the outer corner of Moroni's left eye to his chin had turned a bright white. When her father was upset, his face tensed so that the scar changed in color. The scar always made Kiah feel uneasy. Her father had received it two years earlier in his defense of the city of Mulek. He had been seriously wounded. It was the closest she had ever come to losing him. She did not like to think about it.

"Our people have become hard. Wicked. If they do not repent . . ." The sorrow was all too evident in Moroni's voice. Kiah could only guess at his burdens. He had sworn to protect his people, to the giving of his own life, but they in turn dishonored his oath by failing to keep even the simplest of commandments.

Moroni looked at Kiah with surprise, as if he had forgotten that she was in the room. "I have to take what men I can to the other cities so that they will not fall as well."

Moroni paused, expecting Kiah to respond. Usually when her father announced his departure, she begged to travel with him, to let her fight. But things had changed since her encounter with Jeran. She had gained a new respect for her father and his men. Kiah realized that she had never known real conflict, had never been in real danger. She had finally tasted fear and could not imagine it multiplied by ten thousand if she had to face an entire army of Lamanites. War no longer seemed as romantic as it once had, and Kiah had discovered she was much more fearful than she could have imagined herself to be.

"Are you leaving tonight?" she asked, bending down to help collect the maps made from fig tree bark. She ignored Moroni's probing look.

Moroni nodded. "I'm going to camp with the men outside the city, and we will leave at first light."

Kiah walked over to her father and hugged him. "I will miss you." She knew her father had no idea how much. Ever since her brother Moronihah had married Shabana, her world had turned upside down. Her home was no longer her own. Her father's sister, Linoah, tried as much as possible to keep the peace, but both Kiah and Shabana were too strong willed to back down.

Moroni kissed the top of her head before releasing her. "So, do you have anything to tell your father?"

Kiah's guilty conscience overwhelmed her. Was there any way that her father knew about Jeran? "Anything to tell?" she echoed in an attempt to stall him.

"Any young men that I should know about?"

She turned away from him. Kiah wondered why her father didn't realize how much it hurt her that every time he came home from battle, he asked her the same painful question. "No, Father. There is no one."

"When I was your age . . ." Moroni said as he placed the maps into a thick basket to be carried out.

"I know, I know. You already had two children," Kiah interjected with a moan. She knew where this conversation was headed.

"Look at Moronihah. He has given me two grandchildren."

"Yes," Kiah scoffed. "Moronihah is a shining example to us all."

"Kiah," Moroni warned, and Kiah knew that she had pushed too far.

"I am sorry," she said, even though she wasn't.

"Have you given any more thought to Corahan's offer?"

"No," Kiah immediately replied. "I will not marry him. He is ancient."

"Ancient?" Moroni let out a half laugh. "He is only a few years younger than I am."

"I know," Kiah teased. "Ancient." Kiah didn't know if she should go further, but she wanted to make her feelings on the subject as clear as she could. "Father, there's something about him that isn't right. I just . . . I don't know how to explain it. But the thought of being married to him makes me ill. I would rather spend the rest of my life unmarried than to be his wife."

Moroni shook his head at his daughter, hefting his basket of maps onto his back. "Your aunt tells me that I have always been far too lenient with you. But I only want you to be happy. If Corahan will not make you happy, then I don't want you to marry him." Moroni turned to give instructions to the servants her family employed. He wanted to make certain they provided the family with sufficient supplies in his absence—wood, water, and food from the marketplace.

When he finished, he said to Kiah, "Come, walk me out to the street."

"Did you love my mother?" Kiah knew the answer before she asked the question, but she lived to hear about the mother she barely remembered, the one who had died when she was so young.

"Very much," Moroni said, the pain of his loss evident in his tone.

"That's what I want," Kiah told him as she slipped her arm through his. "I want a man to feel that way about me. I don't want it to be a merger of families or about my dowry. I want to be loved the way you loved my mother." She knew it was a nearly impossible request. Moronihah had married Shabana to forge a political alliance between their families because Shabana belonged to one of the most influential and powerful families in Zarahemla. Kiah knew that her parents had been unusual to marry for love, but now that she had been around a couple who'd married for convention, there was no question which she preferred. Of course, someone besides Corahan had to want to marry her first.

Moroni tied the straps of his head plate under his chin. "Then I promise that is what you will have." Moroni kissed his daughter on her cheek. He then uttered the same thing he always said when he left for war. "Be good, little one."

Kiah gave him the same response she'd given him since she was six. "Come home safe, and I will be." She watched him walk to the end of the street, where four bodyguards fell in step with him to accompany him outside the walls to the camp. Kiah stood there until he was no longer visible.

She turned to go back into the house and stumbled into someone. "I'm sorry," she said as she got up and dusted herself off. Kiah had to hold back a gasp when she saw who it was. "Corahan," she said, trying to keep the disgust out of her voice.

Corahan was a small, wiry man with thin, greasy hair and dull brown eyes. It wasn't just his appearance that made Kiah feel uneasy. She had a vivid memory from years ago when she had eavesdropped on some of her father's captains. They talked of the things Corahan had done in battle. She didn't know if her father was even aware of them. The mental images had always stayed with her, and as a result, she didn't like to be around him. He scared her.

"Kiah, might I speak with you?" Corahan asked in his watery voice.

"No, my aunt is waiting for me. Perhaps another time." Kiah fled into the safety of her home as quickly as her feet would carry her.

* * *

"Taken a fancy to Captain Moroni's young daughter, have you?"

Corahan spun to see a tall, elegant man with a curved, beak-like nose walking toward him. The man's red tunic extended to his ankles and was richly embroidered with golden thread along the hems. A turquoise cape with a border of yellow fluttered softly around him. Silver bracelets on his wrists gleamed in the waning moonlight, and a high, feather-adorned headdress spoke of the man's elevated social status.

"I don't see where that's any of your business," Corahan said and turned to carry out his duties by checking on the soldiers at the east wall.

"I have made it my business." The man smiled and fell into step beside Corahan. "There are other ways to power, you know."

That made Corahan stop. "Power?" he repeated.

The wealthy man's sinister smile pushed farther up his face. "Yes. Why else would a man of your age want to marry Moroni's only daughter?"

"Because . . . because it is time I married and started a family," Corahan stammered, shaken that this man had so easily read his true intentions. After years of slaving away in the army with nothing to show for it, he was ready to move up, to get the respect and position he knew he was rightly owed. He had done everything he could think of to show Captain Moroni what an excellent soldier he was. Despite Corahan's best efforts, he had never obtained the rank of captain.

The man let out a low, slippery laugh. "With what land? What name? What money?"

Corahan narrowed his eyes and tensed his hands into fists. The man put his palms out in a placatory gesture.

"Wait, wait," he said. "I did not come here to anger you, only to make you an offer."

"You have no offer that would interest me," Corahan said, whirling back toward the east wall.

"Your loyalty lies where? With Moroni?" the man called after him. It was enough to make Corahan stop again.

"The same Moroni that leaves you here in Zarahemla while he goes to get glory and prestige in the east?" the man continued. "Why did he leave you here and not take you with him? Few men have as many years of service or battle experience as you. You should be at his right hand."

"Moroni trusts me. That's why he left me here," Corahan sputtered, disliking the doubts and questions he had silently harbored being said aloud by someone else. How many others thought the same thing?

"Yes, he trusts you," the man practically purred. "That's why he left you in charge of the safest city in the land, the impenetrable fortress. Because of his deep and abiding trust."

Corahan's face turned a sickly shade of white, and his entire body started to tremble with anger. "I will hear no more of this."

The man stepped in front of Corahan to stop him from leaving before he had finished. "I offer you more. I offer you power and wealth. I offer you the chance to get everything you have ever wanted. I can even give you Moroni's daughter if you want her." The man gestured to a bald and shriveled man who looked like an avocado left too long in the sun. The man had been hidden in the shadows. Corahan flinched, not having even noticed him. The servant scurried over, holding a wrapped bundle in his arms.

"A token of my esteem," the nobleman said to Corahan, handing him the gift. "My name is Pachus. My family's home is in the northwestern section of the city. It will be very easy to find me once you choose to do so."

Pachus bowed slightly and made a sweeping motion with his cloak. He turned and strode away. The servant ran to keep up with him.

"That went better than I hoped. It will not be long before Corahan is under my control." Pachus tapped his fingers together in eager anticipation. "I will finish what the king-men failed to do five years ago."

Pachus glanced over his shoulder to see Corahan unwrapping the silver and jade dagger. "He will be my unwitting pawn."

"And what will you be?" the servant asked in a tone that suggested he did not care but knew he was supposed to ask.

"What will I be? I will be king."

* * *

Kiah could hear the River Sidon babbling somewhere to the west as she approached the hidden pool. The sun poked through the forest canopy with long, dusty columns of light. Kiah pushed through the riot of greenery that made up the heavy underbrush in the jungle wilderness. Two quetzal birds flittered past, their iridescent green tails brushing the top of Kiah's head. They called noisily at her from their safe perch in a mahogany tree.

The quetzals were not alone. The jungle was alive with a chorus of birds and insects and the chattering of other unseen animals. The familiar sounds gave Kiah continued courage.

She didn't know why she was afraid. She didn't think Jeran would hurt her. Kiah didn't know if she had the right words for how she felt. There was fear, but not for her life. She was nervous, excited. It was different from anything she had ever experienced.

When she finally broke through the tree line at the pond, she saw Jeran sitting on a rock near the water's edge. He seemed to be picking at a piece of wood with a knife. He heard her approach and gave her another one of those smiles that left her a little breathless. She had forgotten how handsome he was, and her heart did a funny flip. Jeran threw the wood into the jungle and put the knife back in his bracer.

"I didn't know if you'd come."

"Neither did I," Kiah confessed, feeling even more awkward than she did yesterday. Jeran seemed oblivious to her anxiety, bringing his spear to her.

"Ready to start your lesson?" Jeran asked. When she said yes, Jeran held the spear in front of him, and Kiah went to take it. At the last second, Jeran pulled it back toward his body.

"Wait. You have to make me a promise."

"A promise?" Kiah repeated skeptically, raising one eyebrow.

"You have to promise that if I show you how to use this, you aren't going to try to kill me with it."

Kiah saw the teasing in Jeran's bright blue eyes. She sighed dramatically. "I suppose I will try to refrain."

Jeran grinned. "Let's get started."

* * *

"Good," Jeran said, and went to pull the spear out of the tree where Kiah had thrown it. She had been much closer to the makeshift target that time. "You have a natural talent."

Kiah was bent at the waist, resting her hands on her knees. This was exhausting and the hardest work she had done in months. She pushed the sweat from her forehead back to her hairline.

Jeran handed her the dull end of the spear, and Kiah assumed the form that Jeran had taught her, spear hefted up to shoulder level on her right. Kiah cleared her mind and focused. She heaved the weapon again with all her might, and this time she was successful—she hit the target dead center.

"You did it!" Jeran whooped, thrusting both arms straight up in the air and running over to her. He picked her up in a big hug, whirling her around. Kiah laughed and clung to his neck.

Jeran stopped spinning and put Kiah down. His face was a short distance from her own, and his eyes smiled into hers. Kiah forgot to let go and stood with a strange anticipation, wondering what he would do next.

He finally released her and walked quickly over to the spear. Kiah furrowed her eyebrows. She was confused. For a moment she had thought Jeran might kiss her. She was embarrassed by her thoughts, embarrassed that she had let Jeran hug her, that she had been more than willing to let him kiss her, and even more humiliated that Jeran seemed so repulsed that he had to walk away. *What's wrong with me?* she wondered.

"So, is the Nephites' new war plan to arm their women?" Jeran asked with his back to her as he carefully edged the spear out of the tree.

"No. Just me," Kiah said as she walked into the pond until the water came up midcalf. She reached down and splashed the water on her face, trying to not only get rid of the sweat and grime, but also to cool down her reddened cheeks.

"Why is that?"

"I was spoiled, I suppose. At least, that's what people like to tell me. My mother died when I was very young, and my father couldn't bear to leave me behind when he went to train for battle. He brought me with him and taught me how to fight."

"It doesn't sound to me like you were spoiled," Jeran said. "It sounds to me like your father loves you."

"He does," Kiah said as she walked around in the shallow end of the water, kicking at pebbles.

"Well, I don't know what more I can teach you."

Kiah looked at him. Jeran had placed one end of the spear on the ground and leaned casually against it. The sentence that he had just uttered didn't seem to be upsetting him too much. Kiah's mind raced. There was no proper or modest way to ask him to see her again. She didn't want him to think she was too forward. Or desperate, for that matter. Even if she did feel a tiny bit desperate at the thought of never seeing him again.

Though it hadn't occurred to her until just then, her mind quickly seized on an opportunity that now seemed so obvious. It had the added benefit of soothing her guilty conscience—if he accepted, she would be doing the Lord's work. Having to sneak out to teach Jeran about the teachings of the prophets didn't seem as bad as sneaking out just to see him. Kiah whispered a quick prayer of gratitude.

"Perhaps it's my turn to teach you. Will you meet me here again tomorrow so that I can tell you about the Church of Christ?"

THREE

"Ow!" Kiah shrieked, her hand flying up to her head, where she grabbed at the colored strips of leather her aunt wove into her hair.

Linoah swatted her hand away. "Stop. I'm almost done."

Kiah put her hand back down on the ground and gritted her teeth as her aunt yanked at her hair with a comb. She yelped again.

"Didn't anyone ever tell you that you must suffer to be beautiful?" Linoah asked. Kiah tried to remember why she had wanted her aunt to fix her hair, and immediately Jeran came to mind. They had been meeting together for weeks now, and there had been so many times, so many chances, for him to kiss her or to say that he had feelings for her. But he never did. She thought that perhaps if she got dressed up, he might feel differently. But Kiah decided this was, by far, the stupidest idea she'd ever had. She was certain that she would see blood dripping from her abused scalp at any moment.

As if it weren't enough that she was dealing with this kind of torture, the tinkling sound of bells alerted her to her sister-in-law coming across the open-air courtyard to where Kiah and Linoah sat. Shabana always wore an excessive amount of decoration when Kiah's father and brother left the city. Shabana enjoyed flaunting her wealth and her petite beauty.

Shabana placed her balled up fists on the hips of her fine-twined silk tunic. "Where do you think you're going?"

"What do you care?" Kiah retorted.

"I don't care," Shabana hissed back. "But if something happens to you while you're off traipsing through the jungle, I'm the one who will be held responsible."

Kiah felt her aunt patting her head. "Are we done?" Kiah asked, and when Linoah nodded, Kiah jumped to her feet. In the beginning Linoah had tried to intercede during these fights, but now she said nothing and turned back to her weaving loom attached to a hook on the wall. She used a long piece of wood to tighten the already woven strands. From how hard Linoah hit the nearly completed blanket with the shuttle, Kiah understood that Linoah was unhappy. Linoah hated confrontation. Kiah wondered if Linoah wanted to get away from Shabana's tyranny as badly as Kiah did.

"While your father and brother are gone, I am the head of the household. You will stay home today and help us here," Shabana said. "You will not go running around the city."

"I know how frustrating this must be for you," Kiah said as she towered over her sister-in-law, "but you cannot control me, no matter what you do."

A storm of rage passed over Shabana's features. Kiah knew that more than anything, Shabana wanted to be master of every situation. Everyone Shabana considered to be a lesser personage had to do what Shabana said. Kiah also knew that Shabana was infuriated that Kiah didn't care who Shabana's family was.

Kiah sighed inwardly. She'd been so happy these last few weeks. Happy in a way she hadn't dreamed possible. She wanted to hug everyone she saw and share her joy with them. She knew that Jeran made her feel this way, and she hated the thought of Shabana unknowingly trying to keep them apart. Kiah knew she should be nicer. It was just that Shabana made it so difficult.

"You think you are so brave and so smart," Shabana said. "You think you don't need anyone. But you do. Someday you might even need my help, and then what are you going to do?"

"I'm going to pray that things never get so bad that I would have to ask you for anything," Kiah said, her anger renewed, and she brushed past her sister-in-law. She would never need Shabana's help. She didn't need anyone to help her.

"Good-bye, Aunt Linoah." Kiah waved and set off across the courtyard, deliberately ignoring Shabana. She could hear Shabana yelling at her to come back as she walked through the open doorway toward the marketplace.

Kiah was tired of the constant fights with Shabana. She wanted to leave this house, to have a house of her own, to feel safe and secure in her own environment again. Shabana's parting words ran through Kiah's mind. She wondered what would happen if her life were in Shabana's hands. She shuddered at the thought and hoped she would never have to find out.

As the early morning sun continued its slow ascent in the sky, Kiah joined the stream of people heading outside of Zarahemla to begin their daily labors. The air hung heavy with the scent of cooking fires set throughout the city to prepare the first meal of the day. All around her she could hear the soothing sound of stone being scraped across stone as women rolled out their maize for breakfast. She turned a corner and was greeted with the sight of the bustling central marketplace, five times larger than normal in preparation for the harvest festival.

Kiah smiled at the scene that spread in front of her. The chief marketplace was located in the city's main plaza outside of the temple complex. The noise was overwhelming—each merchant was calling out for buyers to come and see what they had for sale. There were makeshift booths and stalls made out of wood, with thatched overhangs. Some sold their goods from the front of lean-tos. Others had no such shelter and simply laid their wares on the limestone courtyard on blankets and mats. What might appear as total chaos and confusion to an outsider was actually organized in a grid pattern of absolute order.

She could see the food merchants to her right, and the air was pungent with the mixed scents of all the things that were offered—potatoes, maize, squash, nuts, cacao, fish, beans, peppers, oysters, pumpkins, melons, amaranth, manioc, eggs, tomatoes—there were too many tempting things for Kiah to mentally list them. All these mingled with the delicious aroma of meat being roasted and smoked. Despite having already eaten breakfast, Kiah felt her stomach growl. She planned on bringing some treats from the market to Jeran.

She somehow managed to make out the distant gobble of a distressed turkey from the quarter of the market where merchants offered various animals for eating and breeding. They had a vast assortment of tapirs, peccaries, small dogs, rabbits, deer, and birds, some of which were sold only for their ability to produce feathers.

Kiah approached a vendor and indicated that she wanted several balls of popcorn and some honey-dipped fruit. While the vendor wrapped her purchase, Kiah opened the small leather satchel attached to her belt. She pulled out four cacao beans and offered them to the seller, who indicated that they would be an acceptable exchange.

It was an easier sale than so many going on around her. Merchants calculated exchange rates in the dirt using stones and twigs to write out numbers. Others used greenstone beads, feathers, chips of jade, or measures of salt or silver. Sellers and buyers argued over measurements being used for the trades, whether boxes for measuring maize were the right size or if the clay jars for measuring liquid had been made too thin. One very tall, large male buyer argued with a smaller female vendor over the true measure of an armload or fistful. Kiah heard someone scream, "Two senines of silver for that? Are you serious?" She knew, however, that everyone would agree that haggling at the market was part of the fun.

She made the decision to avoid the weapons and armor quarter altogether, knowing that once she went in, she might not want to leave. It was easy enough for her to pass by the woodcarvings, the jade engravings, the clay vases, the leatherwork, the feathered head-dresses. Silver chains, and bracelets and earrings made of shells, turquoise, jade, and rock crystals did not tempt her either.

Kiah walked behind women carrying their goods on their heads and backs while their barefoot children scampered at their feet. Many of the boys played games with rubber balls, coming dangerously close to knocking over tables and pottery, and nervous merchants yelled at them to have more respect.

Popcorn balls were one of her favorite foods, and she stopped to eat one. She noticed that she had come to rest in front of the builders' market. Their period of recent peace and prosperity had allowed for the building of many new structures. Now the stonemasons worked on creating a building—galleries with rows of rooms lined with columns with multiple courtyards—for the more costly items in the market. She watched as the masons shaped the large slabs of limestone with chisels and wooden mallets. The masons then smoothed the final wall surface by applying thick plaster to make it watertight.

Kiah licked the sticky, sweet honey from her fingers and continued on. She took a sharp left and found herself surrounded by the cloth merchants. Bolts of cotton in every color imaginable spread out in all directions as if a rainbow had fallen to the earth and shattered. There were also countless skeins of yarn and thread. One particularly loud seller managed to get Kiah to wander over to her booth. She ran her fingers over the thread the merchant was offering; it was especially fine. Kiah hardly listened as the woman extolled the virtues of her wares. Kiah's gaze settled on a skein of thread that was a brilliant and intense shade of blue—the exact same shade as Jeran's eyes. The merchant noticed her interest. "It was dyed using attapulgite clay and indigo. Excellent choice."

Kiah heard someone say, "Moroni's daughter." Kiah twisted her neck to see three women in matching red and yellow huipils looking at her and whispering. Loudly.

"Why is she alone? What sort of girl travels by herself?"

"The kind who wears weapons," the second one said. "I hear she is still unmarried."

"I don't know of any man who would want a wife that could defend her home but not clean it." The women laughed and walked away. Kiah's cheeks burned. She could be a wife. She could.

As if to prove her thoughts, Kiah arranged to purchase the thread and have it delivered to her home on credit. She tried not to think about Shabana's reaction when the package arrived. Instead, she gave the merchant a cheery wave as if the women's words had not affected her and headed toward the main causeway out of the city.

What was she going to do with the thread? She ran her fingers idly over hollowed-out gourds that were being sold as rattles, and gave a pat to a taut drum next to them. She shook her head as the instrument merchant tried to show her bone whistles and wooden trumpets.

Kiah started to imagine what sort of pattern she would make. It was the one wifely duty that she excelled at—for some reason she had always been exceptional at embroidery. She thought about embroidering a gift for Jeran and wondered if it was appropriate.

She was nearly to the exit, passing by farming implements and seed that were being sold, when there was a sudden jerk on her arm. Someone yanked Kiah into an alleyway.

"Let me go!" she yelled, and pulled her arm away once she'd gotten her bearings. Her heart had leaped to her throat, and she was shaking. A sour taste filled her mouth when she saw it was Corahan. She wanted to wipe the imprint of his fingers off her arm, but she refrained. Kiah backed into the wooden wall behind her, pressing against it. She looked to her left, to her right. No one could see them. Kiah pushed down the queasy feeling that was weaving its way through her body.

"What do you want?" Kiah asked as Corahan stared at her.

"I want to know if your father has spoken to you about my offer."

Kiah's eyes went wide. She would never have thought Corahan brave enough to ask her something so directly. She didn't know how to respond, how to turn down his offer of marriage without being rude. Kiah was filled with pity for him as she tried to find the right words. She looked down, dragging the toe of her sandal along the ground. "Corahan, I . . ."

But he didn't let her finish. "I was wondering if Captain Moroni had mentioned when our marriage was to be arranged. Your father had said something about talking to you first, but of course, that's nothing more than a formality," Corahan said, letting out a little laugh. "It's not as if any father would let a woman, daughter or not, make a decision like that."

Kiah's head jerked to attention. All the sympathy she had been feeling for him flew away with that insult. "My father has let me make the decision," she said. "And my decision is no. I will not marry you."

Corahan's jaw hung open like a gaping fish without water. He snapped his mouth shut, his eyes blazing. He grabbed her arm in a tight, viselike grip. "Yes, you will marry me."

Kiah shook her head in anger and tried to get her arm free. "I will not. Not now, not ever." Kiah struggled against his hold.

"Release me!" she ordered with a bravery she was far from feeling. Corahan had latched on to both of her arms and was pressing himself against her, pushing her back into the wall.

"You will marry me," Corahan whispered in an ominous voice that frightened Kiah more than anything else he was doing.

Her heart was pounding in her ears, and she could hardly think, let alone move. Some small part of her mind wondered what Jeran would do. Kiah remembered what he had done when they had first fought. She pulled her right leg free and in a backward motion, kicked out at Corahan's feet while simultaneously wrenching her arms loose and pushing at his shoulders. She knocked him off balance, making him fall. She fled back through the marketplace, back toward the causeway. She knew she could outrun Corahan, and if nothing else, she would soon be in the dense jungle. She would definitely lose him there.

* * *

Corahan felt his blood surge. Never in his life had he been so insulted. Never had anyone dared speak to him the way that Kiah just had. He yelled as he punched the wall in front of him, slamming his knuckles against the wooden posts until he bled. Corahan watched as some drops of blood ran down his hand and splattered in the dirt. A girl. A lying, deceiving, disobedient girl had pushed him down. The humiliation was too much to bear.

When he looked down, he saw that one of his knives had fallen. He picked it up, turning it over, its silver hilt gleaming in the light. He looked at the jade squares that lined the handle.

It was as if something had been wound too tightly inside him and suddenly broke. Corahan thrust the knife back into its sheath.

He knew what he had to do. He knew where he had to go.

Within minutes he stood in front of the home of Pachus in the wealthy Mulekite section of Zarahemla. Weeks ago he had found out everything he could about the nobleman, including where he lived, and had returned to this spot several times to weigh Pachus's offer in his mind. Today, Kiah had forced Corahan to accept. If Pachus could do all that he promised, she would never dare treat Corahan that way again. He thought about how he would make her beg him to forgive her, about the ways that he would punish her for her insolence.

He went up the steps to the open doorway, waiting to be noticed. Corahan recognized the small bald man approaching him as the same servant who had accompanied Pachus on his first meeting with Corahan. The man came over and asked Corahan to follow him. The servant looked up at Corahan only for a half second, but it was enough to make Corahan take a step back. The servant's eyes were filled with pure, unmistakable hatred. The servant bowed his head back down and in a shuffling gait led Corahan toward his master.

They passed through a series of rooms, each one more elaborate than the last. They found Pachus in the largest room of all. In the dim light, Corahan could see that the walls were painted in an array of colors, with scenes of battles and warriors. Although the pictures looked as if they encompassed a long history, they had to be recent additions. The Mulekites had no literacy before the Nephites came. It did not matter to Corahan, because he could not read the words anyway. He had been taught along with his peers at school when he'd come of age, but he hadn't had much use for what he had learned since then, and the skill had withered.

Corahan saw a giant ship depicted crossing the ocean from their ancient homeland. He did not recognize the name of the foreign people who had brought the Mulekites, but he did know the name of the city they had come from. Sidon—the same name given to the river here in the promised land. There were also pictures of ascensions, of great victories. The scene of a warrior pointing his spear at a captive's eye grabbed Corahan's attention.

As he gazed at the murals, Corahan noticed a strong and unidentifiable floral scent, and it took him a moment to locate the red clay vases of purple orchids scattered throughout the room. Hearing the sound of someone clearing his throat, Corahan looked away from the paintings. Pachus lounged on large pillows and watched a beautiful, scantily clad woman dance for him. Pachus seemed unsurprised to see Corahan.

"I was wondering how long it would take you to accept my offer," Pachus said as he took a drink of what smelled like balche. It couldn't possibly be balche—outside of religious ceremony, all alcohol was forbidden.

Corahan said nothing as Pachus waved the girl away, his rings glinting in the candlelight that illuminated the windowless room. The girl bowed and hurried off.

"You're bleeding, I see," Pachus stated, and clapped his hands together. "I would prefer you not bleed on my floor."

Two men came in the room with rags and water and set about cleaning Corahan's wound. Corahan noted the way the men were dressed, how short their hair was. He looked at Pachus in surprise. "You have slaves."

Pachus shrugged as if the answer were obvious and unimportant.

"But Captain Moroni and Helaman would never allow anyone to own . . . If Pahoran found out . . ."

Corahan was cut off by Pachus. "But Moroni and Helaman aren't here, are they?"

The men finished their ministrations, bowed, and left. "Please sit," Pachus offered.

Corahan sat on the floor across from Pachus. Pachus ignored him, giving all his attention to the melon on a plate in front of him. Pachus carefully cut the melon into tiny slivers.

When Corahan felt like he could no longer bear the silence, Pachus spoke. "Has something changed? Have you come to join me?"

Corahan nodded.

Pachus smiled before putting a piece of melon into his mouth. He chewed it slowly, deliberately. He raised a linen cloth to his mouth, dabbing at the corners. Corahan instinctively understood that his patience was being tested and remained silent.

"Do you know of the king-men?"

Corahan blinked several times in surprise. Of course he knew of the king-men. He had been in the battle five years ago when the king-men had put Zarahemla in jeopardy by refusing to fight the invading Lamanites. Four thousand king-men had died when they would not take the oath of the Title of Liberty and support the current government.

Some of those king-men had been the remnants left in Zarahemla from ten years previous when Amalickiah had tried to overthrow the chief judges and make himself king. Captain Moroni had stopped the attempted revolution, and Amalickiah had been forced to flee. Corahan had been among the number that chased Amalickiah to the edge of the mountains. Amalickiah had joined the Lamanites, and through manipulations, treachery, and murder, he had become their king.

Amalickiah had led the Lamanites against the Nephites, not content with being king over the entire Lamanite nation. He still had to have Zarahemla. His greed and lust for the city were his undoing. Teancum, one of Moroni's captains, sneaked into Amalickiah's tent in the middle of the night and put a javelin into Amalickiah's heart. Amalickiah's brother Ammoron had taken over the Lamanite throne after Amalickiah's death. And it was Ammoron against whom Moroni now led his armies.

Pachus nodded in satisfaction at the comprehension on Corahan's face. "Not all the king-men left Zarahemla or were killed. Some are still here, waiting to finish what they started." Corahan said nothing and tried to absorb what he was being told.

"Who leads them?" Corahan finally asked, already knowing the answer.

"I do," Pachus confirmed.

"But you took the oath. You fly the Title of Liberty on your tower."

"Sometimes forced allegiances have, shall we say, unpredictable results."

"Why do you want to be king?" Corahan wasn't sure why he had asked the question; it just seemed to slip out of his mouth. The system of judges and chief judges that the Nephites had in place worked well for the people. They had no need for a king.

"For the same reason you chase after Moroni's whelp. Power. Position. You know what it's like to have to take something by force that should by all rights belong to you." Pachus gave Corahan a nasty grin before standing up and walking over to a tapestry of his ancestry that hung on the wall. "I am a descendant of Zarahemla, descended from Mulek and Zedekiah. My ancestors were kings of Israel before Nephi was born. The blood of true kings runs through my veins. For generations my family has stood to the side as those peasant chief judges have ruled over Zarahemla. No more. It is my birthright, and I must restore my family to its rightful place."

Corahan tried to understand the logic. "But, you have no children."

Pachus returned to his cushions and with great show reseated himself. "My brother's daughter has two sons. I will have an heir," he said, waving his hand airily as if to dismiss the matter. This confirmed to Corahan that Pachus's desire to be king had nothing to do with restoring his family's name and everything to do with gaining the throne for himself.

"What does any of this have to do with me?"

"We want you to join us." Pachus picked up his knife and

turned his attention to his plate once again.

"Me? Join the king-men? Why?"

Pachus cut himself another piece of the melon, studying it before he ate it. "Because I have need of your special . . . talents."

As Corahan waited for Pachus to continue, the only things he heard were Pachus chewing his food, a motmot bird hooting in the distance, and his own breath sounding harsh and labored. A stone had begun to sink into his stomach as he feared that he knew exactly what Pachus wanted him for.

Pachus set aside his utensil and food and picked up a piece of cloth to wipe at his mouth and to clean his fingers. He put the napkin on top of his plate and looked up at Corahan with cold eyes.

"I need you to kill someone."

"K-kill someone?" Corahan stammered as he tried to swallow his panic.

Pachus let out a short, barking laugh. "Oh, come now, why this fear? This hesitation? You've killed hundreds of men on the battlefield. What's one more?"

Corahan suddenly realized what a precarious position he was in. Pachus had told him a very shocking secret in revealing that the king-men still existed—that they still plotted to overthrow the chief judges and reinstate a king. Corahan was smart enough to know that it was unlikely that he could simply refuse Pachus's request and leave.

"Who?" The question was close to a whisper.

Pachus studied Corahan with a detached reptilian gaze, as if trying to take the full measure of him. Corahan felt a bit like one of the pieces of melon that Pachus had been eating. He worried about what would happen when Pachus swallowed him whole.

"Ontium."

Ontium? He was Corahan's superior officer in Zarahemla. Pachus wanted him to kill Ontium?

"Why?"

The smirk that had been Pachus's expression for much of their meeting slid off his face. His mouth pressed into a thin, tight line, fury lacing his voice. "I will be your king, Corahan. And your king does not like to be questioned. It is not for you to know why. It is only for you to do as you are commanded."

Corahan nodded, not wishing to provoke Pachus further. Corahan had started to sweat and could feel each individual bead form atop his skin. What had he gotten himself into?

"You will bring to me the dagger I gave you with Ontium's blood on it. You have three days." Pachus picked up some documents and began reading them in what Corahan recognized as his dismissal.

Three days? How could he kill Ontium in three days? Corahan seized on the opportunity to retreat. He turned to walk back through the door and across the courtyard to get as far away from this madman as he could.

"One more thing, if you please."

Corahan stopped, not even daring to turn back around to look at Pachus.

"You now know far too much. You have no choice but to join the king-men."

Corahan still could not face Pachus but instead looked down at the ground, understanding the threat that Pachus issued.

"Either he dies or you do."

There was only one thing he could say to leave the room alive. Corahan nodded and glanced back at Pachus long enough to say, "He will be dead in three days."

FOUR

Kiah climbed up on the large boulder that bordered the Sidon. The bright noon sun shone down on her, and she tipped her head back to welcome the rays. The sun had burned off the haze of clouds that had clung to the volcanic peaks to the south, making the sky clear and beautiful. Despite the ugliness of her morning, she was happy to be there, happy to be with Jeran.

"Are you sure you don't want to play *bul* with me?" she asked.

Jeran stood on a rock in the middle of the river, trying to catch a fish. "Not right now."

"Then I'll just have to play for you." Kiah took out her small, even-length twigs and began to line them up. She removed the kernels of corn she'd brought in her pouch, taking out first the ones she'd burned holes into on one side. She used the rest as her and Jeran's "warriors" in the game, dividing them up and placing them at opposite ends of the sticks.

She threw her four kernels, and after calculating the number of holes showing, she moved her warrior three spaces. She rolled again, and this time it was Jeran's warrior that moved two spaces. Kiah's mind wandered as she played this game of chance. She glanced down at Jeran. Her chest felt a little tight as she looked at him, that familiar funny feeling stopping up her throat. Sometimes Kiah would forget just how handsome Jeran was, and then it would rush back to her in a moment like this.

"Any news from your father?" Jeran called up to her.

Kiah tried to control her thumping heart, tried to command her breathing to be even. "No, nothing recently." Kiah looked away, unable to meet Jeran's gaze. The guilt that surrounded questions about her father was too much. At least she was being partially truthful with him. She had not received any word from Moroni or Moronihah in quite some time. It was strange to not hear from them at all. She quickly changed the subject by asking Jeran how he had learned to spear a fish.

"My father," he said with a smile, and Kiah felt worse. A deep despair began to settle in her stomach. It was like someone was prodding her to tell Jeran who her father was. But she was afraid. Maybe it was arrogance on her part to assume that he would even know who Moroni was. On the other hand, it was entirely possible that her father had fought against Jeran's family in battle. What if Jeran blamed her father for the death of his kinsmen?

This wasn't like her. She didn't lie. Kiah moved her kernel warrior a few more spaces, capturing Jeran's warrior. The lie had started the third day they were together. Kiah had been unable to refrain from asking Jeran if he was a slave. When he had heartily laughed and asked why, Kiah had pointed out his short hair. Jeran's expression immediately changed, as if he were shutting himself away. He stayed silent for several minutes and finally answered that no, he was not a slave. He then asked her if her family kept slaves. Kiah told him her father would never allow slaves in their home. Jeran had asked more about her father, and Kiah found herself lying to him, saying her father was a farmer and a soldier. She had made up a false name.

Even now Kiah was hard pressed to figure out why she had lied. She supposed it was a bit out of selfishness, because she worried that things between them would change if Jeran knew who her father was. She also knew that she did it to step out of her father's shadow. Just once, Kiah wanted someone to know her for being Kiah and not for being Moroni's daughter. Besides, it was before she knew she could really trust Jeran. She could trust Jeran now with her father's identity. But it was too late. If she told him the truth . . . maybe it was better to say nothing.

Even as she thought it, Kiah knew she was wrong. She knew she had to tell him about her father. *Tomorrow. I'll tell him tomorrow.* She pushed the guilt aside to deal with later. There would be plenty of time.

* * *

Kiah said, "Are you sure you don't want to play with me? You're losing."

Jeran grinned at her. "I'm losing?"

"Very badly," Kiah assured him.

"I should probably stay down here. Somebody's got to get a proper meal for us."

Kiah nodded and went back to her game. Jeran crouched on a rock in the middle of the River Sidon, holding his spear aloft, waiting for a fish to swim by. He had chosen a spot where the rocks created a small, shallow pool. Several fish had already swum into this area and had left just as quickly. He would have caught one hours ago if he hadn't been so distracted by Kiah. He sneaked another look at her, perched on top of a large boulder, sunning herself like a giant cat.

Jeran again turned his back on her, knowing he had to keep his distance. It wasn't because he wanted to, but because he had to.

He could see what being so easily distracted by her had cost him. Moroni and his men had left before Jeran had a chance to find him. Now Jeran had to wait for Moroni's return to seek out his help. He stole another look at Kiah. She caught his eye this time and smiled. Jeran felt his stomach explode into a thousand butterflies, each trying to flap its way free.

The fish, the fish, he reminded himself. *Pay attention!*

But Jeran was finding it more and more difficult to do anything but think about Kiah. He had been trying to keep her at a distance, but as time wore on, he was finding that harder to do. There had been many moments between them where he could have kissed her, where he wanted to kiss her more than anything.

But he didn't. Every time, it was Jeran who walked away, Jeran who broke the magic between them first.

He did it because he had nothing to offer her. He had no family name, no lands, no means to support her. He knew their friendship would end sooner or later, and he would never see her again. Kiah would find someone else and get married. A stab of jealousy shot through him, causing his heart to constrict. Jeran shook his head. He couldn't think about that.

Jeran just knew that none of it was fair. It wouldn't be fair to kiss Kiah or hold her or say the things he wanted to say to her. It was better for them both if he kept their friendship light and made it so that neither one would have any regrets when their eventual parting happened.

But on days like today . . . it was so hard to remember that resolution. She had deliberately done her hair up in a way that he had never seen before and wore a beautiful light green tunic with blue-embroidered edges. Her honey eyes glowed with happiness. Jeran wanted nothing more than to scale the boulder himself and kiss her senseless.

Jeran already felt selfish enough. It was his loneliness that had initially prompted him to keep seeking out her company. He never expected to find her such a kindred spirit or to so thoroughly relish being with her.

His left hand drifted to the upper part of his right arm, checking again to make sure that the cloth band was tied tightly in place, that there was no way Kiah could see what lay beneath it. It was better to keep things platonic, he reminded himself for the thousandth time. Better for her, better for him. It was the only sensible thing to do.

Jeran made a stab in the water, but the trout dodged the attack and swam away. The splashing sound caused some nearby turtles to scurry off their rocks and into the river, which made the remaining fish scatter. He wished he had some unripened fruit from a black sapote tree to throw in the water. The fruit stunned the fish and made them rise to the surface. But he had no fruit, and if he didn't start concentrating soon, he and Kiah would go hungry. He clamped his teeth together, trying to strengthen his resolve.

"I win!" Kiah called out triumphantly from the large rock.

"You don't mean I lost, do you?" Jeran said in mock horror.

Kiah nodded. "You are a terrible player. Next time I'll have to make sure to find a more worthy opponent."

There was a slight rustle from the top of a palm tree behind her. Kiah and Jeran both looked up to see a bright green parrot flap its way out of the tree and settle onto a boulder near Kiah. The bird cocked its head at her, as if trying to see her better.

"I think it smells the maize," Kiah said, and they watched the little bird as it made small hops toward the boulder she sat on.

"He must have been someone's pet," Jeran commented. "He's not afraid of you at all."

Kiah gathered up the corn in her right hand and offered it to the bird. She put out her left hand for a perch, the way she had seen bird handlers do in the marketplace. The parrot flapped up and landed on Kiah's outstretched fingers. She let out a laugh of delight as the bird began eagerly consuming the offered corn.

"Isn't he beautiful?" she asked.

"Beautiful," Jeran echoed, unable to even see the parrot.

The bird ate all the corn Kiah had, spread out its wings, and flew away. "I'm sorry, but it looks like there isn't going to be a rematch since he ate the game," she said.

Kiah climbed down the boulder, and toward the bottom she lost her footing. With a yelp, she went down to the ground, landing in the leafy undergrowth.

"Are you all right?" Jeran asked, even though he already knew the answer.

"Fine, I'm fine," Kiah said as she stood up and dusted herself off. She hadn't gone three steps when she tripped over a vine and was back on the ground.

Jeran could only grin. This was Kiah. She was such a charming bundle of contradictions. She was often clumsy, but she moved with incredible grace and elegance in battle. She could be sweet and full of light in one moment and fierce and deadly in the next. There were times when he felt like he could see into her soul and others when he felt like she was keeping a thousand secrets from him. Open yet mysterious. Sweet but temperamental. Innocent yet wise. Jeran realized he could happily spend a lifetime trying to understand her.

Before he had time to really ponder his last revelation, Jeran saw Kiah trying to walk on the rocks across the river to him.

"Careful!" he warned.

"I am being careful," she retorted as she tried to maintain her balance on the slippery steps.

"I don't want to have to dive in after you. I don't want to get my hair wet," Jeran said, and Kiah threw him a dirty look. Jeran had been teasing Kiah about her hair since she arrived. Jeran had wondered if she'd done her hair for him. He was touched by the effort, but he liked it better when she wore only a headband. He loved to watch the way her hair moved and shimmered in the sun.

Jeran stood on a flat-topped stone, and there was not really enough room for Kiah to join him, but she did.

"What are you doing?" he asked.

She gave him a pert smile. "I want to learn how to fish."

She was crowding him. Jeran wanted to back up but couldn't. His mind searched for something, anything, to ease the tension he felt. "Uh, did you want to continue your lessons?"

A look he couldn't describe crossed Kiah's face but was replaced with a smile. "Where did we leave off?"

"With Zenos's prophecies concerning Christ's death," Jeran said, and turned as if to search for more fish.

"Right." There was a tone in Kiah's voice Jeran didn't recognize. It almost sounded like disappointment, but Jeran wouldn't allow himself to dwell on it.

Jeran remembered Kiah telling him about how she had listened to her friend Helaman orally recite the prophecies of Christ over and over again. It was how members of the priestly families learned scripture in addition to having to read and write it. From the time they were small, boys in these families learned to master the sacred works. Kiah had explained that many of the things she knew had come from helping Helaman to learn the teachings by heart.

"And the rocks of the earth must rend; and because of the groanings of the earth . . ." Kiah faltered in her recital. "Two days of darkness or three?" she said more to herself than Jeran.

Jeran replied, "Three days of darkness." Jeran immediately realized his mistake. He saw that Kiah understood it, too.

"Do you mean to tell me . . . you, you . . ." It was like Kiah couldn't finish her thought. She looked very angry.

"Kiah, I can explain . . ."

"Why did you do it? Why did you meet me out here and pretend like you didn't know anything about the prophecies or scriptures or Christ and let me go on and on teaching you about them?" Kiah's eyes flashed at him.

Jeran could hear the hurt in Kiah's voice. "I never said I didn't know anything about it. You assumed I didn't, and I let you assume it."

"Why?" Kiah demanded.

"You don't know?" Jeran thought it impossible that she couldn't tell how much he liked her, how important their time together was to him. He searched her face, her eyes, and saw that she did not know.

Jeran sighed. "It was because I wanted to see you again. And again and again."

"Oh." The noise was a small, surprised one.

"I know what I know because my mother was a member of the Church and believed it with all her heart. She taught me the same faith and knowledge. I have always believed it; I know the things my mother taught me were true. I would have joined the Church long ago had there been anyone in the Lamanite nation with the authority to baptize me," Jeran confessed, glad to have it out in the open.

A heavy silence hung between them, broken only by the sound of cicadas singing in ten-part harmony. "Your mother was a Nephite?" Kiah finally asked.

"Yes." Jeran had told her that his mother had died, but nothing of her origin. They had both been reluctant to share much about their parents for different reasons.

Jeran held out his left hand to her, a wordless gesture. Kiah paused and then put her own hand in his. Jeran squeezed her hand and allowed his thumb to run lightly across her knuckles before he withdrew his hand. In a move that he did not expect, Kiah took a step closer to him.

Too close! Jeran backed up without realizing he had nowhere to go. His back foot stepped out onto water, and he lost his balance. With both arms flailing, Jeran went backwards into the shallow pool.

Kiah let out great big peals of laughter that seemed to fill the whole valley. "Are . . . are you okay?" she finally managed in between laughs.

Jeran had to grin back at her. He loved to hear her laugh. Even if it was at his soggy expense. He held out a hand to her. "Want to help me up?"

"Oh no." Kiah giggled. "You'll pull me in there next to you."

She knew him far too well. "When I talked about wanting to be baptized, this wasn't quite what I had in mind."

Another strange expression flitted across Kiah's face. "I forgot to mention it, but I have some, um, family things over the next couple of days, so I won't be able to meet you until after that."

"I'll be here," he responded. With a mischievous glint in his eye, Jeran scooped a handful of water and flung it up at Kiah.

She let out a small shriek, trying to dodge the spray and turned to run back toward the shore before Jeran could catch her.

FIVE

He couldn't do it.

Corahan had been Ontium's second in command for the last three years. Ontium was a good soldier. Corahan slowly exhaled, stirring up the dust from the ground next to him. His reed mat in the barracks needed to be replaced, but Corahan ignored the rocks digging into his back, the beetles crawling across his leg. His mind was on more important matters. The sun's first beams began to shine through the barracks doorway.

Sunrise. The third day.

If Corahan didn't kill Ontium today, he would never live to see another sunrise.

Corahan again considered his options. He could try to get a message to Moroni. It might even improve his position within the military if he could reveal Pachus's plot. He started cracking his knuckles. Pachus would have thought of it already. Corahan glanced at the sleeping men surrounding him. One of them could be watching him, spying on him, ready to report back to Pachus. Or worse, ready to kill him. If he tried to leave the city himself, it would be certain death. He could dispatch someone else with a message, but whom could he trust? Even an epistle would most likely be intercepted.

Corahan did not know how many king-men there were, or how extensive Pachus's network of allies was. It was impossible to look at someone and see their allegiance. Every man in the room could be one of the king-men waiting for Corahan to make a false step. There were so many ways to kill a man. Undetectable poison in his food or drink. A dart in the back in the middle of a crowd. A mistake in the practice field.

He also had the feeling that he had been approached at the end of Pachus's plans, not at the beginning. Pachus wouldn't be making such a bold move unless he were ready.

Perhaps he could approach Ontium. Maybe they could come up with some sort of plan to stop Pachus. He dismissed the fanciful notion at once as being unrealistic. Ontium was in the same situation Corahan was. Ontium would not know who among his soldiers would follow his commands and who would be ready to force him from his position. There was Pahoran, the chief judge. But Corahan knew that with the bulk of the army gone, Pahoran could wield little power. He doubted that Pahoran could protect him.

Corahan went to turn on his side and was stopped by a painful jab. He pulled the dagger that Pachus had given him loose, looking at his reflection in the silver hilt. Corahan let himself imagine what it would be like if he lived in a big house like Pachus's. A luxuriant bed. Extravagant meals made to his liking. Slave girls to dance for him. Underlings to jump at his command. Money to buy whatever he wanted. Power to do whatever he wished.

A large, metallic-green beetle scurried up Corahan's legs toward his torso. When the beetle got to his chest, Corahan picked the bug up with his free hand. The beetle flailed its legs wildly while Corahan slowly squeezed. He squeezed until the bug exploded into a sticky mess. Corahan tossed the beetle carcass to one side, absent-mindedly rubbing his fingers across his tunic to clean them.

Corahan imagined Pachus crushing him just as easily. Pachus had been frighteningly clear—kill or be killed. And Corahan enjoyed breathing.

It was not as if he'd never been in death's presence before. His profession demanded it. And as Pachus had said, honestly, what was one more death? Corahan had killed scores of rebellious Nephites and Lamanites in battle.

Didn't it all just come down to a matter of perspective? Who was to say that Moroni's cause was more just than Pachus's? Maybe he just needed to think of this as one more battle, a fight for the control of Zarahemla. If he helped Pachus, perhaps it could be an easy and conflict-free transition. Wasn't it better to take one life than to let thousands die? Captain Teancum certainly hadn't had any trouble sneaking into King Amalickiah's tent and killing him in his sleep to stop a war. *What's to prevent me from doing the same?*

Turning his thoughts from the greater good, Corahan centered in on what it meant for him. What choices remained for him if he didn't do what Pachus said? If he were somehow able to thwart Pachus and stop the king-men, then what? Would his life change for the better? Would he gain wealth? Be given the rank of captain? Would he have Kiah?

Corahan began clenching and unclenching his dagger in anger. Kiah. Initially, he had only wanted to marry her to ensure a better future for himself. But it had all changed and spiraled into something different after what she had done. He wanted to punish her. He could not allow any woman to humiliate him the way that she had. Corahan thought of Pachus's promise to give him Kiah if he helped the king-men.

He was toying with ideas on ways to humiliate her the way she had humiliated him when a soldier pushed aside the door curtain and stepped into the opening. The sun shone brightly behind the man, blocking out his features. He looked like an inky shadow.

"Corahan?" he called out. Corahan propped himself up on his elbow to show the soldier where he was.

"You're wanted out front. There is someone here to see you."

Pachus. A small wave of fear passed over him. He would have to keep his wits about him when dealing with that man. Time was running out. A decision would have to be made. It was either Ontium or him.

Corahan got to his feet and went to the doorway, trying to prepare himself to face his fate.

* * *

"Is it much farther?" Helaman the Younger asked, nearly out of breath at the pace that Kiah set. The animal trail they followed was narrow, forcing them to walk single file. It was obvious that someone had cleared this path recently, but the jungle was trying to reclaim it.

Kiah held her wrapped bundle tighter. "We're almost there."

Helaman swatted a palm frond from his face and had to quickly duck to avoid a low branch that Kiah neglected to warn him of. Kiah hurried ahead before he had a chance to complain to her about it. They entered the small clearing that was fenced in by trees and undergrowth. Kiah saw Helaman survey his surroundings, looking at the clear pool of water that emptied from the Sidon. Helaman stopped short when he saw Jeran.

"You mean there really is a Lamanite?" Helaman asked more to himself than anyone in particular.

"Of course," Kiah said. "Did you think I was joking?"

"Who's this?" Jeran asked, gripping his spear tightly.

"This is Helaman," Kiah said, stepping in between the two men. "His father is the leader of the Church in Zarahemla."

Confusion caused Jeran's brow to furrow. "Why did you bring him here?"

"I brought him here to baptize you." Kiah's eyes danced with delight over her surprise.

"Baptize me?" Jeran repeated in disbelief. He looked down at his frayed clothing. "But I couldn't . . ."

Before he could finish his sentence, Kiah handed him the bundle she'd been carrying. "Open it."

Jeran pushed aside the coarse cloth. Inside lay a thick, brilliantly white cotton tunic. He shook the tunic free of its covering, letting it unroll to its full length. The edges were intricately embroidered in a bright shade of blue. Jeran admired the tunic and turned to Kiah. "Did you make this?"

Kiah shrugged as if embarrassed. "My Aunt Linoah made the tunic, but I did all the embroidery."

"Kiah," he breathed, running his fingers over the stitches. "You're an artist." Jeran raised his gaze back to Kiah, locking eyes with her. "Thank you."

Helaman cleared his throat. The small sound indicated how uncomfortable he felt. "There are some questions I need to ask you before I baptize you." Once he made certain that he had Jeran's full attention, he continued. "Do you believe in God, the Eternal Father, in His Son Jesus Christ, and in the Holy Ghost?"

"I do," asserted Jeran.

"And are you desirous to come into the fold of God, to be called His, to stand as a witness of God at all times and in all things and in all places, and are you are willing to enter into a covenant with Him to serve Him and keep His commandments?"

Jeran again nodded. "Yes."

"Then you should probably go get changed," Helaman directed with a smile, unclasping his cloak at his neck and handing it to Kiah. Jeran grinned back and darted into the jungle from beyond view.

"Is something wrong?" Kiah asked Helaman. He seemed nervous. He kept looking around him as if he expected something to happen. Kiah wondered if he was concerned about more Lamanites showing up.

"What? No, nothing. Just a small matter. I will take care of it once we are done here." Helaman waded out into the water until it was to his waist. Kiah saw him bow his head and guessed that he was praying. She sat silently so as not to disturb him.

Kiah's mind began to drift as they waited in stillness. She remembered her own baptism, how sad she'd felt that her mother couldn't be there. She smiled at the memory of her father telling her that her mother *was* there. Kiah just couldn't see her. She wondered if Jeran's mother would be watching over his baptism.

Jeran emerged from the jungle and went out into the water until he stood next to Helaman. The two men began talking in low, quiet voices. Kiah strained to hear what they were saying, but the wind blew in the wrong direction. She watched Helaman directing Jeran to hold onto Helaman's left arm. Helaman raised his right arm to a square behind Jeran. Kiah bowed her head, listening to the words of baptism being spoken. Helaman eased Jeran backward into the water, burying him beneath the sparkling surface. Once he made sure that Jeran was totally submerged, Helaman pulled him back to his feet.

"Welcome to the Church," Helaman told him, clasping his forearm. Jeran enthusiastically returned the gesture.

A sensation of joy intermixed with a complete sense of peace overtook Kiah. Kiah whispered words of gratitude for the blessing of the Spirit, for the witness it bore, and for the comfort it offered her. She saw the looks on Jeran's and Helaman's faces and knew they felt the same things. Kiah could not have asked them to describe how they felt any more than she could describe it to them—in that moment words seemed inadequate.

Jeran turned and waded back to the shore, Helaman close behind. Kiah stood waiting with a woven blanket for a dripping-wet Jeran to wrap around himself. Helaman toweled off the lower half of his tunic and retrieved his cloak from Kiah, putting it back into place.

"If you will excuse me," Helaman said, and before Kiah or Jeran could even thank him, the jungle swallowed him up.

"Well?" Kiah asked, feeling as if she would never stop smiling. "How does it feel to be baptized?" Kiah sat down on a fallen log near the edge of the pool. Jeran sat next to her, pulling his wrap around him tightly.

"Unreal," Jeran said, and Kiah could hear the amazement, the wonder in his tone. "I feel . . . new. Like I'm a different person." He paused, then turned toward her. "Kiah, I can never thank you enough for doing this." Drop after drop of water gathered at the ends of his short black hair and fell onto the blanket.

"Don't thank me. Thank Helaman. When we find him, I mean."

"Here, I want you to have this." Jeran reached up and untied his necklace. It was a mixture of shells, beads, and wood, with a silver sun in the center. He had worn it every day since she'd met him.

"No, I couldn't," Kiah protested as Jeran tied the necklace on her.

"You gave me something, and I want to give you something back." Jeran adjusted the necklace until the knot he'd tied lay on the back of Kiah's neck. "I want you to have something to remember today by." He pulled his blanket around his shoulders again, as if he were cold, or as if he were closing himself off to her.

They sat for a few moments, listening to the usual sounds of the jungle—the hoot of a spider monkey, the grunt of a peccary, the trill of a toucan. Kiah ran her fingers over the necklace, memorizing the texture, wishing she could see what it looked like on her. It was the first gift she'd ever received from a man, and she was thrilled.

"I'll never forget today." She almost whispered it, not meaning to say it out loud.

"Neither will I," Jeran said. Kiah heard something different in his voice, a tone she hadn't heard before. She wondered what it meant.

She didn't have to wonder long. Jeran took one hand out from underneath his blanket and reached up to softly stroke the side of Kiah's face. Kiah jumped at the strangeness of his touch and then relaxed into it, even leaning a little into his open hand.

And then Kiah knew. Jeran was going to kiss her. Half of her was excited, the other half desperately afraid. She watched as his head moved closer and closer to her own, wondering what it would feel like, whether she should be sensible and stop him.

She let her eyes flutter shut and waited. Kiah could feel him a heartbeat away, could feel his warm breath on her face.

The next thing she felt was Jeran being yanked away from her.

Her eyes flew open to see several Nephite guards pinning Jeran to the ground.

"Wait!" Kiah said. "You don't understand!"

Jeran was struggling in earnest, trying to get his captors to release him. But there were too many. She ran over to the guards, trying to pull one away. "He's not an enemy! Stop!"

The soldier elbowed Kiah, and she fell abruptly to the ground with a hard thump. Before she could get up or protest again, she saw a figure detach itself from the shade of a moss-laden gumbo-limbo tree and come to stand before her.

"You," she said in a mixture of trepidation and revulsion.

"Excellent work, Kiah. Just the way we planned it," Corahan said as the guards pulled Jeran to his feet. At Corahan's words, Jeran had gone still.

"What?" Kiah said, unable to make sense of what was happening.

"I just wanted to thank you for helping with this capture. One less Lamanite for us to worry about."

Kiah's eyes widened as she suddenly realized what Corahan was saying. Her head snapped to look at Jeran. He was staring at her with a look of disbelief and betrayal. No! He couldn't possibly believe a snake like Corahan.

"Jeran, I didn't have anything to do with this." Kiah got to her feet and tried to walk in Jeran's direction. She stopped when Jeran took a step back.

"Corahan! Tell him the truth!" Kiah pleaded. The look in Jeran's eyes was stabbing tiny sharp blades into her heart.

"The truth is you're a much better liar than even I thought possible. How did you manage to fool him so completely?" Corahan walked over to Jeran, studying him.

The soldiers were heavily armed. In order for them to fight, she had to get to Jeran's weapons. She had the blade hidden in her tunic, but it wouldn't be enough to take on Corahan's men. Her eyes settled on Jeran's belongings. If she could just edge herself over to where they were without drawing the guards' attention . . .

Her plan was interrupted by Corahan's question. "Well, what is this?" Corahan was pointing at the band encircling Jeran's right upper arm. He went to remove it, and Jeran began thrashing around.

"Hold him still." Corahan whipped out a knife and cut through the cloth effortlessly. He took in a sharp breath at the colorful tattoo on Jeran's bicep. "I've seen this symbol in battle often enough." His cold, beady eyes flicked up to Jeran's face in surprise. "You're Amalickiah's heir. Look what we've done, Kiah. We've caught a prince."

"Jeran?" Kiah asked, not even sure what the question was. She didn't know how it could be true, how Jeran could bear the mark of the House of Amalickiah on his arm.

"Enough!" commanded Corahan. "Take him back to the city."

"Jeran?" Kiah said again, wanting him to look at her, wanting to understand. Jeran finally lifted his gaze to meet Kiah's, his eyes brimming with a defiant sadness.

"How could you do this to me?" was all that Jeran said as the guards led him in the direction of Zarahemla.

"No!" Kiah called after him in desperation.

"This is what you rejected me for?" Corahan's voice was a low growl behind her. Kiah whirled to face him. "You won't marry me, but you'll let some filthy Lamanite put his hands all over you?"

"Get away from me," Kiah said, willing herself to sound brave and confident. She was all too aware of how they were alone, of how she was unarmed, and of how dangerous Corahan was.

"I don't think so," Corahan leered. "Not this time." He reached out an arm, but Kiah was ready for him. She quickly knocked it away, crouching into a defensive position.

A look of the most intense anger she'd ever seen filled Corahan's face. He let out a curse under his breath and turned slightly away from her, as if he were leaving.

"Kiah!"

Kiah instinctively turned toward her name being called, giving Corahan the opening that he needed. He swung his thick arm around and hit Kiah in the face, forcing her to the ground. Stars exploded behind her eyes, and the world went temporarily black.

SIX

"Kiah!" Helaman ran toward them.

Kiah held her hand against the spot where Corahan had punched her, trying to soothe the stinging sensation. She gaped up at Corahan as Helaman rushed to her side.

Corahan looked stunned. "Kiah, I'm . . . I didn't . . ."

"What is going on?" Helaman demanded, putting his arms protectively around Kiah's shoulders.

Corahan didn't answer. He ran into the jungle without looking back.

"I saw him hit you," Helaman stated in disbelief. Kiah nodded miserably, trying to get to her feet. The world began to spin around her, and she quickly sat back down.

"Oh, Kiah," Helaman said, as he sat down on the ground next to her, his head hanging low. "This is all my fault."

"Your fault?" Kiah repeated in disbelief. "How?"

Helaman said nothing for a moment and then sighed. "When you told me about Jeran, I thought this was a trap, that you were in danger. I thought he was trying to lure you and me out here. We'd be valuable captives because of who our fathers are."

Kiah's eyes stung while her head throbbed unmercifully. "He doesn't even know who my father is."

"I went to Corahan this morning and asked for his help. He was supposed to wait for a signal. I never gave it, because after I met Jeran, I prayed about the situation and received confirmation that Jeran was a good man and that the Lord was pleased with his desire to be baptized."

"Just like that? You prayed and knew?"

Helaman looked at her quizzically. "All we have to do is ask in faith, and it will be revealed to us." Helaman pulled Kiah's hand away from her face to inspect the mark Corahan had made. "I left quickly so that I could find Corahan and his men and let them know that they could leave. I didn't want you to know that I had . . . I'm sorry." Helaman brushed at the dirt that was clinging to his wet clothing, his words laden with regret. "I was trying to help you avoid a trap, and instead I walked you right into one."

"I understand why you did it. But we need to get back to the city. Corahan is dangerous. There's no telling what he'll do to Jeran."

Helaman stood up and offered his hand to Kiah in a gesture that was both helpful and reconciliatory. Kiah paused only a second before taking his hand and allowing him to assist her to her feet. She swayed when she stood, but Helaman caught her and pulled her upright. Helaman started to lead her in the direction of the trail.

"Wait." Kiah walked unsteadily toward Jeran's belongings. She couldn't leave them out here. She bent over and picked up his weapons and his woven pouch. The top wasn't latched properly and something heavy fell out.

Curious, Kiah picked up the wooden object. When she flipped it over, she saw it was a parrot. Jeran had been carving the bird out of a piece of ceiba wood and was only halfway done. Kiah caught her breath. Even though it wasn't complete, she knew it was the same parrot from their day by the river, the one that had eaten out of her hand. It was the most beautiful, lifelike statuette she'd ever seen.

She had to fight to keep the ever-present tears from falling down her cheeks. Why would Jeran be carving this? Did he . . . had he felt the way she did on that day? She let her fingers run down the smooth edges that formed the feathers on the right wing.

She would not let Corahan ruin it. She wouldn't. She would go back to the city and get Jeran away from Corahan and explain to Jeran what had happened. If he wasn't willing to listen, she'd have to find a way to make him understand. Kiah had never backed down from a fight in her life, and she wasn't about to start. With strong resolution, she thrust the unfinished bird back into the bag. "Let's go."

* * *

Corahan ran blindly through the foliage, liana vines snapping and whipping across his face. He didn't know where he was going, and at that moment, he didn't care.

Helaman had seen him. He had *seen* him hit Kiah. Moroni might be known as a caring and compassionate man, but Corahan knew that no father would take kindly to his daughter being back-handed.

When his chest began to burn from his panic, Corahan slowed to a trot, his ragged, desperate breaths filling his stinging lungs.

It meant the end of everything. The end of his military ambition. The end of his hope for an alliance with Moroni's family. There would be no positions open to him. No one that would help him. He would be shunned, an outcast.

Corahan tore through the thick brush like an animal, with his sword slashing a path, when the jungle suddenly closed in on him.

He hadn't meant to do it. It had just happened. He had wanted to apologize, but he'd been so shocked that he actually hit her, and then Helaman was there . . . It had all gone so wrong. This was not how he had imagined things going this morning when Helaman had awoken him to ask for help in protecting Kiah. He had pictured himself the triumphant hero who would save her. He envisioned Moroni's gratitude and finally being given Kiah as his reward. What had made this happen?

"That Lamanite," he growled to himself. Amalickiah's heir. He was the one responsible for this. If it hadn't been for him, Corahan never would have lost his control, never would have hit Kiah. It was his fault this had happened. Corahan stopped and looked to the west. He wanted to turn back to Zarahemla and give the Lamanite prince the punishment he deserved for ruining all of Corahan's hard work.

But that would certainly mean a death sentence. Either from Moroni or Pachus. Death seemed inevitable.

With a howl of frustration, Corahan swung his sword with all of his might into the trunk of a nearby cedar, and the tree shuddered in protest. Corahan slumped to his knees, pressing his hands against the lushly carpeted forest floor.

He had no time to react when he heard a slight hiss and the thump of a young brown-and-black snake with a yellow-tipped tail as it fell from a tree branch above.

Corahan's heart thundered in his chest as he slowly straightened his torso, immediately recognizing the deadly markings. A terciopelo. There was no time to escape. The snake would not coil in warning, nor would it flee. It would bite him, and he would die.

He wanted to run but knew it was pointless. The snake's striking movements would be faster than his standing to his feet.

A strange sense of ease overtook him. His breathing slowed, his heart calmed. *So this is how it will end,* he thought with an air of detachment. Not on a battlefield, not from a conspiracy, not at the end of Pachus's sword. Here, by a snake that would kill him because Corahan had been fool enough to disturb the wrong tree.

He would have some time to live before the venom caused swelling, bruising, and blistering. Then the pain would become unbearable, and shortly thereafter his life would end. He had seen it happen before. He might have had a chance with an adult— they would bite and slip away. Unfortunately, a young terciopelo like this would sink its inch-long fangs in and not let go, emptying all of its venom into his body. Corahan hoped it would be over soon.

The snake did not seem to be accommodating him. The whispered hiss cut Corahan to his core and caused his entire being to tense. The terciopelo flicked its forked tongue in and out as it inched toward him. Then it smoothly climbed into Corahan's lap.

Corahan briefly wondered if snakes played games the way men did before they killed their prey. He considered provoking the snake to have it over but held still.

The snake continued its exploration, shifting its triangular head back and forth, hissing in soft delight as it moved across Corahan in what seemed like small, reptilian caresses.

Seconds stretched into what felt like hours as Corahan waited for the fate nature had dealt him.

And then the snake was gone. Corahan felt it slide from his body and slip away into the sheltering foliage. He sat there dumb-founded, trying to make sense of it.

Corahan wasted no time getting up. He left his sword in the tree, not willing to risk disturbing any other creature living in its boughs. He pointed himself in the direction of the city.

His life had been spared. The snake had spared him. There could be no logic or reason to it, he decided. The snake had slith-ered away, granting him his life. In one second Corahan had been prepared to die, and in the next, he was willing to do whatever it would take to live.

Corahan knew then that he would do anything to save his own life. Including taking someone else's.

Moroni could not give him a future. But Pachus could.

He knew what had to be done. And he had until sunset to accomplish it.

As Corahan searched for an animal trail that would lead him back to Zarahemla, he had the sudden and uneasy awareness that perhaps the snake had left him alone because it had recognized a kindred spirit.

* * *

"Please," Kiah begged her aunt. "Don't make me go over the story again." Kiah had curled up on the padded bench facing the wall, but she found no peace. Helaman had instructed her to go home, telling her that he would go to the prison to see what could be done. He reminded Kiah that the judicial courts were closed in time of war, so there would be no immediate trial. Jeran could be locked up for a long time unless they figured out a way to free him. Helaman had thought it would be easier for him to gain access and information on his own.

She'd had to go home and explain the bruise on her face. Kiah had hoped that perhaps if the servants were still in the house, there would be no confrontation and no scene, since none of the women would want such private business aired in public. Unfortunately, her family's few servants had left for the night to attend to their evening meal. The whole, long tale had to be spilled out to her sister-in-law and aunt.

Kiah knew how angry Shabana and Linoah were. Linoah covered it better, and Kiah felt her concern. From the corner of her eye, Kiah watched Shabana perfunctorily perform her nightly task of putting corn ears into a lime-and-water solution to separate the kernels from the cob. Then Shabana slammed a covered clay pot in the midst of the three-stone hearth to start the vegetable-and-quail stew cooking.

Shabana went into the courtyard with a bowl of water, angrily sprinkling it onto the ground instead of lightly shaking it there. Her two sons chased one of their pet ducks, kicking up the dirt that their mother was trying to wet down. She didn't seem to care and muttered unintelligible words under her breath.

"Did this boy ever . . ." Linoah let the words trail off. Kiah violently shook her head. "Never. He treated me with nothing but respect." Her fingers flittered up to the necklace he had given her, finding strength from it. "He is my friend."

"Friend," Shabana snorted. "This is what we get for letting you run wild. Disgrace and dishonor on the whole family." Shabana flung another handful of water onto the courtyard, just missing her youngest child. "When your father gets back . . ."

"When my father gets back," Kiah retorted, "he will fix all of this. He would never let Jeran sit in that prison. He has done nothing wrong. Corahan wants to punish me. That's the only reason he's there."

Shabana stopped her water throwing and faced Kiah. "And why would Corahan want to punish you?"

"It's too complicated," Kiah groaned. "I don't want to talk about it anymore. I just want to sleep."

From the corner of her eye Kiah saw Shabana slam the hollowed-out gourd that she used as a bowl onto a nearby table. She squared off toward Kiah, obviously ready for a fight. Thankfully, there was a call of greeting from the front entrance, and Shabana stalked away to answer it.

Linoah brushed the ends of Kiah's hair, but Kiah ignored the entreaty to roll over and look at her aunt.

"Are you all right?"

"I'm fine," Kiah said. "It will be all right. I know it will."

"Do you love him?"

That made Kiah turn around. Kiah looked at the sweet, kindly face of the woman who had been her mother after her own had died. A lump rose up in her throat, making it impossible for her to answer. Kiah's mind fluttered with confusion. Did she love Jeran? She knew what it was like to love a father, a brother, her nephews. But what did it mean to love a man the way Linoah meant? Kiah tried several times to speak, to work out her answer, but there were no words.

Then Kiah heard a soft sound, something akin to a muffled scream. The skin on the back of her neck turned cold as a flicker of apprehension shot through her. "Did you . . ."

Before Kiah could finish her sentence, Linoah stood to help the boys get the quacking duck back into its pen.

"Wait," Kiah whispered, tugging the hem of Linoah's tunic. "Do you hear that?"

"Hear what?" Linoah asked.

Kiah cocked her head to the side and concentrated. Linoah's eyebrows shot up in surprise when Kiah grabbed her short swords. "Get the boys. Go into the back. Don't come out until I call you."

She sprinted toward the front entrance and saw what she had feared. A short, hairy spider of a man had one hand over Shabana's mouth and an arm wrapped around her waist. Shabana had been emitting muffled screams, the sound that Kiah had heard and followed.

"What's this?" the man asked when Kiah moved through the shadowed hallway and stepped into the front foyer, the descending sun gleaming off her swords. The man's gaze fell on the weapons. He tightened his grip on Shabana and hissed, "You said there were no men . . ." Kiah stepped into the light, and the man visibly relaxed. "Bah. Just a woman."

"I may be just a woman," Kiah informed him, readying her weapons. "And there are no men here. But I will kill you just the same."

The man let out a harsh, grating chuckle. "Will you? I'd like to see you try."

"Let her go, and I'll be glad to." As she'd been taught, Kiah quickly assessed the situation. His emaciated frame suggested that he didn't possess a great deal of physical strength. Kiah held the advantage by having at least six inches on him. While he was taller than Shabana, he would be no match for Kiah.

Knowing the fight would end quickly and in her favor, Kiah experienced none of the fear she had with Corahan or Jeran. Thinking of Jeran made her heart twist apart, and Kiah's hands shook slightly. She hadn't been able to protect herself or Jeran from Corahan. But she could certainly protect her family from this man.

He smirked at her and pushed Shabana toward the hallway. Instead of running as Kiah had expected her to, Shabana moved against a pillar and waited.

Kiah bent her knees. She positioned her left foot forward and planted her right foot behind her as a base, shifting her weight to the back.

The spidery man crept slowly toward her, and Kiah held still, hoping to lure him into a false sense of security. "Come here, girl," he said, and Kiah could see that several of his teeth were missing. "I won't hurt you . . . much."

When the man reached for Kiah with his left hand, she flicked her sword out and nicked the inside of his hand. He pulled his left arm back, gasping in surprise. He lunged for her again with his right arm, and Kiah cut the palm of that hand, too. The man held his hands in front of him as if unbelieving of what he saw. He drew his own poorly made weapon and Kiah nearly laughed. The curved, dull hardwood sword would barely chop down maize. Her swords would cut it in half.

And the second he slashed toward her with it, that's exactly what Kiah did. She swung, crisscrossed her blades, and hit the sword from both sides. The man's sword split and landed with a pitiful clank on the floor. Kiah landed a superficial wound on the man's chest. The lecherous gleam in the man's eyes disappeared and was replaced by a look of pure terror as he stumbled backward.

"You have overstayed your welcome. I'm going to have to ask you to go," Kiah said with an easy smile. "And it is only because of my father's belief in the sanctity of life that I will not kill you—if you leave now, that is."

"This isn't over," the man told her, edging toward the front entrance and freedom.

"Yes, it is," Kiah told him lowly. "If I ever see you near this house, me, or my sister, I will kill you before you can lay one finger on us. And if I'm not here to do it, my father, Captain Moroni, will make sure of it."

If Kiah had thought the man looked scared before, he looked absolutely terrified now at the mention of Moroni. He ran until he gained the street and continued to run as quickly as his spindly legs would carry him.

Kiah stepped through the corbeled archway to watch him run and to make certain that he left. He ran all the way to the end of the street and then disappeared from her line of sight when he fled into someone's private fruit grove.

A strong medicinal scent hit Kiah's nose. Looking around her, Kiah spotted bags full of herbs against the front steps and wondered that she hadn't smelled them before. The man had left his goods behind. She saw that each bag had its name and properties written on it. Kiah picked up the bags and went back into the house. As she dropped them in the front foyer, she saw Shabana slide down the length of the column until she collapsed on the floor.

"He . . . he was some sort of merchant . . ." Shabana said in a shaky voice. Kiah could hear the bells at Shabana's wrists tinkle as Shabana shivered in fear. "He . . . he asked to see the man of the home . . . and I told him . . . I was so stupid." Shabana drew in several deep breaths. "He could have . . . he was going to . . . my boys!"

Shabana turned to find her children, and Kiah saw Linoah leading them out into the courtyard. Linoah carried a sword of her own, one that Kiah knew Linoah had retrieved from her father's armory. Linoah was trying to send the boys into the rooms at the back of the house, but they were clinging to her skirt.

"They're fine," Kiah reassured Shabana. She should have known that Linoah would never have stayed put.

Kiah noticed that Shabana held a large rock and gripped it so tightly her knuckles had gone white. "Here. Give that to me. You don't need it now. He's gone." Kiah managed to pry the rock free from Shabana's hand and tossed it aside.

"Are you all right?"

Shabana looked at Kiah with dazed, brown eyes. "Yes, I am. Because of you," she whispered as if she didn't believe it. "Why did you do that?"

"Do what? Save your life?"

Shabana nodded.

Kiah shook her head as if Shabana had asked something silly. "You may be annoying, but you are my sister. No matter what, we are family."

There was a pause as Shabana stared straight ahead with a dazed expression. "Would you really have killed that man?"

"To stop him from hurting us? Yes." Kiah wiped the blood off of her swords with a cloth that had rested on top of one of the man's herb bags. She dropped the rag back onto the bags when she finished.

"I'll go check on the boys and let Linoah know everything is fine," Kiah said. "I'll come back and clean up this mess in a little while. Stay here until you feel better."

Shabana started to say something, but Kiah stopped her. "Don't worry, that man won't be back. He's a coward."

"No," Shabana protested. "I wanted to . . . to say thank you."

Kiah knelt down, squeezing her sister-in-law's shoulders to provide some comfort, trying to infuse Shabana with some of her own strength. She surprised Shabana with a quirky smile. "Next time you're upset about the way I cook, you should think about today and remember that I might have some use after all."

* * *

Jeran heard a man at the top of the stairs say, "I'm here to administer to the prisoners." Jeran had noted the minimal security at the prison when Corahan's men brought him there. He had seen only two guards outside the front entrance and one guard at the base of the stairs. After all, the captives were bound hand and foot. And they had nowhere to go. Even if they managed to escape the prison, they would never make it through the city undetected, let alone survive the jungle that surrounded Zarahemla without weapons and provisions.

Jeran wondered if it was day or night. The prison had no windows. While inside these walls, it was perpetual night.

He tried to stay fully awake, to take in all of his surroundings so that he could plan an escape. There were four other prisoners incarcerated here, the ones whom the Nephites considered most valuable for bargaining. They were the sons of captains and chief captains. And now they had the heir of a king.

Jeran could just make out the soft light of a torch being carried down the stairs. The flame snapped and crackled, the smoke making the air gritty. The man holding the torch gave an order to the guard seated inside to retrieve some water. The guard scrambled up the stairs at the command.

Jeran peered through his badly swollen eyes to see someone that looked like Helaman, the man who had baptized him that afternoon. It seemed like a different lifetime, as if it had happened to someone else. He wondered if he was dreaming or if he'd finally become delirious. Jeran shifted in the dirt, trying to find a position that didn't make his body feel like it was on fire.

He realized he wasn't dreaming when he felt a cool, damp cloth being carefully sponged on his face.

"What—" Jeran croaked through cracked and bleeding lips, not understanding why someone would help.

"Forgive me," Helaman asked while trying to clean Jeran's face the best he could.

"Not . . . your . . . fault," Jeran managed in labored breaths. "Kiah."

"No. It's not Kiah's fault this happened. It's mine." While continuing his ministrations, Helaman recounted to Jeran all of the events of the day that had led to Jeran's present circumstances.

Despite the pain that flamed through his body, Jeran felt a sense of relief. He knew Helaman spoke the truth, that this had been a misunderstanding, a mistake. Much of the pain he felt had been not only from the beating, but from the belief in Kiah's betrayal. To find out that she had done nothing to hurt him, that his trust in her had not been misplaced as he'd feared . . . It made everything seem a bit better and brighter.

"Nothing to forgive," Jeran murmured before Helaman poured some clear, pure water into his dry mouth. Jeran tried to keep it down but let out a few barking coughs before Helaman gave him more water.

"It is my fault that you're suffering and that you're here." Helaman gestured to the darkness that surrounded them, held at bay only by the light from Helaman's torch.

"I've been through worse," Jeran grumbled as he struggled to get up to a sitting position with Helaman's help. "I'm a fast healer."

Jeran saw the look of confusion on Helaman's face. But Jeran was in no mood to explain his life history to the other man. "Do I look the way I feel?"

"Yes. But we're going to do what we can to get you out of here. I don't know how long it will take. The courts have been closed until the war is over. I'll have to find another way to reach the chief judge and get him to release you."

Jeran knew such a thing would never happen. His family—their greed, their ambition, their bloodthirstiness—was the reason for the recent wars. People weren't usually prone to reason or justice when faced with a chance to exact some revenge. He gave Helaman a weak smile and thanked him.

After Helaman had cleaned Jeran as much as possible, he called again to the inner guard and instructed that a healer be immediately brought to help Jeran. When the healer arrived, Helaman said his farewells to Jeran, promising to visit him the next day.

"One thing," Jeran said in a low voice. "Please. Don't let her see me like this."

Helaman grimaced when Jeran's body shuddered in pain as the healer applied a poultice. Large drops of sweat mingled with the healer's herbal treatments to Jeran's open and festering wounds.

"I won't. I'll be back soon. Rest."

It barely registered with Jeran when Helaman left the prison, the pain from the healing too excruciating to let his mind function right.

Jeran realized that he must have blacked out, because when he awoke, the healer was gone. He flexed his muscles, shifting his body, and found that already the pain had lessened. He could only hope that Helaman would be able to keep both of his promises—to get him out of this prison and to keep Kiah from seeing him.

With nothing else to occupy him, Jeran had the time to explore the feelings for Kiah that nagged at him, even though he tried to suppress them. It did him no good to try to deny what he felt for her. He knew why it was so important to him that she stay away and not see him in this condition. He knew why he had risked so much to spend time with her despite his mission in coming to Zarahemla. He also knew that if anyone could make him break his oath, it would be Kiah. And that made her dangerous to him.

Jeran let his eyelids drift shut, welcoming the healing sleep that waited for him. A smile twitched his chapped lips. It shouldn't be too hard to stay away from Kiah while he remained in prison. These feelings he had would just have to run their course. He would get out, and Kiah would marry another and have the life she deserved.

Even as he thought it, in that last moment between sleep and waking, Jeran knew that his feelings would never change. He knew as strongly as he had ever known anything in his life that he would never stop loving Kiah.

* * *

Corahan strode with purpose through the waning crowds in the marketplace as the vendors closed for the night. He wondered if Pachus's men had already begun their search for him, if he would be allowed to complete his mission before they captured him.

He knew Ontium would be manning a tower near the west side of the city at this time of night, checking on the guards, looking for any sign of enemy armies outside of Zarahemla. Corahan laughed to himself as he thought how ironic it was that Ontium focused on the outside, failing to look within the city for the revolution that would begin with his death.

In the dusk, Corahan was just another soldier, no different from the dozens that he walked past on his way to the wall. A slight breeze blew down from the mountains, but it did nothing to cool his feverish temperament. He hardly noticed the dull and muted conversations of soldiers at their posts as he continued with single-minded purpose. The air had a strange silver taste to it, as if he could feel the anticipation swirling around him like a living thing.

Finally, Corahan found his quarry. Just ahead, Ontium conversed with a man of inferior rank, giving him instructions. The tower was only a hand's width away from the city wall. Corahan waited, melting into the shadows. Ontium finished with his commands, and the soldier nodded and made his way down the gently sloping side of the earthen mound. Ontium turned to again observe the lands surrounding the city walls.

Ontium was finally alone. This was the moment—Ontium would die now, or Corahan would. When Corahan made a decision, he carried it through to the end. And he had made the decision that he wanted to live. Nothing would deter him. Having reconfirmed his choice, and with his heart thumping wildly in his chest, Corahan walked silently toward Ontium.

Corahan walked as normally as possible, not wanting to alarm Ontium needlessly. His mind ran frantically over his plan, trying to make sure that he executed it perfectly.

"What is it?" Ontium asked without turning around. Corahan hesitated. He had to go through with it. *Him or me.* Corahan's mouth went dry, and then with a surge he seized on Ontium's fatal mistake—had Ontium turned to face Corahan, he might have had a chance.

Ontium only had time to make a slight gurgling noise as Corahan plunged Pachus's dagger into Ontium's back. He pulled it out and heaved Ontium over the city wall. Given the height of the tower and the subsequent force of his body's impact on the sharp, almost razorlike surface of the rocks below, Ontium's knife wound was certain to be lost among the other wounds that resulted from the fall. Corahan leaped from the wooden platform and ran down the hillside.

What have I done?

SEVEN

The guards in the watchtowers along the wall were looking toward the wilderness for an invasion. No one's attention would be focused where Ontium fell. Corahan counted on their being distracted.

His breath sounded so loud that he was sure he would wake half the city with it. Corahan gained the shadows and willed himself to calm down, trying to regulate his breathing. He skulked through the darkness, avoiding every person he saw. He walked into the city and away from the wall.

What have I done?

No alarm had been sounded. No one had seen him commit his crime.

Corahan wrapped the knife in the cloth he had brought with him for this purpose. He stuck the dagger into the back of his belt, where it would be safely hidden. His cloak would cover the bulge from any prying eyes.

It had to be done. There was no helping it. No undoing it, not even if he wanted to. Death was always permanent. Corahan swallowed the taste of bile and pressed the back of his hand to his mouth. He closed his eyes. Pachus had made a murderer of him.

Corahan forced his thoughts away from Ontium. He locked the incident in a tiny part of his mind and pressed it down. He wouldn't think on it anymore. It would do him no good to dwell on it. His self-preservation instincts kicked in. Corahan had to make certain that no one suspected him. He had to take charge of this situation so that the blame would not be pointed toward him.

He waited for twenty minutes and made a show of walking back toward the tower. Corahan called out to several soldiers, giving them meaningless assignments. He called a nearby soldier and asked where he could find Ontium.

Corahan's throat constricted, and he desperately hoped that the soldier couldn't see his distress. The soldier told Corahan that Ontium would be at the apex of one of the towers. Corahan ordered the soldier to accompany him, and when they saw that Ontium was not atop any of the nearby towers, Corahan told the soldier to begin searching for the captain. They walked in opposite directions speaking to each guard, asking for Ontium's whereabouts.

Corahan ordered a search, and since there had been accidents in the past, several soldiers climbed high towers and leaned over the side with torches to see if they could detect anyone outside of the wall. A guard finally located Ontium's body, a battered and bloody mess.

"Take some men outside the city and retrieve him. See if he's alive." Corahan hoped his voice didn't betray the fact that he absolutely knew Ontium was dead. "We need to bring him back in the city. If he's still alive, he needs to be tended to. If he isn't . . . I don't want the beasts to find him."

"Who was the last man to see Ontium alive?" Corahan questioned the small band of soldiers that had executed the search. A guard called out a name, and Corahan presumed it was the name of the man that he had seen speaking with Ontium before the attack. "Bring him here for questioning. We have to find out what happened."

"Should we alert the judges?" a different soldier asked.

Corahan's heart dropped at the prospect, and he struggled to gain control. He tried not to scowl at the man. "There is no need for that. This could have been nothing more than an accident. If we find that something is amiss, I will speak with Pahoran myself."

The soldiers scrambled to follow Corahan's dictates. Corahan would make certain to personally oversee the investigation where it would be determined that Ontium's death was an accident.

As Corahan stood there, still willing himself not to think of what he had done, a soldier barely out of boyhood approached him.

"Captain?"

He realized that the boy spoke to him. In the rush of carrying out Pachus's designs he had forgotten that with Ontium's death he was now in charge of the Zarahemla troops. *Captain.* A smile hovered at the end of his lips. He certainly liked the sound of that.

"Corahan?" the soldier tried again.

"Captain," Corahan corrected. "Captain Corahan."

* * *

Kiah waited until well after Shabana and Linoah had gone to bed to sneak out of the house. She'd had no word from Helaman and couldn't wait any longer. She had to know what had happened to Jeran.

When Kiah reached Helaman's house, she saw that his fires were still burning. Several soldiers stood outside his home, apparently waiting for something. She announced her presence at the door, and a male voice called for her to enter.

She walked into the house, and her eyes widened at the sight of several servants rushing back and forth packing bags with blankets, weapons, and rations. She rushed down the outer rim of the courtyard to find Helaman.

"Helaman?"

"In here," he called. Kiah went into a room where Helaman sat with men who were writing quickly on parchments.

"What's happening?" she asked.

Helaman finished his dictation and asked the man on his right to hand him the parchment. Helaman folded it up and handed it to Kiah. "Here. You're going to need this."

Before Kiah could ask again what was going on, Helaman told her, "I've received word from my father. He's asked me to join him and his stripling warriors in Manti and to bring as many kinsmen, weapons, and supplies as I can manage. The Lamanites have fled, but my father fears they may attack again soon. He wants to shore up his defenses. The southern cities have to be maintained. I'm leaving immediately. That epistle I just gave you is for Pahoran, to let him know the situation with Jeran. I will not have time to try to speak with him before I leave. I'm sorry. It's the best I can do right now."

"What about Corahan?" Kiah asked.

"I don't think him foolish enough to come back to Zarahemla, do you?" Helaman replied. "I think you're safe enough."

Kiah looked down at the paper in her hand and then back at Helaman. Helaman organized the men around him like the natural leader that he was. He gave instructions to load up the soldiers outside with the goods bound for Manti. As the soldiers began putting the straps of the packs around their foreheads, Kiah was struck with the strange sensation that this might be the last time she saw Helaman. A large lump formed in her throat, and she had a hard time pushing it down. "Please be careful."

Helaman stopped what he was doing to turn and smile at Kiah. "I will be."

He walked over to her, raising his right arm across his chest, and clasped Kiah's left shoulder. Kiah arched one eyebrow in surprise. Helaman bade her farewell in the manner of one warrior to another. She put her right arm across her chest and clasped his left shoulder in return.

"God be with you until we meet again," Helaman said.

"And with you."

And then Helaman and his men were gone. Kiah snapped into action. She would bring the letter to Pahoran immediately. She euphorically thought that Jeran might be released this very night.

She well knew where Pahoran lived, in the large complex housing his home and the judicial courts that faced the temple across the city's main plaza. The structure towered over her as she approached, and Kiah could see why Pahoran's family had celebrated after he had been reaffirmed by election as chief judge by the freemen of the city, despite the objections of the king-men. The building was magnificent.

Pahoran's home was as lit up as Helaman's had been. She could hear a crowd of voices speaking that sounded at once like a pack of peccaries. "Hello?" she called out.

A tall, gangly scribe came to the doorway and pushed aside the door curtain, jotting something on a small piece of parchment. "Yes?"

"I have an epistle here for Judge Pahoran. It is imperative that he read it now."

The scribe reached for the parchment without taking his eyes off his own document. "I will take it."

"You don't understand," Kiah said, trying to keep her frustration in check. "This needs to be taken to him immediately. It can't wait until morning. He has to see this right now."

The man straightened up as if Kiah had insulted him and nipped the epistle from her fingers. "Judge Pahoran is in a meeting, as you can hear, on matters of national importance. I will take your little letter and pass it along. He is not to be disturbed."

Kiah started through the door, but two guards whom she had disregarded stepped in front of her. The man began walking away. She usually hated using her father's name, but she was now going to do it for the second time that day. "Please, I'm Captain Moroni's daughter . . ."

It did her no good. "I'm sure you are. Good night." Kiah saw the man drop her parchment into a basket piled up with letters before the curtain was secured back onto the hooks at the four corners of the doorway.

She wanted to kick something. Preferably that annoying, condescending scribe. Kiah turned on her heel and headed back out to the street. Who knew how long it would take Pahoran to see her letter? Or if he would see it at all? Kiah let out a long, exasperated sigh. She would have to have faith that Pahoran would read it and release Jeran soon.

Kiah suddenly felt very tired and overwhelmed. Maybe she should go home and write a letter to her father. She had to admit that wouldn't do any good either. He obviously had more pressing problems to deal with. She wished she had someone who could tell her how to fix this. She leaned against the white stone of Pahoran's home, the full moon turning it into a soft, vibrant silver. Crickets chirped their insect melodies, and Kiah let the familiarity of her world soothe her.

She pushed away from the wall and turned toward the prison on the other side of the temple. She might not be able to get Jeran out, but there was no reason she couldn't get in.

Kiah brushed away the thought that Jeran might still believe that she had led him into a trap. She would deal with that when she saw him. There had to be a way to convince Jeran that she'd had nothing to do with Corahan's actions.

Her one hope when she arrived at the prison was that the men on duty would know her. She was familiar and friendly with a large number of Nephite soldiers from training with them on the practice fields.

Kiah wanted to clap with joy when she recognized Giddion standing guard at the entrance. She called out a greeting to him, and he returned it.

"What are you doing here this late at night?" Giddion asked her while the other guard eyed her suspiciously.

"I was hoping that I might be able to speak with one of the prisoners." Kiah gave him what she hoped was a winning smile.

"Kiah, you know that isn't allowed. Your father's rules, I might add."

"Giddion, please trust me. My father would break his rule in this instance. It's really important."

Giddion's mouth twisted up as if he were uncomfortable with the situation. "I don't know, Kiah . . ."

"Please," she softly begged.

Something in her voice must have won him over. "Give me your weapons." Kiah handed them over as fast as she could. "Five minutes," he told her and gestured toward the stairs leading down into the prison. While she went down the steps, Giddion called to the inner guard, asking him to come outside. She was grateful to Giddion for allowing her to speak with Jeran in private. She brushed past the guard as he ascended the steps. When she got to the foot of the stairs, she reached up for the torch that hung on the wall. If there were prisoners in the room, she couldn't see them.

"Jeran?" she called out, walking into the darkness.

Her heart exploded in fear when a figure jumped threateningly in front of her. She reached for her sword with her free hand before she realized she didn't have it. She put both hands on the torch, ready to wield it like a club.

"What do you want?" the man growled. He looked menacing—he must have had a shaved head once, but now his hair grew back in scraggly clumps. A shell nose plug reflected Kiah's light back at her. A number of welts, bruises, and scars covered his body.

"I want to speak with Jeran," Kiah answered, not sure what she should do. It was then that she realized the man was bound at his ankles and wrists and could do little more than slam into her. She relaxed.

"What business do you have with the prince?" the man demanded.

"Not 'the prince,' just Jeran. It's all right, Lamonti. She's a friend."

Kiah's stomach did a funny flip when she heard the rich timbre of Jeran's voice. She began walking toward the sound.

"No, stop," Jeran ordered.

Kiah frowned at the darkness. Why would Jeran say she was a friend but not let her come any closer?

"You heard the prince. Stay where you are."

She turned toward the man Jeran called Lamonti. "Who are you?"

The man lifted his chest. "I am Lamonti, son of Zamir, captain of ten thousand. My father served the true Lamanite king, and I serve the prince."

"Bodyguards in prison?" Kiah asked the darkness.

"One of the many benefits," Jeran dryly replied. He went silent for a few moments and then asked, "Why are you here?"

Why was she there? Wasn't it completely obvious? "I'm here to see you. To make sure that you're all right."

"I'm fine."

Kiah finally realized what was wrong—she heard a slight and unfamiliar raspy sound at the edge of Jeran's voice. She pushed past Lamonti and walked forward until she found Jeran. She gasped and dropped the torch. She bent down to pick it back up and moved across the dirt until she was sitting directly in front of Jeran. He was propped up in the corner with his hands tied behind him, his bound ankles tucked underneath him. She felt like someone had punched her in the stomach. Jeran's body was covered in bruises and cuts. Kiah wanted to reach out to soothe him but realized that her touch would probably make him feel worse.

"Who did that to you?" Jeran asked her with a seething fury in his voice that she'd never heard from him before. Kiah must have looked confused because Jeran clarified. "That bruise on your face."

Kiah's free hand flew up to touch the forgotten bruise, the one that now seemed so insignificant, considering the ones that covered Jeran's entire body.

"Did Corahan hit you?"

She nodded. Jeran let out a litany of angry words that was breathtaking in its intensity.

"I'll be fine. You're the one who needs help," Kiah reminded him. "Did Corahan beat you?"

"He didn't do it himself. He had his men do it for him."

"I feel so useless," Kiah said. "I wish there was something I could do to make you feel better."

Jeran avoided her gaze. "Being near you makes me feel better."

Kiah became aware of the Lamanite prisoners who watched them just beyond the range of her torch's light, and she felt self-conscious.

"Lamonti is the only one who speaks your language," Jeran said, as if he could sense her uneasiness.

"I was trained in the palace alongside the prince," Lamonti announced, still hovering over them like a large bird of prey.

A palace and a prince. Kiah still had a hard time digesting the fact that Jeran was a prince, the heir to a throne—a throne belonging to those who would kill her family, her father, all her kinsmen.

"Are you in pain?" she finally asked, wanting to move her thoughts from their current course.

"Only when I smile," Jeran told her, a slight smile playing at the corners of his mouth.

She wanted to roll her eyes. Only Jeran could joke in a situation like this. His teasing reminded her of their time together earlier that day by the river.

"I want you to know that I had nothing to do with what happened today with Corahan," Kiah told him, but Jeran cut her off.

"I . . . I know you didn't help him. You don't have to explain. Helaman told me."

Helaman had been to see Jeran? Helaman should have told her what condition Jeran was in. Kiah sat in the silence, letting the darkness envelop them. She tried to find the right words to say, wanted to tell him how sorry she was. But she saw in his eyes that he already understood without her saying anything at all. Kiah studied Jeran in the torchlight. She saw that he still wore the baptismal tunic she had made for him, but it was torn and stained with dirt and blood. Her gaze traveled over to his right arm, and she stopped at the tattoo of Amalickiah.

"Amalickiah swore to drink my father's blood," she blurted out.

"Your father's?" Jeran asked sharply. "Wait. Is Moroni your father?"

When Kiah nodded yes, Jeran started to laugh softly.

"Why are you laughing?" she demanded.

"I came here to find your father. To seek his help. I was so busy spending time with you that I didn't get to speak with him before he left. If I'd known from the beginning . . ."

"None of this would have happened," Kiah finished. Not only the bad things, but the good things too. It sounded like he wished that he hadn't spent time with her. Her shoulders fell inward.

"I don't regret any of it, Kiah," Jeran told her as if he could read her mind. "I wouldn't trade what we've shared for anything. But why didn't you tell me?"

"You didn't exactly tell me about Amalickiah," Kiah countered. "I didn't know if I could trust you."

"I understand about not trusting people," Jeran said with a tone that made Kiah imagine that he was speaking about something else. "I think we should make a pact to start trusting each other from now on by being totally honest."

"Agreed," Kiah said. Some strange, new feeling surged through her. She felt in that moment a deep and inexplicable bond with Jeran, one that she had never shared with any other person, not even her father. It was like she had been homesick for years and hadn't realized it until she'd met Jeran. When she was with him, she felt like she had finally come home, as if being with him was where she belonged. Even in this awful prison.

She reached out to push a lock of hair from Jeran's forehead when there was a loud crash outside. Kiah's head snapped up to look toward the stairs. Giddion would have called for her. Something was wrong.

"Someone's coming," Jeran whispered. "Put out the torch."

Jeran gave directions to the other Lamanites in their native tongue. She caught one of the words. Blankets. Jeran directed Kiah to where the Lamanites were crawling along the floor to gather their blankets together. Kiah retrieved the blankets from the Lamanite prisoners. She stamped the torch out with her foot and headed to the corner opposite of where Jeran sat, bumping clumsily into the stone wall twice. The blankets reeked of sweat and urine, but she threw them over herself and curled up into a ball.

"Where's the light?"

Kiah had to fight back a wave of nausea. Corahan. She would recognize his voice anywhere. He had returned to Zarahemla! If he found her here . . .

Even through the blankets Kiah could tell when a torch had been brought into the room. She wished she were invisible.

"Well, well. What do we have here?" Corahan asked.

EIGHT

Corahan knows. He knows, Kiah thought.

Kiah's whole body tensed, preparing for a fight.

His steps moved away from her and toward Jeran. Her corner was plunged back into darkness as Corahan approached the crouching Lamanites. As quietly as she could, Kiah shifted the blankets until she found a hole that would allow her to see what was happening.

"I understand you had a visitor today," Corahan sneered, staring down at Jeran. Jeran returned his gaze, unafraid.

Kiah, however, felt an overwhelming anxiety. Corahan knew she was here, knew she had come to see Jeran. He was toying with them both. Kiah was defenseless, as were the Lamanite prisoners. Corahan would be able to do anything he wished to all of them. The fear deadened her limbs, and she had to force her mind to relax, to pay attention and figure out how to deal with Corahan and his guards.

Corahan seemed to be waiting for Jeran to speak, and when he didn't, Corahan raised his hand to hit him. Lamonti jumped up, pushing himself in front of Jeran. Obviously displeased with Lamonti's actions, Corahan balled up his fist and struck Lamonti in the face. Kiah put her hand over her mouth to keep from crying out.

She heard Lamonti grunt as he collapsed against the floor. A second later Lamonti spit out the tooth that Corahan had hit loose. He strained to get up into a kneeling position.

"I will kill you for what you have done," Lamonti stated in a low, matter-of-fact tone.

"Threatening me?" Corahan jeered.

"Promising you."

Corahan folded his arms across his chest and grinned. "You might find that hard to accomplish while you are in here and I am out there."

"It will not always be this way," Lamonti told him.

"It will be this way, or you will be dead," Corahan said. "Things have changed in Zarahemla. I am the captain of the city now."

What had happened to Captain Ontium? The blackness of the prison seemed suffocating, and Kiah's frustration mounted. How had Corahan come to be in charge of Zarahemla? Kiah had thought he would not dare to return to the city after he'd hit her. She had clearly underestimated him. She could not make that mistake again.

"Your judges do not give you the power to rule the city," Lamonti scoffed.

Corahan grinned again, kneeling down until he was eye level with the man. "You're right. *They* don't."

Kiah tried to make sense of what Corahan was saying but couldn't. There was an obvious insinuation in his tone. If the judges did not give him power, was he saying another did? Who?

"It does not matter," Lamonti told him. "I swear by the Great Spirit that I will escape this prison, and I will not rest until I find you."

Corahan let out a laugh. "You might want to reconsider such a serious vow. I know how you Lamanites are about making oaths. I would hate to be responsible for you breaking one." He stood up and kicked Lamonti in the chest, slamming him backward.

"Where were we, Your Highness?" Corahan asked as he walked back over to Jeran. "Ah, yes. Your visit with the priest. Was he coming to check on his newest convert? How is your eternal soul?" Corahan mocked Jeran and his baptism. Kiah let out a breath she didn't know she was holding in. Corahan didn't know she was there. Corahan had been talking about Helaman visiting Jeran.

Jeran still said nothing.

Corahan studied Jeran. "You don't have anything to say for yourself? That's fine. We will continue this discussion another day." Corahan lowered his torch to better see Jeran. "And then you will explain to me why you have the mark of Amalickiah on your arm."

"No," Jeran finally said.

"No?" Corahan said. "I don't think I like your answer." He shrugged. "No matter. You can say no now, but you will say yes when I bring Kiah here and torture her until you give me the answers I want."

Kiah's throat clamped shut at the image. Jeran made as if to stand, but Corahan pushed him back down, laughing. "I thought you might be persuaded."

"Sleep while you can," Corahan told the prisoners. "You have been treated too well. I plan on rectifying that situation."

Corahan spun on his heel and left with the guards. Kiah waited for what felt like hours, not daring to come out from underneath her blankets. Her mind raced over what Corahan had said, mixed with thoughts of Jeran and memories of that day as she tried to puzzle it out. She wondered if they would be in this position now if earlier that afternoon Jeran had tried to resist his captors. She started to turn over to ease the ache in her shoulder but went still at the sound of feet on the stairs.

"Kiah?" Giddion called out in a loud whisper. "He's gone. You need to go. Hurry."

Kiah threw the blankets off. "Coming." Her eyes adjusted to the dim gloom with the help of the faint light from Giddion's torch. She scampered back over to Jeran.

"I will find a way to get you out," Kiah said while checking over her shoulder to make sure that Giddion stayed at the stairs.

"Helaman will take care of it. I want you to leave Zarahemla and get away from Corahan," Jeran told her.

She turned back to look at Jeran and shook her head. "Helaman is gone. He was called away today to fight. There is only me. I can deal with Corahan. You have to trust me."

Jeran looked at her for a long moment then said, "I trust you."

Kiah began to stand up and then hesitated. "Before I go . . . earlier today, why didn't you help me fight our way out of this? I was going for your weapons. Together we could have defeated Corahan and those guards, and then you wouldn't be here."

"I couldn't."

"Why?"

"Because I would have killed someone."

Corahan being dead didn't seem like a particularly bad notion to Kiah. "And?"

"And I made an oath," Jeran said, turning slightly away from her. His tone indicated that the matter was finished.

"Kiah, hurry!" Giddion urged. With no time for a proper good-bye, Kiah took one last look at Jeran and then fled into the darkness.

* * *

Corahan resisted the urge to fidget, holding himself still against one of the pillars surrounding the courtyard while Pachus, clad in a blue-green tunic with silver stitching, chatted with a group of noblemen. Corahan had been waiting for nearly an hour while Pachus lectured his guests. Corahan could make out bits and pieces of the conversation here and there but was too far away to get the majority of it. He knew, however, that Pachus was carrying out his plan to turn the people of Zarahemla against Captain Moroni, Pahoran, and all freemen.

Pachus posed a striking contrast to the lesser judges who hung on his every word. The lower judges were fat, useless men caught up in idle and luxurious lifestyles. Pachus, on the other hand, was physically fit and more than capable of combat. The people of Zarahemla would only support a king that could stand at the head of the army and fight alongside his men. Anyone without that kind of prowess and ability was considered weak and would be permanently removed from ruling.

In addition, not one of these judges had even a fraction of Pachus's ambition. As an ambitious man himself, Corahan had to admire the same trait in others. Technically, Pachus had no claim on the kingship. The Mulekites had no king when the Nephites arrived and joined them. The land of Zarahemla was filled with the descendents of the last Nephite kings, Benjamin and Mosiah. Their claim would be stronger and truer than Pachus's. Pachus overcame this shortcoming through flattery, treachery, charm, greed, manipulation, and sheer force of will.

Corahan shifted his weight and tried not to sigh. He knew that Pachus let him stand under the blistering sun deliberately. Pachus was reminding Corahan who was in control.

Had Corahan possessed the ability to care about anyone beside himself, he would have been impressed with the cleverness of Pachus's actions, Pachus's ability to exert his authority in any situation. Corahan had found that he craved such power. He liked the way his soldiers lined up and followed all of his orders without hesitation, liked knowing that he now had no commanding officer to answer to. He saw the look of respect in the soldiers' eyes. He was important. He mattered. He was someone.

Pachus's dismissive attitude toward him deflated his feeling of superiority, and it irritated him. He wanted to leave this house and get back to commanding his troops. And he wanted to collect on the reward that was promised him. Kiah.

He had placed two guards outside of her home last night, and they reported this morning that while other members of the family had come and gone, there had been no sign of Kiah. Either she was hiding inside, or she hadn't come home at all last night. Corahan grew tired of waiting.

Pachus's party finally began to break up, and the noblemen drifted as a group to leave Pachus's home. When the courtyard had cleared and quieted, Pachus motioned for his slaves to attend him.

The young girl that Corahan had previously seen dancing for Pachus rushed to his side, bringing him a drink. Pachus took a sip with one hand while using the other to run his fingers up and down the maiden's arm. Suddenly the bald slave that seemed to loathe everyone, including Corahan, materialized at Corahan's side. Corahan saw that the man carried a tray with various types of food and drink. The slave stared at Pachus and the girl. The girl sent a furtive glance in the slave's direction and then looked away. The older man gripped the tray so tightly the containers rattled. Corahan had only a moment to again wonder at the source of the slave's anger when Pachus called him over.

Pachus ambled over to his menagerie, expecting Corahan to follow. Well-kept cages of different sizes lined the south wall of the courtyard. Corahan saw and heard birds of all colors and shapes, coatimundi, snakes, an ocelot, lizards, a peccary, kinkajous, rabbits, some chattering monkeys, and even a young capybara that barked loudly.

Pachus opened one of the cages and selected a bright red bird with yellow and blue feathers across its wings. Corahan twisted his mouth to keep from laughing at the sight of Pachus whistling to his scarlet macaw as Pachus placed it on his shoulder. The bird gave Pachus's ear a playful nip and screeched its happiness. Pachus continued to ignore the humans around him and spoke softly to his macaw. He motioned that the slave girl should leave. She bowed at the waist and disappeared.

Corahan stood at what he hoped was a respectful distance while Pachus continued chatting with his bird.

"You have something to tell me?" Pachus finally asked, not bothering to look at Corahan while he fed his animals with the food that the bald slave brought to him.

Corahan tried not to stare at the bird that moved back and forth across Pachus's shoulder. He removed his wrapped dagger, the white cloth turned brown from Ontium's dried blood. He threw it at Pachus's feet. "Yes. It is done."

Pachus glanced down at the cloth bundle and then looked at Corahan. "I already know." Corahan blinked twice quickly, knowing he shouldn't be surprised but not able to help it.

"I have come to collect my reward," Corahan announced, feeling foolish as Pachus continued to talk to his macaw and feed him seeds.

"Reward?" Pachus looked puzzled. "You mean the girl?"

"Yes, the girl."

Pachus shook his head negatively. "There will be no time for that now. There is much to do. You must join the brotherhood. We have to coordinate the gathering of king-men into Zarahemla. Find out which soldiers will ally themselves with us and begin to send those loyal to the freemen away on assignments. Everything must be timed exactly and with great subtlety and care so that no one is made aware of our plan."

"But you said . . ."

"All in due time," Pachus said as he opened another cage and picked up a fluffy white-and-gray rabbit. The rabbit nestled down into Pachus's cradled arm as Pachus stroked its fur. "We must concern ourselves with things that hold more import. The girl is not going anywhere. When it is time, you may have her. We cannot risk alerting her family by abducting her. You will wait."

The command was clear. Corahan felt his jaw tense, then release, then tense up again. This was not their bargain. He resented Pachus talking down to him. But he knew he had no choice. He had fully and completely committed himself to Pachus's cause. Corahan had committed murder for him. There would be no turning back. He would have to do what he was told.

The red bird on Pachus's shoulder flapped its wings and squawked. It didn't appear to like the competition for its master's attention. It reached down and bit one of the rabbit's ears.

"Now, now," Pachus said. "That was not very nice. We must all learn to get along." Pachus thrust the rabbit toward his slave, expecting the man to catch the rabbit and put it back in its cage. The slave wasn't quick enough.

The rabbit fell hard onto the ground and skittered underneath a nearby cage. The slave started apologizing as Pachus coaxed the rabbit back out, soothed it, and returned it to its pen. Corahan saw the reason for the slave's fear and stammered apologies as Pachus reached up for a length of heavy, thorn-covered rope that hung on the wall. Without hesitation Pachus began whipping the slave across his back. The slave fell to the ground, and Pachus continued with the beating.

Corahan averted his eyes until the slave's cries had stopped. He looked up to see Pachus return the rope and direct the bird onto his finger, where Pachus began to pet it. Corahan felt the beating had been as much for his benefit as it was for the slave's. The warning was clear.

Pachus owned Corahan the same way he owned these animals. Corahan was not kept in a cage, but he could feel the strain of Pachus's leash against his throat. Corahan had become powerful, but only as powerful as Pachus allowed him to be.

"You may leave," Pachus said to Corahan as the slave huddled on the ground where he had fallen, rocking back and forth.

Corahan nodded, grateful for the reprieve.

"I would suggest not leaving the city. We have too much to do." Pachus opened up the cage and put the bird back. "If you were foolish enough to try to leave, to cross me, there are people who witnessed you murdering Ontium."

"And I suppose that even if I hadn't killed him, there would still be witnesses saying I did?"

Pachus gave Corahan a slight smile. "At last we are beginning to understand one another."

* * *

It worried Kiah that she could no longer see the guards. They had been in front of her home for two days and had just disappeared.

She knew no one would question the two guards' presence at the house—her father's military position guaranteed that the home was usually bursting with soldiers. Besides, by now Shabana had probably told an overly exaggerated tale of being attacked to all the women in nearby homes. The neighbors would surmise that Moroni or Moronihah had placed the guards themselves to protect their family.

It made her uneasy that she couldn't find the guards or Corahan. She had searched for them these last couple of days, to find out their location so that she could avoid them. She had wanted to enter the barracks but knew it would be too dangerous.

She did overhear that Captain Ontium had died in an accidental fall and that Corahan had taken control of the city's army. Knowing what she did of Corahan, Kiah suspected it had been no accident. With Corahan as captain, she thought it would be easier to find him, but it wasn't.

Her twin cousins, Joshua and Caleb, searched with her. The threesome had split up, and Kiah waited for them to return to the designated location. It was pointless to continue searching since the darkness of the night provided too many hiding spots.

Kiah had gone to Joshua and Caleb's home the night she left the prison. She didn't think that Corahan was aware of her mother's family. Her aunt welcomed her in and accepted her short and uninformative explanation of why she sought refuge. Kiah didn't think there was any reason to alarm them, and she let them believe what they wished. Anyone who knew Shabana wouldn't blame Kiah for wanting to leave her home for a few days.

She had alternated her time between watching the prison and watching her home. She had recruited Joshua and Caleb to help her. Both of them had received serious leg wounds during battle, and they had been brought back home to recover. They were nearly mended and ready to return to fight with her father. When Kiah confided the truth to them, they had agreed to help her. After weeks of recuperation, Joshua said they were ready for a little adventure.

Both Joshua and Caleb made better followers than leaders. Usually you just had to point them in the right direction and let them beat up whatever stood in their path.

There had been a flurry of activity and guards for two days, and then it abruptly stopped. Kiah couldn't decide if Corahan was now ignoring them, which she thought was unlikely, or if he was just being craftier.

A thought occurred to Kiah then that she hadn't considered before—what if the reason she couldn't find the soldiers was because they were inside the house? Surely Corahan wouldn't go so far as to hurt her family, would he? A picture of Corahan's guards torturing her nephews seared her mind. She froze in a moment of fear while her heart began to pound, and then Kiah jumped to her feet and started running for the house. While passing through an alley, Joshua and Caleb caught sight of her and started running too.

Aware that she now had assistance, Kiah headed for the entrance to her home.

Before she could climb the steps, Caleb grabbed her and pulled her to one side of the house.

"What are you doing?" he asked.

"What if the guards have been inside the whole time?" Kiah said.

A look passed between Joshua and Caleb, and Kiah knew they were communicating without words as they seemed able to do.

"If they're inside . . ." Joshua began, and Caleb finished with, "They'll be expecting you. We have to surprise them."

Kiah nodded her agreement. "You two go through the front. I'm going to climb up the south wall and drop into the courtyard."

The twins went around to the front while Kiah ran to the back of her large home. The wall at the south end was older and the stones were more jagged. She had no trouble finding hand- and footholds and scaled the wall quickly.

She made an opening in the thatch to get inside the steeply sloped roof. She ran along a sapodilla wood lintel that made up the bottom roof beams. When Kiah reached the opening of the court-yard, she nearly fell and had to fight to regain her balance. She found a space between the awnings that covered the courtyard, lowered herself down, let go, and dropped the rest of the way.

She had barely gathered her breath when a loud, piercing scream rent the night air.

Kiah ran in the direction of the scream and found Shabana standing in the middle of the courtyard as Joshua and Caleb approached. Kiah put her hand over Shabana's mouth to stop the sound.

"Shabana, it's me," Kiah whispered. "Stop! You'll wake the entire city."

She eased her hand off of Shabana's mouth. Shabana turned and hit Kiah in the arm. "Where have you been? Your aunt and I have been worried to death about you!"

Linoah, awoken by Shabana's scream, came into the courtyard, and Kiah ushered them into a nearby windowless room. She lit a pine splinter candle and explained what had happened to her over the last few days, and about her knowledge that Corahan wanted to hurt her and the suspicion that he had done something to Ontium. Linoah looked concerned, Shabana terrified.

This was not like Shabana. She had softened some toward Kiah immediately after the attack, and Kiah had thought it was out of guilt. Now she saw that it was out of Shabana's own fear. Shabana must have been more unsettled by everything than Kiah realized. Shabana was usually so in control, not afraid of anything. Now she looked like some sort of timid rabbit ready to flee.

"Something is going on, and I have to find out what," Kiah said after finishing her tale.

"No, not you," Shabana said, crossing her arms and gaining some of her old spirit back. "Your cousins can find out."

In a sense Shabana was right. They would cover more ground if more than just one of them searched for Corahan. Joshua and Caleb had also offered to try and speak to some of the soldiers here in Zarahemla, but they had agreed that it might cause more problems than solutions. Right now Kiah needed to know that her loved ones would be safe from that monster. Joshua and Caleb could do a better job of protecting them together than she could by herself. Besides, twins were supposed to be lucky. Her family could certainly use all the luck they could get.

"Joshua and Caleb could go," Kiah nodded. "But I thought it might be better if they stay here to protect you."

Linoah shook her head, smoothing out a wrinkle on her long, dark skirt. "I do not like this, Kiah. It's too dangerous. Joshua and Caleb should be with their own family."

"My father may be considered too old to fight, but he is not too old to protect his home if he needs to," Joshua disagreed. "I don't think that Corahan knows about them, which will keep them safe."

Caleb nodded. "Joshua and I will stay here and help. If we leave the house now, someone might discover our identity, and then we definitely would be putting our own family at risk if the situation is as bad as Kiah says."

Linoah turned to Kiah and tried again. "Then we should write to your father and brother."

Kiah walked over to her aunt and held the older woman's hand. "Something must be done. We don't know who to trust anymore. We could write a letter to them, but what if it was intercepted? It would put all of our lives in jeopardy. I think pretending ignorance is the best path for us. We continue on with our lives as if nothing has changed. And I will do what I can to discover what is happening." Kiah couldn't admit that she was concerned not only for her family, but also for Jeran. The thought of something happening to him made her feel like someone had kicked her in the stomach. She had to do what she could to ensure safety for all of them. And as she had told her family, she knew there was no one else to do it.

"Will you at least stay here tonight?" Linoah asked, tightening her grip on Kiah's hand.

"I will stay tonight," Kiah agreed. "But tomorrow I will find out what Corahan is up to."

NINE

Despite being tucked away in a shadow against a cool wall, Kiah reached up to wipe away the line of sweat forming at her brow. The hot and miserable day was made worse by all the clothing Kiah was wrapped up in. She didn't dare leave the house without some sort of disguise on. She covered her head in a turban like some married women did and wore ankle- and wrist-length clothing, in addition to the multicolored scarf tied at her waist and the shawl slung over her shoulders.

Three days had gone by, and despite a diligent search, Kiah had not been able to find Corahan. She had waited by the barracks, scouted out the walls and towers to catch a glimpse of him, and the result was always the same. Nothing. Part of her hoped that Corahan had simply fled the city, that he had been found out and chased away. But the realistic part of her knew that he was out there somewhere, biding his time before he would strike.

Today Kiah waited outside the prison. After another fruitless day of scouring the city and trying to get in to see Pahoran, where she was once again turned away by some low-level bureaucrat for being a "stupid woman" that dared try to waste the time of the great chief judge, she ended up where she always ended up. Back at the prison. Back to where Jeran was. Her hand absentmindedly outlined the shape of the silver sun on Jeran's necklace hidden underneath her shawl. She knew it was dangerous to be here, but she couldn't help it. Just to be near where Jeran was being held was enough.

Kiah snapped out of her reverie at the sight of the guards going down the stairs of the building. Something was happening. They emerged a few minutes later, leading the Lamanite prisoners, including Jeran, out. The bindings at their feet and wrists had been cut. Confused but resolved to know what was going on, Kiah started following them at a discreet distance.

The guards and prisoners exited Zarahemla via the causeway. Kiah pushed through the throng of people who were entering and leaving the city, determined to see where the prisoners were being taken. She didn't allow herself to think about what the guards' intentions were. She couldn't consider the possibility that they were being led out to be killed.

On the west side of the city, she saw a large number of Lamanites digging outside the wall. The unimportant Lamanite prisoners of war were kept in prisons in nearby villages. They were already hard at work digging the trench and reinforcing the earthen city walls. She knew her father had a policy of using prisoners for manual labor, and she felt a sense of relief wash through her. Jeran and his fellow prisoners were being led out to help the other Lamanites dig the trench.

But why were they creating the trench defense at Zarahemla in the first place? Maybe the war wasn't going well. Perhaps there had been word of the Lamanites planning to attack Zarahemla. It wouldn't do her any good to ask the guards. They were most likely just following orders. There would be one person who would know. Corahan.

Kiah watched as the Lamanite prisoners were handed tools and ordered to begin digging. She wanted to get closer, to talk to Jeran, to make sure he was all right. Her heart leaped with an anticipated sense of joy when she finally saw him. She allowed herself to take the sight of him in, to revel in the happiness she felt.

Some time later she noticed movement to the right of the prisoners where the guards and other Nephite men were standing. A group of women moved through the diggers. She saw that they carried skins with water, giving the thirsty men drinks.

Kiah tried to move as inconspicuously as possible to where the water was being handed out. She accepted several skins and moved to the Lamanite prisoners. This was almost too easy. None of the guards questioned her; none of them was even paying attention.

The soldiers had nothing to worry about with their prisoners—the Lamanites were far too conspicuous. Even if one of the Lamanites tried to flee, they would have to cross the open valley floor to gain the jungle and would pass every farmer working his field, every villager coming in or out of Zarahemla to trade, every man tending his flocks, and not one of them would hesitate to stop an escapee. Even if a prisoner somehow managed to make it to the jungle, survival would be unlikely for a man without a sword. Perhaps these guards had made the prisoners swear an oath that they would not escape, knowing the Lamanites did not break their word.

She moved through the prisoners, saying the Lamanite word for water. The men stopped what they were doing and greedily drank from the proffered bags. Jeran was at the end of the line and had not seen her yet. While the other prisoners drank, Kiah wondered what was wrong with her. Jeran was a prisoner. They were in a life or death situation. But all she could do was admire the way the muscles in Jeran's arms moved as he dug up dirt. She sucked in a sharp breath. He was so handsome, so tall, so . . . everything. It was more than just a physical attraction she felt. It was his honor, his inner strength, his intelligence, his sense of humor, his bravery, and now, his compassion. She saw another woman giving the water skin to Jeran, but he kept passing the water along to his Lamanite brethren instead of taking any for himself.

As if he sensed that he was being watched, Jeran turned. When he saw her, he knew her despite the disguise. He gave her one of his dazzling smiles, and his blue eyes danced. The expression on his face looked the way she felt, like he wanted to grab her and hold her. The sharp ache in her chest made her realize just how desperately she had missed him.

"What are you doing here?" he finally asked in a low whisper when she approached him. "If Corahan finds you . . ."

"I wanted to make sure you were all right."

"Much better. See?" Jeran held out his arms for inspection. The bruises and cuts that had marred his body and face were nearly gone. There was hardly any evidence of the abuse he had suffered. She used the opportunity to inspect as a chance to admire.

Jeran took a long, deep gulp from the water skin Kiah gave him. He handed it back, letting his fingers brush against hers, and Kiah nearly dropped the water. Jeran picked up his tool and began to dig again. "Where is Corahan?" he asked.

"I don't know," she confessed, keeping an eye on the guards and giving water to Lamanites near Jeran. "I haven't been able to find him. He put guards outside of our home and then took them away. It makes me worried. Like the quiet before the storm."

"He hasn't been back to the prison either. The guards have been almost . . . kind to us without him giving orders to the contrary," Jeran told her, flinging a pile of dirt to one side. "It doesn't make any sense. What would be keeping him away?"

* * *

Jeran's eyes scanned the horizon, wondering if Corahan stood somewhere nearby watching. He saw a large group of Nephites gathering not too far from where they worked. A man stood on a flat rock in the center of the group.

"Who is that?" Jeran asked, shading his eyes from the sun to see. Kiah shook her head to indicate that she didn't know.

The man's voice carried over to them on the hot winds that blew down from the mountains. While the workers dug, some soldiers talked with one another, a couple were even playing an impromptu game of *bul* with rocks and sticks. A few of the guards turned their gaze from the Lamanites to listen to the commanding voice.

"We have had enough of this war. Enough sacrifice of our sons, our brothers, our fathers, your husbands. It is a war we cannot win!

"The judges and captains have lied to you. They would have you believe that the Lamanites will kill you, rape your women, enslave your children. The Lamanites only want to reclaim what is theirs. If we have the right leader, a strong leader, a king, a treaty can be reached. Peace can be obtained."

"Pachus," Kiah said the word in a breathy whisper, as if she couldn't believe it.

"You know this man?" Jeran asked.

"Yes," Kiah said. "He was one of the king-men that tried to take over Zarahemla five years ago. He swore an oath of allegiance to my father." Kiah squeezed the water skin she held, and water seeped through the seams. Jeran sensed there was more than what she told him, but he didn't probe further.

"How do you know this?" a voice in the crowd challenged Pachus. "The Lamanites cannot be trusted." Several voices murmured their agreement.

"Ammoron, king of the Lamanites, has already sent word that a treaty is possible. We could continue to live our lives in peace as a free people." The wind shifted, and they could no longer hear Pachus.

"That's a lie." Jeran spat the words out in anger. "Ammoron would never let the Nephites live in peace or freedom."

Jeran's angry tone made a guard a stone's throw away turn toward them. The guard looked as if he might investigate, but then another soldier called him over to join them in their game. The soldier trotted away and left them virtually unguarded. It had been too close. Kiah couldn't risk being discovered. She should go. But Jeran wanted Kiah to stay. He had missed her. He knew she should leave, but perhaps there was a way . . .

"Here," Jeran said as he surveyed the land around them. He piled dirt on top of a small mound next to him. "If you hide on the other side of this we should be able to talk, and you can stay a while longer."

Kiah laid against the wall on the opposite side of the mound, which protected her from the eyes of the only guards who might be close enough to notice her. While some of the Lamanite prisoners gave them strange looks, no one said anything. Lamonti had been sure to pass the word that he would personally take care of anyone that interfered with the prince's activities. While he'd been embarrassed at the time, Jeran was now grateful for the privacy it afforded him and Kiah.

Jeran did not see any soldiers on her exposed side. Everyone on his side of the mound seemed to be interested in their own activities or in what Pachus had to say. Jeran was disappointed that he could no longer see her but was glad that he could at least be near her. That was something.

He heard the name *Ammoron* again from Pachus, and he slammed the top of his digger into the ground in frustration. "Ammoron. He would butcher innocents until his bloodlust was sated and then enslave every man, woman, and child within Zarahemla's walls."

"How do you know Ammoron?"

Jeran could hear the deliberate casualness in Kiah's tone. He looked down at his right arm, at the mark that told the world of his birthright. The tattooist had drawn the symbol and then made deep cuts along the lines so that the tattoo remained on his arm in scars and ink. He sighed, not wanting to share what Amalickiah and Ammoron had done to him, but knowing that he would have to tell Kiah the whole truth. She trusted him. It was time for him to totally trust her.

"He is my uncle."

"Your *uncle?*" Kiah didn't manage to hide the surprise in her voice from Jeran. He was glad for that pile of dirt between them. It kept him from having to face her.

"Amalickiah planned for years to take over Zarahemla, to displace the chief judge as a king with the help of his followers. But he was a very cunning man. Amalickiah always had a secondary plan in case the first one didn't succeed."

"Too bad he didn't have a secondary plan for getting killed in his sleep."

Jeran allowed himself a half smile at Kiah's dry wit and then continued. "Amalickiah wanted to make certain that if he failed with the Nephites, he would have the support of the Lamanites."

"How did he do that?"

Jeran looked up to see where the guards were focusing their attention. "He met my father outside of Zarahemla many years ago. My father was a traveling merchant who got closer to the city than he intended to. Amalickiah discovered who his family was and made overtures of friendship with him. Amalickiah brought him back to his house, and that is when my father met my mother, Adinah. She was Amalickiah and Ammoron's sister. Amalickiah gave her in marriage to my father, and my father brought her back to live in the city of Nephi with his family. His *royal* family." Jeran paused, coughing out some dirt that had flown into his mouth. "My father was the brother of the king of the Lamanites."

Kiah let out a soft gasp, but Jeran pushed on. Now that he had started, he wanted to finish it. "When Amalickiah and his followers fled Zarahemla after being defeated by your father, they came to the city of Nephi. My uncle, the king, welcomed them with open arms, treated them like his family, because that is what he considered them to be. Amalickiah bided his time, plotted against the king, assassinated him, and blamed it on the king's servants."

"Those servants came to my father for help and told him what had happened."

Jeran nodded, even though Kiah couldn't see him. "Amalickiah married the queen and took over as the king of the Lamanites. I didn't know any of this until I was much older. I was raised in the royal household because my father was always gone. And then my father didn't return from his travels. It was assumed that thieves had killed him. But now I think . . ."

"You think Amalickiah had him killed so that he wouldn't threaten to take the throne."

Jeran stopped in surprise that Kiah had finished his sentence. It was almost like she could see into his mind, his soul, and read what was there. Jeran had spent so many years hiding his true feelings and beliefs to keep himself safe, and now Kiah was acting as if it was nothing to know what he would say next.

"Y-yes," he stammered, not liking the feeling of being off balance. Kiah had this effect on him, and while at times he enjoyed it, at times like now he felt a little overwhelmed.

"Amalickiah had no children." Jeran took in a deep breath, trying to calm himself, as well as fighting down the sick feeling of retelling his story. "And Ammoron had only daughters by his wife and one illegitimate son, Tubaloth, by a concubine. I was the only legitimate male heir in the family."

"So Amalickiah made you his heir."

Jeran stopped shoveling and leaned against the long handle. He blinked at the dust swirling up in front of him and traveled to a different time and place in his mind. "Yes. And when Teancum killed Amalickiah in battle, the Lamanite elders called upon me to take my rightful place as king. Ammoron resisted. He thought he should be the next king, especially since I didn't want to be king. Do you know what happens when a new king is coronated? How many innocent people are slaughtered as sacrifices? But my desires did not matter. There were discussions, debates about what should take place. That was when my mother fell ill."

He attacked the dirt then, trying to rid himself of the emotions that welled up in him with the physical labor. He dug for several minutes before exhaustion took over. Looking to make certain that the guards were still more involved with Pachus's speech than with watching the prisoners, Jeran chanced ceasing his labors to finish with his account.

"Ammoron would do nothing while my mother lived. When she . . ." Jeran's voice caught, and he cleared his throat a few times before he continued. "When she died, his tolerance for me died with her. Ammoron took control of the army with lies and planned to kill me." Jeran's right hand reached up to feel the ends of his hair. "First he humiliated me by shaving my hair as if I were a slave and parading me in front of the court after tying me up and beating me. My aunt, the queen, did nothing. There was nothing she could do. Ammoron made a public announcement that he would kill me in the square the next day for the whole city's amusement.

"That night Lamonti's father, Zamir, smuggled me out of the palace. He was still loyal to my Lamanite uncle and my father, considering us to be the true kings of the Lamanite nation. He gave me weapons and supplies and took me outside the city. I tried to live in other Lamanite cities and villages, but Ammoron was furious at my escape, and he put a price on my head, a literal king's ransom, worth more if I were already dead. Within weeks every home in the Lamanite nation had a description of me and the lure of a great reward. Everywhere I went, people were suspicious. I couldn't live among my own people, and I certainly couldn't live among the Nephites. I lived in the jungle for a while, and then I decided to come here to find your father, having heard of his reputation as a righteous and fair man. I thought he might be able to help me, give me refuge." Jeran took a deep breath and wiped off the grime he could feel building up on his cheeks. "If I ever tried to live among the Lamanites again, I would immediately be killed."

There was a long silence before Kiah asked, "Why didn't you resist Ammoron? I've seen you fight. You're one of the most skilled warriors I've ever known."

"Ammoron knew of my oath. He knew I would not engage in a fight where I would kill him." Jeran's voice sounded as cracked as the baked earth beneath them.

Jeran felt Kiah's hesitation and knew what her next question would be. But he had shared enough of himself this day and could bear no more.

Pachus's voice boomed in the distance, startling them both. "Isn't it treason to speak the way he is?" Jeran asked.

"We have the freedom to speak as we want in Zarahemla. We are allowed to believe what we wish. Pachus has a right to hold different political views as long as he holds to the oath he made to the judges and my father." Jeran could tell that she was trying to sound unconcerned, but he knew her well enough to know that even as she spoke, she felt uneasy about Pachus and his speech. Her casualness was a cover for what she truly felt.

Jeran tried to resume digging. He found that he barely had the strength to do so. His confession had taken a physical and emotional toll on him. He looked back at Pachus and was struck by how much Pachus reminded him of Amalickiah and Ammoron. He sucked in his breath sharply at this impression. This was bad. Worse than anything Jeran could have imagined. This went far beyond Corahan and being imprisoned. Perhaps it was the effect from being raised near greedy, grasping, murderous men, but Jeran recognized a play for power when he saw it.

"Something isn't right here."

"You sense it too?" Kiah asked in a quiet voice.

He did not answer her. He couldn't. He didn't know what to say. Again his family had cast a long shadow across the land, corrupting everything in their path. Pachus stood there now because of what Amalickiah had done ten years ago. Jeran felt cursed, as if he could never truly put the past behind him. Amalickiah still reached from the grave to ruin lives.

"Do you think Pachus is trying to gather the king-men to take over Zarahemla?" Kiah asked with a strangled voice. "If he is, who would I tell? How would I get help? I don't think Judge Pahoran would see me without proof."

"I think it is entirely possible that the king-men are plotting to rise again. There must be someone else you can tell. They can convince your judge."

"I can do it." Jeran could hear the hurt pride in Kiah's voice. "Don't you think I can do it?"

Jeran sighed. "I know you can do it, Kiah. That's not the point. Corahan will hurt you if he can find you, and I can't stand the thought of . . ." Jeran broke off, his voice laden with fierce passion. Not caring about the guards or anyone else seeing them, Jeran stepped around the mound of dirt that kept Kiah hidden so that he could face her. He had to refrain from reaching out to try to shake some sense into her.

"I want you to leave the city tonight. Take your family and leave."

Kiah's golden eyes looked confused, hurt, then angry. "These are my people, my kin. I have to do what I can to help. It is my duty."

Jeran wanted to shout that her duty was to stay alive, that he didn't know how he could go on if something happened to her. He had to turn away from her, not wanting her to read from his expression what he felt. When had she so completely infiltrated his heart? Jeran struggled within himself until he felt calm enough to face her.

He saw the confusion in Kiah's eyes again, but he would not explain himself to her. *She deserves a better life,* he reminded himself, ignoring his heartache.

"I will find a way to make Pahoran listen to me. And when he does, I will get you out of prison, and we will find my father together. If the king-men are trying to take the city, he will be able to stop them." Kiah was so earnest, so endearingly sure that she could save them all. Jeran wanted to take her in his arms, hold her close, and never let go.

Instead he grabbed his tool and went back to his task, hoping none of the guards had noticed his momentary lapse of control, his inability to stay away from Kiah. Jeran knew there was no way he could stop her, knew there was nothing he could do to protect her, and it was driving him mad. He also knew what Corahan would do to Kiah if he caught her. There had been talk of what some Nephite soldiers did to Lamanite women when they took them as prisoners, and with no one here to control Corahan, Jeran was sure that Corahan would do worse to Kiah if he could.

Pachus had finished with his speech, and the group around him had started drifting away.

"You need to go," Jeran said in a low voice. "The guards will be watching us again." He heard Kiah stand and brush dirt from her clothes.

"I still have to find Corahan and see what he's doing," Kiah responded quietly.

Jeran squeezed his eyelids shut, trying to will away the images of Corahan capturing Kiah. How could he keep his oath to the Lord when a monster like Corahan existed? His shoulders sagged down since he knew there was no choice—the only way they had hope of surviving was to know what was happening so that they could fight against it. Kiah was right.

He knew her well enough to know that once she had set her mind on a goal, she wouldn't relent until she'd met it. If she felt there was something that needed to happen, Kiah would move heaven and earth to see it done. From what he had heard of Captain Moroni, it was a trait she'd inherited from her father. Short of getting a rope and tying her to him, there was no way to keep Kiah from looking for Corahan. Jeran would have to help her the best that he could within his limitations and pray that she would be kept safe.

"If Corahan is playing the fool, you can be sure that Pachus is playing his master," Jeran said as he looked in Pachus's direction. "I think that if you follow him, you will find Corahan." He heard Kiah moving behind him as if to go. She stopped and placed a hand on his bare upper arm, squeezing it softly. His skin flamed up like a rush of fire at her touch. Jeran stiffened his shoulders, unconsciously rebelling against a feeling that he knew he could not act on.

But a moment later she was gone, and only a whisper of skirts and a tingling of the skin on his shoulder indicated that she had been there at all.

TEN

It was easy enough to follow Pachus through the city—not only did the man have an entourage of six men, but each dressed like a brightly colored parrot in mating season, eager to display his plumage. Their vanity ensured that Kiah could hide easily and not lose the group. The sun had begun its descent into the horizon, and Kiah found herself shedding the outer layers of her disguise, dropping the shawl, turban, belt, outer cape. Her whole body sighed with relief. Kiah stealthily moved through large groups of people, hiding behind homes, trees, or pillars as the group traversed the city streets.

As it often did, her mind turned to Jeran. She knew that Jeran thought of her as a friend, that today he had proven he did trust her. She wondered if his feelings ran deeper, the way that her own did. After he had opened up to her today, Kiah realized that Linoah was right. Kiah did love him. And she didn't know what was worse, not being able to see him at all or seeing him but not being able to help him.

She had these moments when she caught Jeran looking at her with an expression in his eyes that she couldn't identify, and then he would turn away from her. She thought she had witnessed it again out at the trench. Today he had seemed so happy to see her, as happy as she was to see him. Did he feel something for her beyond friendship? Could he ever love her the way she loved him? Kiah's insecurities ate away at her until she reminded herself that there were more important issues to worry about.

Kiah had assumed that Pachus would be going to his home and felt mildly surprised when he did not turn into the wealthier part of Zarahemla but instead went to the barracks. Would he raise an insurrection right there in the middle of the city for all to see?

She soon discovered what Pachus went to the barracks for—Corahan. She flattened herself against the wall, expelling all the air in her chest in one short breath. She wanted to make certain that Corahan did not see her. Pachus most likely wouldn't know who she was, but Corahan certainly would.

Corahan spoke briefly to Pachus, and Pachus gestured that Corahan and a handful of soldiers should follow them. Kiah thought they would head to Pachus's house, but the growing crowd turned back toward the walkway that led out of the city. Corahan walked at the head of the large group alongside Pachus, and Corahan swaggered through the streets as if he owned them.

Her heart pounding in her ears, Kiah continued to follow them. They went through the market, bypassed the merchants entering and leaving Zarahemla, moved past the hunters returning with their prey, and continued on, passing the Lamanite prisoners still hard at work, through the ten-foot-high corn that had not yet been harvested, fruit orchards, the beekeepers and their singing hives, and past farmers burning their fields to keep the jungle encroachment at bay and to make way for new crops. The group stopped long enough to build portable fires of green wood used to ward off the ever-swarming, bloodthirsty insects. They continued southeast, toward the mountains and straight into the jungle.

Kiah continued to stay a good distance behind them as they headed into the dense foliage. They were easy enough to follow. They weren't even attempting to hide their passage. It was like tracking a stupid, lumbering animal, which in Corahan's case was more than apt. Kiah drew her short swords. Her father had taught her constant preparedness in the jungle—to let your guard down for even a second was to risk death.

Tiny rodents scampered out of her way as she moved carefully across the thick green growth under her feet. Not protected by the smoke of Pachus's men, Kiah swatted at the mosquitoes that landed to feast on her exposed flesh. She regretted having dropped her bulky costume earlier.

She strained to hear what the men were saying as they walked, but the general cacophony of the jungle, undisturbed by its human intruders, continued on as loud as ever. She could catch only snatches of their conversation above the howls of monkeys, the buzzing of insects, the caws of birds.

The happy thought occurred to her that the men might be abandoning Zarahemla. It would make everything much easier if Corahan had left the city behind for good. Perhaps the king-men had failed, and they were headed to Manti or the mountain passes in the south to get to the lands of the Lamanites.

Her smile faltered when she saw that the men were not leaving the city permanently, but had another destination in mind. They walked with purpose to a high, rocky outcropping. It looked as if a sword had cut the tall hill down the middle, leaving its innards exposed. The hill's craggy face was pocketed with openings that Kiah presumed led to caves. The men gathered in front of a sharply slit entrance that would only permit one person to pass at a time. Kiah crouched behind a large fern, peering between its long fronds as one man after the next disappeared into the fissure between the rocks. One of the men looked like a Lamanite, but he entered the wall too quickly for her to be sure.

Kiah waited, her ears straining to catch any predator sounds that might mean danger behind her, her eyes focused on the cave for the danger that waited in front of her. The last man passed through the entrance.

Pachus and Corahan did not leave any guards to protect the cave.

They were either foolish or arrogant, and Kiah guessed it was the latter. Such confidence worried her. They did not fear intruders. It indicated they most likely thought they were too clever and too powerful to concern themselves with someone discovering their plans.

The sun reached the horizon, and darkness began to descend. Kiah did not like the idea of being in the jungle at night. She wanted to find out now what Corahan's plans were. Keeping low to the ground, Kiah sprinted over to the opening. She leaned against the rocky limestone wall, gripping her swords tightly. She inhaled and exhaled slowly and then went inside the cave.

The ground in front of her was cut into rough, uneven steps. Torches in braces blazed along the extremely narrow cavern walls, making it easier to negotiate the stairs.

Kiah stepped carefully, afraid of dislodging even a small pebble and drawing attention to herself. Her leather sandals made no sound as she crept along the slimy steps that went deeper into the cave. The cave had a musty, earthy smell, and as she ventured further underground, she became aware of the sound of dripping water.

She was in a deep cavern that contained an underground spring. Kiah stopped short when she realized it. She knew what these were used for by unbelievers. The Lamanites considered them sacred, and she had heard brief snatches of discussions in her father's home of what happened in places like this one, of the ungodly ceremonies that took place here.

An icy, immobilizing fear gripped Kiah's heart, urging her to turn around and run back up the wet steps. But she pressed on, driven by her need to protect her loved ones and finally discover the truth.

Kiah touched her fingertips to the cold, damp limestone that formed the walls around her, using them to keep her balance as the stairs became steeper.

She was about to make another turn when she heard low, male voices. She stopped and crouched on the ground, her breathing harsh and erratic, sounding like two stones scraping against each other. Kiah was certain they would descend on her at any moment.

Her breathing slowed as she became aware that the voices were coming from the other side of the thin limestone wall. From her vantage point, Kiah saw a slit in the wall that she had missed while standing. It gave her a limited view into the room beyond.

Deep red limestone stalactites dripped water into the bluish green pool in the center of the cavern. Next to the stalactites, the pale white roots of trees had broken through the top of the cave and were worming their way down to the pool like eerie fingers. In the center of the thin crust that made up the cave's roof, a small circle of earth had collapsed into the water below, allowing a beam of fading sunlight to hit the water beneath it, making the room luminescent.

She could see men moving back and forth, none of them staying in front of the slit long enough for her to make them out. Then a conversation drifted up to where she sat. She heard Corahan's unmistakable voice, and after today's public spectacle, she recognized the other as belonging to Pachus.

"Is everything in place to take hold of the city tonight?" Pachus asked.

"Yes," Corahan replied. "On your command, you will become king of Zarahemla and the entire Nephite nation."

Kiah blinked rapidly, trying to fight off the pounding pain that suddenly took control of her head. It was as bad as she and Jeran had thought. The king-men were back. And they were planning to take control of Zarahemla.

And there was no one to stop them.

No one but Kiah.

"And has the letter to Ammoron been sent indicating that we wish an alliance?"

"The messenger is already on his way," Corahan told him. An alliance with the Lamanites? Then Pachus's speech today had been legitimate. He had to be mad. Jeran had given her a clear enough picture of what would happen when Ammoron gained control of Zarahemla, Pachus or no Pachus.

"What of the girl?" she heard Corahan ask, and knew with a drowning feeling that she was the girl in question. A heart-rattling shiver rushed from the base of her spine, traveling up and breaking out into a cold sweat at the nape of her neck.

"When we secure the city, she is yours."

"It will be quick," Corahan said. "I think we will encounter little resistance, particularly since you've cut off all communication in and out of Zarahemla. There will be no reinforcements coming for those who would fight."

They stopped talking to let Pachus laugh at his own cleverness. Kiah now had the answer for the unusual silence from her father and brother—Pachus's men had taken their incoming letters as well as the outgoing ones she and her family had written. Kiah felt a fervent gratitude that she'd been careful to say nothing incriminating in her letters.

There was a pause, and then Corahan asked, "What do you wish to do with the Lamanite prisoners?"

"Whatever you wish," Pachus said. "Kill them, return them to Ammoron as a sign of loyalty—it does not matter to me." They ceased speaking until Pachus said, "The sun has finally set. It is time to begin your induction ceremony."

The water dripped all around Kiah while her throat felt like it was closing in. Corahan was going to kill Jeran. Whether he did the task himself or returned him to the Lamanites, Jeran's life would be over. She couldn't let that happen. But she didn't know what to do to stop it.

A low rumbling sound worked its way up from the bottom of the cave, and for a second, Kiah feared an earthquake. She realized it was the dozen or so men in the cave, chanting words in unison in a language she did not recognize. She feared the words they spoke. Two of the men began a heavy, rhythmic banging of drums. The chanting continued, and Pachus stepped in Kiah's line of vision in front of a stone slab table. He had put on the mask of a screaming monkey, its teeth bared and mouth wide. He held his hands up and said words in the same language the men were chanting. It sounded ancient. Evil.

Pachus stopped and then, perhaps so that Corahan would understand, said, "This night of the full moon we welcome Corahan into our brotherhood. This is where we honor the god of this world, the god of wealth, the god of power. Our god."

Corahan went forward to where Pachus stood and then knelt at Pachus's feet. Someone else was dragged into view—the Lamanite whom Kiah had seen earlier. Someone had painted him blue. She didn't recognize him—he wasn't one of the prisoners that shared a cell with Jeran. She noticed that his hands were bound, his mouth gagged, and he struggled with great force against the two soldiers who pulled him to the table in front of Pachus, stretching him across it. Kiah saw Pachus pull a knife from his sheath.

What are they going to do to that Lamanite? she wondered. *Maybe they're going to . . .*

No. NO!

ELEVEN

Kiah didn't know how she got to the top of the steps, much less how she managed to do so without alerting all the men in the cavern to her presence. The narrow passageway seemed to be closing in on her. She pushed her way clear of the entrance and stumbled forward, closing her eyes as if that would somehow blot out the scene she had just witnessed.

Something grabbed at her neck. Kiah's eyes flew open, and she was too scared to even scream. They had found her. They would sacrifice her next.

She started to struggle, lashing out ineffectually with her swords to get free of whoever was holding her.

When Kiah turned to face her attacker, she had to fight back a hysterical sob. She was being attacked by a tree limb. Kiah dropped her weapons. She yanked herself free, scratching her neck in the process, and fell down onto the ground.

She knelt in a prostrate position, palms flat out to support her, her forehead touching the ground. Waves of nausea passed through her, and she began to dry heave.

Her terror made her hyperaware of her surroundings. The brightness of the full moon, the grunts of a scavenging tapir, the sweet pungent smell of nighttime orchids, the bugs that bit at her relentlessly and caused little red bumps to appear all over her skin. But she did not feel any pain. Only fear.

Kiah knew she should run away. But her panic had locked her limbs into place as she rocked back and forth, unable to find the strength to push herself to go on.

Jeran was right. Not that she had doubted him—it was just so incomprehensible to imagine the level of destruction he spoke of. The Lamanites would descend like locusts and kill every man, woman, and child they came across. Those that were not killed would be faced with a lifetime of slavery. And that fiend in there would act as the gatekeeper, letting the Lamanites in to slaughter his own people. Pachus would rule supreme in a hellish nightmare. Pachus and the Lamanites would rob them of everything—their lands, their religion, their freedom.

Great sobs welled up in her chest that she dared not release, afraid that someone would hear her. The darkness closed in on her, smothering her senses, making her feel suffocated. She heaved great breaths in and out, finding it increasingly harder to breathe.

Father, her soul cried, and she didn't know if she anguished for the earthly or heavenly one to help her. Both, she supposed. But there was only one whom she could talk to in that moment.

Father, she pleaded. *I don't know what to do. How can I stop them?* Kiah waited, listening, struggling to keep breathing. There was a deep, black silence. No answer.

No, she started to cry with tears of frustration, banging her fists on the ground. *Not now. Don't ignore me now. I need Thee to stop them.* In her mind she started picturing wild visions of all the ways the Lord could stop Pachus and Corahan—the ceiling of the cave could collapse in on them. The water in the cave could rise up suddenly and sweep them all away. She imagined the heavens pouring down avenging angels to destroy the king-men. The pictures got confusing and quickly slid from her mind. Despite the improbability, she waited to see if the ground would shake or open up whole to swallow the king-men.

I have to do something. Still silence.

Please, answer me, she begged.

Helaman had said that if she asked in faith, it would be revealed to her. Where was the revelation? Why was she abandoned now?

She'd never felt so alone, so scared. The darkness all around pressed down even harder on her. Everything felt so heavy. *Help me. Help Thy people, Thy faithful servants.*

Was she doing something wrong? Why wasn't He answering?

Her tears still flowed freely, sobs racking her entire body. *I need Thee, Father. I need Thy help. I cannot do this alone.*

Kiah hung suspended in the thunderous silence until the darkness was pulled from her. She slowly came back to herself, feeling every bite on her skin, the tightness in her chest, the rawness in her eyes and throat from crying. And then there was a comfort, a peace unlike anything she'd ever experienced. Warmth covered her entire body, pressing against her like an embrace.

She straightened up, sniffled, and wiped away her tears. She waited.

And then a series of images filled her mind, one coming rapidly after the next. She saw herself and could see and hear everything she was doing. She saw where to go, what to say. The succession of images ended, and she reached out to take hold of her swords.

Kiah stood, resolute, knowing exactly what she had to do.

She sprinted into the jungle, knowing she would be kept safe while she passed through. The moon lit the way for her, and she ran toward Zarahemla.

Go back.

The words were so soft, Kiah barely heard them. She ran hard, deciding she must have imagined it. She didn't even dare to look behind her. She would never go back. She would only go forward.

* * *

She ran first to her house. Kiah had entered the city unchallenged. The Title of Liberty still flew from every tower. Zarahemla was still under the control of the freemen.

Joshua and Caleb were waiting in the courtyard, weapons drawn, when she came running in. As if they were one person, they both immediately relaxed upon seeing her, lowering their swords.

"Where are Shabana and Linoah?" Kiah asked.

"They're visiting some of Shabana's family with the boys," Joshua told her.

It did not change her plans that the women weren't in the house; in fact, it made things easier for her. She wouldn't have to explain to them yet and try to convince them to leave. She would be coming back to the house after her next destination. She could gather them up then and get them out of Zarahemla.

"Did you find him?" Caleb asked.

Kiah nodded. "We don't have much time. Come with me. I'll explain on the way."

She told her twin cousins the story, and their faces colored with shock and disbelief, then anger. They began a rapid exchange that Kiah could only partially make out as they seemed to be ending one another's thoughts and sentences.

Kiah was alert, listening for danger. She heard none. She knew she would not—they were being given time.

The trio arrived outside of Pahoran's large home. Caleb and Joshua stopped arguing when they realized where they were. "We'll never get in," Joshua said with a sound of disgust.

"This is important," Kiah said, facing her cousins, making sure she had their full attention. "You must go with Pahoran and his men. You have to gather as many freemen as possible and get out of the city before Pachus and the king-men return."

"Of course . . ." Joshua began. Caleb added, " . . . we will."

"Do you promise?" she asked. Both men nodded. "Then you will go with Pahoran and not follow me when I leave."

"Wait," Joshua said while Caleb interjected with an, "I don't think so."

"You promised." They tried to argue with her that they didn't know what they were promising, that she needed them to protect her.

"I've done a fair job of protecting myself up to now," Kiah replied in a huff. She tried staring them down, but the twins were unmoved.

"I can't explain everything right now. I just know that you two are supposed to go with Pahoran and help him. My path lies in another direction."

Her cousins exchanged a loaded glance and then nodded. "Fine," Caleb said. "We'll go with Pahoran while you go off and get yourself killed."

"And if you do get yourself killed," Joshua warned, wagging a finger at her, "we're following you into the next world and thrashing you."

"Agreed." Kiah smiled. As always, armed guards stood outside the doorway of Pahoran's vast house. She heard Caleb mutter to his brother, "When did we start taking orders from a woman?"

"Should we take care of those two?" Joshua asked, nodding in the direction of the men.

"No. We don't want to cause a scene out here in the street. I know another way in."

The twins followed Kiah around to the side of the house. There was a window created to let smoke out of one of the rooms, set up high off the ground. Joshua helped boost her up to the ledge. They were still conducting business inside—Kiah could smell the smoky scent from the candles and fires that burned throughout Pahoran's home. She could hear men's voices arguing. Having visited the courtroom inside of Pahoran's house in the past, she had a good idea of the chaos that could exist from people trying to be heard over one another, to make their voice the one that the chief judge heard.

Kiah pulled herself up to the window and slung her legs inside. The scene was just as she had expected—Pahoran sat against a large cushion on a dais above the lowered floor, his head resting on his right hand, looking as if he desperately wanted to retire to his private quarters. Men dressed in somber colors squabbled on the floor like turkeys, pecking at one another over how the recent harvest should be collected, taxed, and distributed. Pahoran was flanked by lesser judges, many of whom were sleeping. One openly snored.

She wondered how she would make herself heard over this din when she leaped down to the floor. She landed as lithely as any cat, and when she straightened up, she leaned too far to the right, pushing over a clay granary pot nearly as tall as she was. Kiah tried to catch it but it was too late. The momentum bowled the pot over, breaking it into a thousand pieces when it hit the floor and scattering maize everywhere.

Kiah cursed her clumsiness until she realized that the room had gone silent. Every eye was fixed on her. Another blessing in disguise.

"I have come to speak with the chief judge," Kiah called out in a loud voice. Men of all shapes and sizes immediately blocked her path, and she heard "not a woman's place," "business going on here," "real problems" coming from the crowd as all tried to speak at once.

"Quiet!" a voice roared, and Kiah saw Pahoran descend from his seat as the men grew instantly silent. They parted like the Red Sea as Pahoran made his way to Kiah.

She had not seen Pahoran in many years, but his face was as she remembered. Pahoran was a man of average height, average build, with dark brown hair. In any other situation he would have been a forgettable sort of person. But there was an air about him, something that drew people's attention to him.

He was a good man, a wise man, an excellent leader. Kiah knew her father held him in high respect, and that by itself was enough to command her respect also.

"You are Moroni's daughter . . . Kiah, correct?" he asked. She nodded.

"I thought so. You have his look about you. Please, come in. Have you heard from your father recently? I have been expecting reports for nearly two weeks, and none have arrived." Pahoran directed Kiah to cushions on the dais, away from the listening horde of overexuberant courtiers. He waited until she was seated before sitting down himself. Kiah saw that Joshua and Caleb took positions nearby to keep the others from getting too close.

"No. He hasn't received any letters from us, either. No messengers are being let in or out of the city." Kiah lowered her voice, wondering briefly if there were king-men in the room. She didn't want anyone to alert Corahan and Pachus to her actions.

"On whose orders?" Pahoran demanded.

"Pachus. Do you know him?"

"By reputation."

"Pachus has gathered the remaining king-men. He has taken control of the soldiers left within the city through Corahan. I think they might have killed Ontium. Pachus has sent Ammoron an epistle, asking for an alliance. Tonight I saw the king-men led by Pachus practicing dark rituals in a cave not far from here." The room was so silent she heard a feather from a headdress land on the ground. Kiah held everyone's attention. She continued on, knowing her message must be delivered even if there were spies in the courtroom. "You must gather all the trustworthy men, supplies, and weapons you can find and leave Zarahemla. I don't know how much time you have, but you have to be clear of the city before Pachus springs his trap."

Pahoran looked ill, his face completely white. But his face never held even a trace of skepticism, despite her lack of proof. She could see that he believed her, as she had known he would.

"Never!" someone shouted from the crowd. "We defeated the king-men five years ago. We can do so again. I say we stay and fight!" Several members of the group yelled their agreement, while some advocated the decision to leave.

Kiah got to her feet. "You defeated them with the full strength of my father's army, which is not here. You have only a few thousand soldiers in the city, and you don't know which ones you can trust, who will be on your side. Fighting is not an option. The only option now is to find my father's army, and then retake Zarahemla."

The lawyers, who made their living debating such things, returned to arguing amongst themselves.

She knelt back down to be at eye level with Pahoran. "You must trust me. Countless lives will be lost if you stay here. You must flee."

Pahoran stayed silent. Kiah watched the various expressions on his face as he weighed the information she had given him and what the best course of action would be.

He stood, looking almost regal, the mantle of his position obvious. He began barking orders for provisions to be collected, weapons to be brought, loyal freemen to be found.

Pahoran turned to Kiah while men began running in countless directions to fulfill the tasks assigned to them. "Fortunately, I have already been gathering men and supplies to send to Captain Moroni to support his troops out in the field. We will go to the land of Gideon. I will send messengers to find your father to let him know where we are." Pahoran clasped his hands on Kiah's shoulders in a sign of solidarity. "We will always resist such wickedness. If we must leave so that we may fight another day, that is what we will do."

Kiah felt the air whoosh out of her as she sighed in relief. She knew that very soon, clouds would cover the moon and stars, allowing Pahoran and his allies to escape and making it more difficult for Pachus and the king-men to trace their steps. Everything was happening the way it was supposed to.

Pahoran had turned to take a list from a scribe and began to add entries to it as Kiah dashed for the window. "I hope you are ready to travel with us. Your father would never forgive me if I didn't bring you to him safely . . . Kiah?" She heard his words as she was dropping out of the window.

In the din and confusion, she had slipped out the way she had come in, leaving Caleb and Joshua with the rest.

Kiah ran through the now pitch-black night, relying on her knowledge of the area to guide her, and betting on the fact that Pahoran would have no time to track her down. They would have to go on without her.

She had a prisoner to save.

TWELVE

Kiah arrived at her father's home winded. The rest of her family had returned. Shabana looked distraught, wringing her hands together, sending off waves of little tinkling sounds.

"Where are your cousins?" Shabana pounced on Kiah as soon as she stepped into the inner courtyard.

For the third time that night, Kiah explained what she had seen and what was now happening.

"You will have to pack up for the boys," she told Shabana after she had finished. "We are running out of time. If the king-men figure out that I am involved, they will come here. I want all of you safe."

"What are *you* doing?" Linoah asked, a statue of grace and serenity in direct opposition to Shabana's hysteria.

Kiah told them her plans as she went in and out of her father's armory. Moroni kept a stockpile of weapons and armor for their poorer kinsmen who had to borrow them to go into battle. She retrieved half a dozen sets of armor and weapons. She quickly packed them into a large bag. Kiah went to her sleeping pallet and extricated Jeran's belongings, including his spear, and put them into her bag as well. Linoah and Shabana trailed after her like baby ducks.

"Where are the herbs from that merchant?"

Shabana pointed toward the cooking area, and Kiah went into the storage room. The room was filled with wooden chests, cotton bags, and pottery. Kiah made her way though the bunches of chile peppers and baskets that hung from the lintels until she found what she was looking for. She sniffed the herb bag, smiled, and put it into her pack. Kiah took several water skins and one skin filled with the wine that Helaman had forgotten so long ago. She also packed all the foodstuffs she could find—food that would travel well—into smaller bags.

"Kiah?" Linoah asked again. Her aunt had followed her, while Shabana stood looking helpless, going back and forth between where her sons slept and where Kiah gathered up what she needed.

"I'm not leaving here without Jeran," Kiah told Linoah. "I will get him out. I need you and Shabana to go to the home of Pahoran. Joshua and Caleb are there. They will protect you and get all of you out of Zarahemla. But you have to leave now. Time is running away from us."

"You love him." It was a statement this time, not a question.

Kiah straightened up, making sure her bag was secure. "Yes. And I won't let them kill him."

"Aren't you frightened?" Linoah asked in that voice that indicated she already knew the answer to her question.

"I'm terrified. But there are enough Nephites to be worried about without anyone being concerned about the Lamanites." Kiah turned from her aunt, willing herself not to cry. What had happened to her since meeting Jeran? She never used to cry.

Linoah turned her back around so that they were facing each other. "You are truly your father's daughter. If there is anyone who can do this, it is you." Suddenly, being compared to her father didn't seem like such a hard thing. It seemed wonderful.

Kiah threw herself into her aunt's arms, hugging her tight. "You have to go. Although I would love to take Shabana with me, I just can't imagine her in the company of Lamanites."

The women laughed softly, and the sound drew Shabana back to them. Linoah left Kiah and Shabana alone, saying that she would prepare for their departure.

"What's so funny?" Shabana demanded.

"Nothing." Kiah smiled. "Come on. I'll help you pack up your things so we can leave. I want to be far from here before Pachus and Corahan realize what has happened. If they know what I have done, they will catch me before I even get past Zarahemla's walls."

"Who did you say?" Shabana asked with a strangled whisper.

"Pachus and Corahan."

Something changed in Shabana's face. The furrowed crease in her high forehead smoothed out. The skin around her eyes relaxed, her frowning mouth evened out.

"We will stay here. There is no need for us to go with you."

Somewhere, in a northerly direction, Kiah heard shouting, and the sounds of a fight. She didn't know what happened, but it felt like a freezing blast of wind had blown over her skin.

It had begun.

"I'm serious," Kiah told Shabana, pulling her bag toward the front entryway. "They will kill you if they come here."

"Nothing will happen to us." Shabana seemed different—there was a confidence about her that Kiah hadn't seen for some time, and strangely enough, a total lack of fear.

Kiah's mind was too overwrought to try to figure it out. She could feel the seconds slipping away from her. She knew she was supposed to save the Lamanite prisoners. There had been nothing in the images to indicate that she was to force her family to leave. Shabana seemed sure enough of their safety. Kiah was torn, the words *hurry, hurry* echoing in her mind.

"I could never live with the guilt if something happened to all of you."

"Kiah, you know why my sons and I will not be harmed."

And in an instant Kiah did know, finally understanding why Shabana felt safe in Zarahemla despite what was happening.

"But if what you say is true," Shabana continued, "we will not be safe if you are found here."

Kiah nodded, putting the strap of the bag from the armory around her forehead to carry the near-bursting pack. Kiah felt a bout of uneasiness. She wondered if Shabana's loyalty would lie with her old family or her new one. She tried to make out Shabana's expression, but Shabana's face was impassive, unreadable.

"Before I leave . . . if someone does come here, I need you to say you haven't seen me."

Shabana went strangely still, her body tense. "You want me to lie?"

Kiah couldn't interpret the tone in Shabana's voice. "Shabana, I know we don't have the best relationship, but if Corahan figures out what I've taken from my father's armory, where I've gone . . . I can't begin to imagine what he will do to me." Kiah closed her eyes, suddenly weary. It was all too much.

"Shabana, please. I've never asked for it before, and I told you I never would, but please . . . I need your help."

Tension emanated from Shabana's small frame. Kiah didn't know if Shabana had even heard her. Shabana's head seemed to nod slightly, as if in agreement, and not wanting to lose any more precious time, Kiah went to free Jeran.

* * *

Corahan emerged from the cave as if being reborn, feeling himself to be a different person. He tried to remember what his life was like before this night and found he couldn't. His face felt stiff from where the blood markings had dried up. He had not bothered to clean himself in the pool as the others had done. He preferred not to see his reflection. It was easier to face what he had done if he did not have look at himself. His body felt neither cold nor warm in the evening air; he only felt numb. He blinked twice, trying to adjust his eyes to the darkness. With the full moon he had expected easy passage back to Zarahemla, but he couldn't see anything more than an arm's length in front of him. Strange that there should be such a thick cloud cover. The rainy season was months away, the new year about to begin. They never had rain this time of the year.

Pachus left the cave and called for torches to be brought. While they waited for this to be done, Corahan saw Pachus take off one of his sandals to remove a rock. As he put his bare foot back down,

Pachus mumbled an oath of pain. One of the king-men brought a torch to Pachus. Pachus muttered that he had stepped on something and bent down to pick it up.

"What is this?" Pachus asked.

Corahan walked over to where Pachus stood, his way guided by the torch's ring of light. Pachus held something that glinted slightly in the torchlight.

"It's a necklace," Pachus said, his voice sounding slightly confused. "Does this belong to anyone here?"

"Perhaps it belonged to the Lamanite," someone in the dark offered.

Corahan took the outstretched necklace, studying it, running his fingers over the various beads and shells. When he got to the center with the silver carving of a sun, he swore aloud.

"What?" Pachus asked in a tone that said his patience had reached its end.

"I know who this belongs to," Corahan informed him grimly.

* * *

Just as she had expected, the soldiers that stood in front of the prison were men she didn't know. Probably king-men. Not allowing herself time to consider her fear, she began to walk in front of them slowly, pretending to ignore them. She stopped when she reached the midpoint on the street between the two men, dropping her pack with an exaggerated moan.

She took up her water skin, drinking from it greedily and letting out a contented and satisfied sigh when she finished. Kiah wiped her mouth with the back of her hand and then dropped the water bag down on the side of the pack furthest from the guards, next to the skin with wine.

"What do you have there?" asked one of the men who had been avidly watching Kiah's performance.

"Wine," Kiah said with an inviting smile. The men didn't take the bait, and Kiah pressed on.

"I would offer you some, but I see that you stand guard. It's a shame I can't share it with you," Kiah said in a voice that she hoped was even remotely enticing.

As if it had been their idea all along, she heard the man on the left say, "It wouldn't hurt to have a little. No one would know."

Kiah adjusted her bag as the two men quickly rationalized their decision to have some of the wine. "Girl! Bring that skin over here."

The picture of innocence, Kiah tried her best to imitate Shabana as she sashayed over to the men, offering them the wine. The man on the left grabbed the skin and downed a large gulp. He passed it to the guard on the right, who also began to take a deep drink.

Before the second man had even lowered the skin, the first guard collapsed into a heap.

"What . . ." the guard on the right said, lunging at Kiah. She had only to step back, and the man crumpled at Kiah's feet, feeling the effects of the drugged wine as strongly and as quickly as his fellow guard.

Kiah grabbed her bag, put it on, and pulled out her short swords. She descended carefully down the stairs leading into the prison, knowing a third guard waited at the base of the steps.

She turned the sword in her right hand around so that the hilt was facing outward. She crept up behind the guard who sat on the ground, his back to the wall with his head turned to the side. He appeared to be dozing. Raising her arm, she hit the man on the back of his head, below his crown, just like her father taught her. The unconscious man slid sideways against the wall. Kiah wasted no time in grabbing a torch and running over to the sleeping Lamanite prisoners.

Kiah put the torch into a bracer on the wall, put her large pack down, and began the task of cutting through the Lamanites' ropes. The men began to stir, as if unsure whether they were dreaming or if their bindings really were being loosed.

She saved Jeran for last, cutting through the tightly woven ropes at his ankles and wrists. He stared at her, asking, "Kiah?" as if he couldn't believe she was there.

"It's me." She smiled, throwing his ropes to one side. "We have to go."

Jeran got to his feet while gazing at her. Then he swooped down, pulling her against him in a tight, loving embrace. Kiah settled into his arms, feeling as if this were where she truly belonged, had always belonged. She could hear the steady thumping of his heart, and she closed her eyes, wanting to stay in the moment forever. It was almost enough to make her forget about Pachus and Corahan. Almost.

She became aware of the other Lamanite prisoners getting to their feet. She forced herself to let go of Jeran, to walk away from his warmth. Kiah had to fight the urge to throw herself back into his arms and let the entire world disappear.

She stepped back and turned her attention to the pack she had brought with her. "Here. Have everyone put these on." Kiah handed Jeran quilted cotton armor with an inner lining of tapir hide and the helms she had gathered together.

The smell of the brine-cured armor assaulted her nostrils. She quickly put on a set of the armor, being careful to tie her hair behind her, tucking the long part down into the back of her outfit. Since the Lamanites were unaccustomed to wearing any armor, she had hers laced up quicker than the others. She got Jeran's spear and his pack. "These are yours."

Jeran pulled his head through the hole at the top of the armor and looked at what Kiah gave him. "You kept my things," he said in a tone of disbelief.

"Of course I did."

"Thank you."

Kiah could only just make out Jeran's face in the muted light, and she decided her anxiety was making her imagine things. The expression on his face . . . he looked like . . . like he loved her.

She gulped down the emotion bubbling to the surface and began to tell Jeran the story of how he had been right—how the king-men were planning to take over Zarahemla. She told him of her actions so far, and Jeran nodded as if they had been the right and smart things to do. Kiah basked in Jeran's approval. She felt a security, a safeness, that she had not felt for a long time just by being with him. Everything would be all right.

"I saw . . . I saw them sacrifice a man," Kiah said as the memory came rushing back to her as if she were still crouched in the stairway of the cave, watching it happen. Her body swayed toward Jeran, seeking his strength.

"A terrible thing to watch." Jeran said the words as if he truly understood what she had witnessed.

When Kiah nodded, he folded her into his arms, holding her more gently this time. She could feel his even, warm breaths against her ear, and she forgot that anyone else existed.

Kiah was brought crashing back into reality when Lamonti loudly informed her and Jeran that they were dressed. Jeran seemed as reluctant to let go of her as she was to be let go of. She turned to the Lamanites and was surprised at how much they looked like Nephites with their disguises on, especially when protected by the cover of darkness.

"One more thing," Kiah said, pulling bows and arrows along with some swords out of her pack and distributing them to the prisoners. She had worried over this decision, not sure if it was the right thing to do. But to send them out to the jungle without a way to protect themselves was akin to a death sentence, and she would not have their deaths on her head. She would give them whatever means they needed to survive. None of them deserved to be defenseless.

"Tell them they have to promise not to kill any good Nephites," Kiah said to assuage her guilty conscience.

Jeran repeated her statement to the men, and one of the prisoners responded. There was a deep round of laughter, the kind that only imprisoned men about to be freed can give.

"What did he say?"

Jeran turned back to Kiah, still smiling. "He wanted to know how we're supposed to tell the difference when you all look the same."

Kiah shook her head and distributed skins of water and food, keeping a set for herself that she put into a smaller bag brought for this purpose, and moved to heft it onto her back. Jeran stopped her and took it, slipping the handle over his head and strapping it into place.

"Let's go," he said.

Kiah nodded and took the lead. When she indicated the street was clear, the Lamanites pulled the two outside guards back into the stairwell so that no one passing by would be suspicious. Kiah lined the men up in twos, putting herself in the middle row so that she would look like one of the men. Jeran fell in place next to her. She gave them quiet directions on which way to go, with Jeran translating, and they began their slow walk to freedom.

Much as she wanted to run, Kiah held herself in check. To run would call attention to themselves, and they would be dead before they gained the walkway. There were guards all around the city, and the guards in the towers located near the entrance would watch for anyone entering or exiting.

The clouded sky made it difficult to see, and more than once they nearly ran into a wall or kicked over a stray pot. The city and its denizens slept, and Kiah didn't want to alert anyone by carrying a torch.

Almost there, we're almost there, she thought over and over as a way to keep her mind focused, to not let herself concentrate on the enormity of what she was doing and how very dead she would be if they were discovered.

Too late Kiah saw the group of soldiers heading straight toward them. There was no time to run or hide. Kiah and her band of Lamanite prisoners could only walk as if they too were just going about their orders.

"Keep going," Kiah said, and Jeran relayed the message.

As the Nephite soldiers came closer, Kiah saw that they carried torches. And that they were led by Corahan.

They were all going to die.

THIRTEEN

Kiah stopped breathing. She tried to force herself to start, knowing she would faint if she didn't. She felt Jeran's fingers brush against her own, and she refrained from grabbing onto him, reminding herself that soldiers didn't hold hands. He was letting her know that he also saw Corahan, telling her to be strong.

She squared her shoulders and continued to march. Kiah could feel the uneasiness in the Lamanite prisoners around her, but they wanted their freedom too badly to do anything to ruin it. They pressed forward, as determined to ignore Corahan and his men as she was.

The space between them became shorter and shorter until Corahan and his soldiers were practically on top of them.

Kiah refused to look in Corahan's direction and would not look at the ground as she wanted to. She kept her eyes trained straight ahead. Kiah felt glad for the weight of her short swords against her hips. She was not defenseless. If Corahan discovered them, she would fight.

Corahan and his band pushed past the Lamanite prisoners. Their cloaks whipped against Kiah's leg as they hurried by, each small smack a reminder of how tenuous their situation was.

She finally dared to breathe when the soldiers were several feet behind them, still intent on their destination. The disguises had worked. Corahan hadn't suspected anything.

A low laugh from one of the Lamanites broke the silence, and Kiah refrained from giggling nervously. Jeran smiled and took her hand for a moment, squeezing it lightly, then let it go. They were so close now.

The ground became elevated as they began their ascent up the passage that led from the city—where it would level out and then descend down toward the open fields and to the safety of the jungle beyond. Kiah thought about Joshua and Caleb. She wondered if Pahoran and the freemen had already left the city, if they had passed this way or found another means of escape.

A horn sounded behind them, and there was shouting. Kiah and Jeran exchanged glances and hurried their pace. Almost there.

A call passed from one soldier to the next. It began as a murmur in the distance and traveled nearer to them like a gathering wave until it crashed down with "The prisoners have escaped!"

The alarm went up to the guards in the towers, the ones that would prevent them from leaving. The guards would not be able to get down in time to stop them on foot, but the expert archers would pick them off one by one from their higher ground. She noticed movement in a tower to her right and realized that Pachus and Corahan had reinforced the troops there—several soldiers with bows and arrows kept watch. There was no way out.

"Who's there?" a guard from the tower called down to them.

What could they say? Kiah opened her mouth to speak and then stopped. It was one thing to dress like a man, but she couldn't make herself sound like one.

Jeran stepped forward. "Numa, son of Benaiah."

"What are you doing?" the guard asked.

"Haven't you heard? The prisoners have escaped. We have been ordered to find them."

A long, deadly silence ensued. Kiah's sweat thoroughly soaked her tunic, despite the coolness of the night. Finally, at a point when Kiah thought she would start screaming and never stop, the guard waved his hand indicating they could leave.

Just put one foot in front of the other. They passed through the open archway between the walls, and Kiah felt the earth sloping down. They were going to make it. The soldiers had believed Jeran. Jeran's quick thinking thoroughly impressed her. He had saved them.

They headed east from the city, toward the River Sidon. Kiah's heart quickened when she heard the rushing water, and she nearly collapsed in relief when they passed through the tree line. They were safe.

Kiah and the Lamanites followed an animal trail, moving deeper into the jungle. The clouds covering the stars and the moon dissipated, making it easy for them to move through the trees. They finally stopped to rest and began to undo the armor they wore, throwing it into a pile. None of them was accustomed to wearing it, and it felt heavy and hot.

The prisoners held a quick conference while Kiah checked on her bag of supplies, noting that she needed to stop at the river to refill the water. Two of the men turned to Kiah, saying Lamanite words she recognized as "thank you." Then they left, running south toward the mountains.

"Where are they going?" she asked Jeran.

Jeran undid the chin straps holding his helm in place. "They are going to return to their people in the city of Nephi."

"Aren't you going home too?" Kiah asked Lamonti. Lamonti stood up and held his sword up in the moonlight, inspecting it.

"No."

Kiah waited to see if he would explain further. Inside a Nephite prison, Lamonti was fairly intimidating, but he was almost menacing outside of one. "Will he get mad if I ask him where he's going?" she whispered to Jeran.

Overhearing her, Lamonti said, "My friend and I are going to track down Corahan and kill him as I have sworn to do. And I always keep my word." Finding their weapons satisfactory, the men took the food that Kiah had offered them along with a water skin. Even though she knew she shouldn't wish such a thing, a part of her did hope that Lamonti found Corahan.

"But he's inside the city."

"He will not stay there forever," Lamonti said with an air of supreme confidence. "We will wait for him. Then we will go north to join my father, Zamir. And we promise not to kill any good Nephites," he said with a grin. Kiah smiled back.

"We will not forget what you have done for us," Lamonti said to Jeran and Kiah.

Kiah raised a hand in farewell as Lamonti and his man left to decide the best place to set a trap for their prey.

"Where to?" Jeran asked.

"We could go with Pahoran and his men to Gideon, but I would like to join my father and brother. Their armies should be in the north, near the coastal cities. I know Pahoran will send for their help, but you know how easy it is for people to get lost in the jungle."

"Yes, I definitely know how easy that is," Jeran said with a laugh.

"So off to find my father, then?"

Jeran adjusted the various bags he carried and grabbed his spear. "As you wish." He held his free hand out to Kiah to help her up. She hesitated, looking back at Zarahemla, seeing the white limestone of the temple lovingly bathed in moonlight. Then she slipped her hand into Jeran's and followed him deeper into the jungle.

* * *

Corahan entered Moroni's house, followed by a small squad of soldiers. He walked through the home looking for Kiah. He thrust a torch into the dark shadows, expecting to find her cringing in a corner.

He entered the sleeping quarters and saw two children and an older woman sleeping, and a young woman sitting up on her pallet quietly staring at him. Her gaze felt familiar somehow, and Corahan backed up, unsettled.

"What are you doing here?" the woman asked, walking past Corahan into the courtyard. She exuded authority, and Corahan found himself following her.

"I have come for Kiah. Where is she?"

In the full moonlight, Corahan recognized the woman as Shabana, Moroni's daughter-in-law. He knew there was no love lost between Shabana and Kiah. Surely she would remember where her loyalties must lie and give the girl up.

Shabana stood as silent as the night and continued to stare at Corahan.

"You're not protecting her, are you?" Corahan asked incredulously. "You know on whose orders I am here tonight?"

"I know."

"Then tell me where she is. Was she here? What did she do? Where is she now?"

Shabana folded her arms across her chest. She turned her face from Corahan to look at her two small boys, sleeping soundly. Corahan called to his men to search the entire home, uncovering all of the hiding places until they found Kiah. But he began to suspect that she was not there, and the only person who could confirm her current whereabouts said nothing.

Corahan waited until his patience ended. He approached the petite woman, determined to get the information he wanted.

"Your uncle has seized the city. He will be king. And your sons will be kings. Think of it! They are heirs to the entire Nephite kingdom."

He thought this enough to motivate anyone to act properly. Pachus, having no children of his own, had declared his niece's sons his heirs. What more could a mother want for her sons than to be rulers of nations? Not that Corahan believed it would ever happen—Pachus was an old man, and these boys were too young to rule. There would be a fight for the throne. Sure that Pachus would name him chief captain once everything had settled, he knew he would be in the best position to take over as king.

Corahan would not let this one stubborn woman badly in need of a beating stand in the way of his desires. Pachus had ordered him to contain the situation, and he needed to know what Kiah had seen, what she'd had heard, whom she had told.

Although he hadn't informed Pachus yet, Corahan knew he would be furious that Kiah had somehow smuggled the Lamanite prisoners out of the city. Corahan wanted to know how she had accomplished it. Upon his return to Zarahemla, he'd gone straight to the prison, guessing Kiah would run to her precious Lamanite once she knew of their plans. He raised the alarm, then gave strict orders that he be notified the instant they were recaptured. He was still waiting.

"I will ask you one last time, and then I will drag you by your hair to Pachus, where you can answer to him. Where is Kiah?"

Shabana tilted her head to one side as if to study Corahan, and her cold, unblinking gaze reminded him too much of Pachus. He took a step back and then cursed himself for acting like a fool. She was only a woman. She was sure to confess everything now.

"She has not been here all night. I don't know where she is."

Corahan's sharp breath whistled through his teeth. "Are you certain that is what you want to tell me?"

Shabana moved her arms so that her fists were balled up and resting on her hips. "I repeat, I have not seen her. I don't know where she is." She said each word deliberately, loudly.

"You will regret this."

"The only thing I regret is that you are in my home. I will ask you and your men to leave now."

"You are choosing the wrong side. Your uncle will not forgive you for this."

Corahan twisted away from her and shouted to his soldiers to fall in. He was walking to the outer side of the courtyard, trying to gain some distance from that infuriating woman, when he saw something shiny on the ground.

He walked over to the object. A head plate. Corahan knew that Moroni kept an extensive armory within his home. It would do him no good to search it; he wouldn't know if something was missing, and Shabana would be no help to him. But if Kiah had taken armor, helms, weapons . . .

The Lamanites would look like Nephites. A group of Nephite soldiers.

Like the one he had run into in his dash for the prison. He had gone right past them.

A mixture of fury, despair, and disbelief mingled on Corahan's face as Shabana came over and stood next to him with a knowing smile, looking like a lioness cornering her prey.

"My husband and father-in-law will return with the might of their armies, with the might of their God—my God—on their side. And when, not if, but *when* they defeat Pachus, we both know what your fate will be, and whom Pachus will blame for what has happened tonight. If there is anyone here that needs to worry about Pachus's unforgiving nature, it is you and not me."

* * *

Pachus hurled a clay cup of wine against the wall behind the dais in the courtroom of the judges, causing the cup to break and wine to drip down the wall.

"You mean to tell me that not only did she free the Lamanite prisoners, but she also alerted the entire city of our coming!"

He picked up a wooden stool and threw it against the same wall, throwing a tantrum like a spoiled child.

Corahan stood still, not wanting to draw Pachus's attention. For all he knew, Pachus would start throwing weapons next, and he had no desire to be the target. Noblemen, soldiers, and other king-men filled the room, talking and boasting of the great victory they had achieved without even having to fight.

He knew that Pachus had brought these king-men to Pahoran's house in order to defeat Pahoran and claim Zarahemla as his own. After his initial shock at finding Pahoran's house emptied, Pachus had grown angrier by the minute. And Corahan's news of who caused all these events only made things worse.

"None of this would have happened if you'd given her to me when I asked for her," Corahan grumbled.

"What? What did you say?" Pachus whirled on Corahan, his eyes flashing furiously, the feathers of his headdress whipping Corahan in the face.

"Nothing, my king," Corahan added, wisely biting back the retort that had sprung to his lips.

His words had their desired effect, and Pachus visibly calmed and called for a map to be brought to him. Corahan knew that so far, nothing had happened the way Pachus had envisioned, particularly not the bloodless change of government.

Pachus took the chief judge's seat, remarking that he would need a throne, not a cushion. Several of the lesser king-men nearby quickly agreed with Pachus, praising him for his wisdom and taste.

The bald, hateful slave who always seemed to be lurking around Pachus came into the courtroom, now Pachus's throne room. He carried a large chest of what Corahan guessed were Pachus's belongings. Pachus had naturally decided to take up residence in the former chief judge's home.

"Do you still want us to unpack?" the slave asked, looking at the ground.

"Of course I do," Pachus snapped. "The only thing that's changed is that now you won't have to get blood stains out of the rugs." The slave gave a small bow and retreated to a corner of the room.

"I don't trust him," Corahan said, wondering why Pachus kept such a belligerent man as a slave.

"He's easy enough to manage. I keep his daughter as a slave as well, and he knows that if he ever crosses me, it will be her death. I keep them separated. They are not allowed to be in the same room together, not allowed to speak." Pachus settled back against the pillow. "I trust him well enough. More than I trust most of the men in this room. I would never keep any slave that I couldn't control."

Pachus's words had physical power. Corahan could feel the shackles being placed on his wrists, could feel his hair being shorn. He thought himself a great man, the captain of Zarahemla, when in reality he had no more power than this slave. Pachus was master to them all.

Pachus raised his hand, causing the lavender jade bracelets he wore to clink together, and again demanded his map.

"Here, my king." One quickly appeared, and it was unfolded for Pachus on a low table in front of him.

"Pahoran and his men will have gone to Gideon. It is the closest city and has the best defenses to withstand an assault."

"Do you want me to send men after them?" Corahan asked.

"No," Pachus shook his head, pressing the tips of his fingers together as he thought. "It would be too risky. He could have sent runners ahead of him, and the entire city of Gideon could be waiting for us in the jungle. The smartest course is to stay here within the walls."

Smartest and most cowardly, Corahan thought.

"We will need to send more messengers to Ammoron and ask for his promised assistance. With the combined strength of the Lamanite army, we will be able to repulse any attacks." Pachus looked particularly pleased with himself.

"Ammoron's men will have to go through the entire Nephite army to get here, and through every city and village along the way. They will never reach us in time. By now Pahoran has sent word to Moroni, and his men are marching on Zarahemla even as we speak," Corahan told him, not wanting to put his own life at risk for the mere sake of petting Pachus by telling him what he wanted to hear. "We cannot withstand the full strength of Moroni's and Pahoran's armies. They will crush us."

Pachus's jaw tensed, and he nodded tersely. He had to know Corahan was right. Pachus stood and began to pace back and forth on the dais, his hands folded behind his back. The chattering in the throne room continued as men discussed what they thought the best solution would be. The anger on Pachus's face lifted as he finally arrived at a plan.

"I want Moroni's daughter found. I want her captured and taken here." Pachus pointed at the map. "To Nephihah. Lamanites control the city, and it is virtually impregnable. We will send runners out to Moroni's camp to tell him that his daughter is being held prisoner in Nephihah. A man as weakened by emotion as Moroni is will surely run to Nephihah to ensure the safety of his child and let lesser men try to take Zarahemla. Moroni already fights a war on two fronts. He cannot stretch himself further. He will lose."

At times like these, Pachus's cleverness surprised Corahan. He was right. Captain or not, a man like Moroni would want to protect his child above all things. He would decide that there were others who could lead the fight against them, and as Pachus had said, they would lose. The king-men had the advantage. They were safe within the city walls, and they would not be surprised. They also had at their fingertips the wealth and resources of Zarahemla. Corahan's chest swelled with arrogance.

"I want her found," Pachus said in a low growl. "She must be taken to Nephihah before she can find protection."

Corahan bowed. "It is already being taken care of. I have sent the Home Guard after her."

A sinister and excited grin spread across Pachus's face. "Excellent. Then it will only be a matter of time until she is caught."

FOURTEEN

"This feels awful," Kiah complained, rolling the mixture between her thumb and forefinger.

Jeran stood in front of the andiroba tree and pulled down another brown nut. He opened it to reveal the oil-rich seeds inside, which he then mixed with pressed reddish orange annatto seeds that he carried with him. "You'll feel worse when you're eaten alive by bugs."

He handed her another gourd full of paste. "We can't carry a fire out here to smoke the mosquitoes away. If anyone is looking for us, they'll see it. This is our only option."

Kiah gave a disgusted sigh and slathered the paste onto her body while Jeran continued to create the mixture.

"It isn't so bad once it hardens."

"I'm guessing you speak from experience," Kiah said, and Jeran nodded.

She felt sticky and tired. Kiah twisted her hair up and secured it with a tie, not wanting her hair to get this paste in it. They both applied the mixture to all of their exposed skin, and Kiah decided that if the oily paste didn't repel the insects, it would at least trap them. She tried not to imagine her skin covered in tiny insect corpses.

They resumed their journey, traveling on a well-worn animal trail. Jeran told her it would be harder to track them here with so many different creatures using the path.

"Do you think they will follow us?" Kiah asked.

"They don't know you were involved."

"But if they find out . . ."

"I don't know what will happen. I hope they won't search for you. If they discover that it was you, Pachus and Corahan will be furious about what you did tonight. Pachus might want to take you to Zarahemla to bargain with your father. And Corahan will want to . . ." Jeran trailed off, not wanting to finish. They both knew what Corahan wanted with Kiah.

They walked on, but Kiah's strength slipped away from her. The day had been a completely exhausting one in every sense, and she had been running on sheer adrenaline for the last few hours. She wanted to rest. Her feet suddenly felt very heavy, and it became difficult to lift them off the ground. She stumbled and pushed against Jeran's right arm.

"Are you all right?" he asked, taking her by the shoulders to help her to stand.

"I'm just tired. Could we rest a little?"

Jeran looked from one side to the next. Then he looked up, and after telling Kiah to wait, he went off the path and into the vegetation that surrounded them, through the wall of vines, plant fronds, and giant leaves. She watched him climb a large, twisted tree, moving as deftly as a monkey.

He used his spear to hit several limbs of the tree. She heard the thumping sound of small creatures falling onto the ground below. Jeran next took a rag from his pack and brushed away the ants and termites that marched back and forth across the branches. He called out for Kiah, and she went over to the tree. Jeran offered her his hand and helped her to climb up to the limbs he had cleared.

Kiah relaxed and leaned back against the old tree, feeling content. Jeran took out some of their food and offered it to her. She waved it away, and Jeran took a corn cake to eat. She knew she should be more worried about being in the jungle this day, just the two of them, but they had no choice. Besides, Jeran had managed to live for four years in the jungle by himself. If anyone could navigate their way to safety, it was Jeran.

The full moon broke through the upper canopy in long beams of light that reached lovingly toward the mossy ground. Kiah smelled the sweet scent of scarlet blossom, indicative of the wild cacao trees clustered nearby. All around them tree frogs chirruped in a soft harmony. Were it not for the fact that they were running for their lives, she thought with a twisted smile, it would have been a very romantic moment.

She looked up at the moon and remembered sitting outside with her mother on a night like this one.

"Do you see the rabbit?" Kiah asked.

"Rabbit?" Jeran asked with a mouthful of food, looking at the ground beneath them. He swallowed down the rest of the cake. "Where?"

"Not down there. Up there. The dark spots on the moon. See?" Kiah leaned closer to him, pointing up at the sky. "They're shaped like a leaping rabbit. My mother used to make up stories for me about why the rabbit had jumped that high."

Kiah realized that Jeran wasn't looking at the moon when she felt his breath moving across her cheek. A tingling sensation moved across her cheek, down her neck, and then spread throughout her whole body. All of her senses hummed in nervous anticipation. Would she ever get used to being this close to Jeran?

She turned her head to face his, and they held each other's gazes for a moment, their lips hovering a heartbeat apart. Then Jeran broke off and moved a little further down onto the limb to lie down.

Kiah fought the urge to push him off the branch and returned to her spot. She folded her arms and willed her heart to resume its normal rhythm. Was she the only one who felt this spark between them?

Jeran had thrown his free arm across his eyes and appeared to be sleeping. Kiah no longer felt tired. She felt restless. Her mind skittered from one thought to the next, until it returned to one of her least favorite subjects. She tried to redirect her thoughts away from Corahan, but the harder she tried to stop thinking about him, the more she did.

"What will we do if they find us?" Kiah asked the question in a probing way, dancing around what little information Jeran had given her. She gathered he'd made an oath that prevented him from killing. She wanted to know why, particularly given their situation. Kiah feared they were approaching a kill-or-be-killed confrontation.

Jeran lifted his arm off his eyes to look at her. "Let's hope they don't find us."

Not getting the response she wanted, Kiah decided she was too tired to play games. She took a more direct approach. "Why did you make an oath not to kill anyone?"

Jeran sat straight up, looking shocked. He blinked a few times and then let out a deep sigh that sounded like he was emptying his soul. He looked like he was struggling with something, making a decision. Kiah wondered if he would shut her out again as a long silence stretched between them. She almost jumped with surprise when he began to speak.

"On my twelfth birthday, Amalickiah and Ammoron decided to take me on a hunt with the men. I was so excited. I had been training for many years, and I was finally going to get a chance to prove myself. They did not tell me exactly what kind of animal we would track. My mother begged me not to go, but I didn't listen." Jeran grabbed a palm-sized spider that had dropped down on a web line from a higher branch and threw it to the ground. "We hunted for hours. The animal kept scurrying through the underbrush, making it nearly impossible to find. We caught sight of it, and my uncles encouraged me to shoot. I took my bow, nocked my arrow, aimed, and shot. I heard a grunt and heard something fall down.

"When we got close . . ." Jeran let out a shuddering breath, "it was no animal. My uncles had me hunting a small man. A slave. He wasn't dead. He asked me to help him. I went to pull the arrow out, but Amalickiah restrained me. Ammoron stepped up and cut out his heart."

Kiah put her hand to her mouth at the image, unable to imagine what it would be like.

Jeran's head whipped up in anger as he relived that moment. "I made a sacred oath then and there to the Lord that I would never again take another person's life. It was why Ammoron knew he could torment me. It's why I didn't fight Corahan when he took me prisoner."

She didn't know what to say. "I'm sorry" didn't seem adequate. It obviously still caused him intense pain.

Kiah reached out, putting her hand on Jeran's arm. "If they find us, I could . . . take care of that part."

"Have you ever killed a man?"

"No," she admitted. "I've never been allowed to fight in battle."

"You can't imagine what it's like," Jeran said in a voice so low that Kiah could barely hear him. "To take someone's life . . . that person—they are somebody's whole world and you destroy it. The ramifications . . . it's horrible. It's sickening. And the worst part of it . . . the worst part of it was watching how much Ammoron and Amalickiah enjoyed killing him . . . and knowing that you could become like them, that you could crave killing the way they did."

Kiah tried again to find the right words to relieve Jeran's suffering. She found nothing adequate, let alone helpful. She could only squeeze his arm in quiet sympathy. Jeran put his hand over hers.

She tried not to tremble or to think about kissing Jeran. "You're right. I can't imagine what it's like. I'm usually too afraid when I'm fighting to imagine actually carrying it through to the end."

Jeran looked surprised. "You didn't seem afraid the day we fought."

"I was terrified," Kiah confided. "But my father always taught me that you don't fight because you have no fear. You fight in spite of it."

"He's right. It's true courage to fight when you're most afraid."

"I don't feel very courageous," Kiah said, looking away from him, too confused over what she felt, what she had admitted to him—something she'd never admitted to anyone else.

Jeran took his hand from hers and placed it under her chin, lifting her face to look at him, running his thumb along her jawline. "You are the most beautiful and courageous person I know, Kiah."

"What?" Kiah's breath caught in her throat. No man had ever said she was beautiful. Except for her father, but that hardly counted.

"You are," Jeran reiterated before he let her face go and again withdrew from her. He extricated himself, moving over on the branch so that they were no longer touching.

Kiah feared that she would start crying. She didn't want their conversation to stop. "Are you ever afraid?"

"There are different kinds of fear."

Different kinds of fear? Like what? "Are you afraid of dying?" she finally asked.

"No." Jeran grinned. "I just got baptized, remember? Things would be good for me in the next life if I died now."

Kiah landed a light smack on his shoulder as they both laughed. "You really aren't afraid of anything?"

The smile died on Jeran's face. "There are some things I'm afraid of."

"Like what?"

"Like . . . how I feel." There was an unrecognizable tone to Jeran's voice, a rawness she was not familiar with.

"Feel?" Kiah repeated, feeling a little lightheaded as her stomach jumped like it was filled with bouncing moon rabbits. She hadn't fallen asleep, had she? Kiah pinched herself and realized she was very much awake.

Jeran had moved his right hand to the back of his neck and rubbed it, ducking his head down and away from Kiah. He let out an angry sigh, straightened up, and then moved closer to her.

"Kiah, there's something I want to say, in case anything happens to us. Maybe it's not fair for me to say it, because I don't want to influence how you . . . it's just that I think you deserve the best and even if . . . look, Kiah." Jeran took both of her hands in his, and Kiah's heart forgot to beat. "I want you to know . . . Do you hear that?"

The only thing Kiah could hear was the blood rushing in her ears. "I don't hear anything. What were you saying?"

"Listen."

Jeran turned southward, toward Zarahemla. Kiah tried to focus but was having trouble doing so.

Then she heard it—a reverberating high-pitched whistle that cut through the night like an obsidian sword.

"No," she breathed. "Corahan couldn't possibly . . ."

"What was that a signal for?"

"The Home Guard. The Order of the Jaguar. They're the most elite warriors of the Nephite nation—my father selects his personal bodyguards from their members." Kiah shook her head. All her numbing fear came rushing back to her. Corahan must truly want her dead if he had sent the Home Guard after her.

"What do we do?" she asked in an anguished voice, a question she had meant to keep to herself.

Jeran gripped her hands tightly. "We run."

FIFTEEN

Jeran and Kiah ran hand in hand along the worn animal path, trying to remain as quiet as possible. Somewhere behind them they could still hear the Home Guard calling to one another with a series of whistles as they sliced through thinner trees and dense bushes, trying to flush them out.

Kiah ran until she thought her heart would burst. She dragged deep and ragged breaths in and out, the exertion almost too much to bear. Her lungs felt as if at any moment they would explode from her chest. Every muscle in her body ached, and a sharp pain in her side began to throb.

Time passed too quickly, and Kiah had no idea how long she'd been running. She only knew she had never run this far and this fast before, and it was killing her.

When she reached the point where she could run no more, as if reading her mind, Jeran slowed down, pulling Kiah to a stop. She bent at the waist, resting her hands on her knees, trying to gather her breath as if she'd been drowning. She started to sit down on a nearby mossy boulder when Jeran grabbed her.

"No, don't do that. Walk around. If you sit, your body will tighten up, and you won't be able to run."

"I don't know if I can," Kiah gasped, wondering how it was that Jeran looked so cool and unaffected. He wasn't even sweating!

"How are you not tired?" she asked as he walked her in a circle.

"I come from a long line of runners," Jeran said, keeping his gaze trained to the south. "That's why my father was such a successful merchant—his ability to run long distances quickly while carrying his goods."

"Well, that and the fact that he was a member of the royal family probably had a little something to do with his success," Kiah said, able to joke some now that the pain had started to subside. Jeran flashed one of his perfect smiles at her.

The jungle, which earlier that evening had struck Kiah as romantic, now seemed menacing. The shrill shrieks and mutterings of unfamiliar and unseen nocturnal animals meshed into a cadence that made the trees around her seem like they were alive, breathing together in concert while they awaited their chance to devour Kiah and Jeran whole.

Jeran's smile faded when a whistle sounded close by. Much too close.

Kiah wanted to give up. She wanted to lie down on the ground and curl into a ball, fall asleep, and awaken tomorrow to find this all a dream. She was tired. Exhausted. She couldn't keep running.

"Come on," Jeran said, pulling on Kiah's hand. "They'll find the trail soon. We have to move."

Her entire body protested as they broke into another run. Kiah thought she heard something behind her and turned her head to look. The path behind them remained empty. She moved her gaze forward again, but not fast enough to prevent herself from tripping over a raised root that Jeran had jumped over. Her left foot caught underneath, and her entire upper body rotated as she tried to free herself, twisting her leg in the process.

"Ow!" she cried out, unable to stifle her cry, and she grabbed at her left ankle. Jeran hushed her and dropped down next to her, testing her foot.

"It isn't broken," he told her, trying to get her up. "Can you walk?"

Tears of pain welled in Kiah's eyes as soon as she put weight on her left foot. "No."

"I'll help you." Jeran put Kiah's left arm around his neck. He wrapped his right arm around her waist and tried to take her weight so that they could continue, but she could only manage a slight hobble.

"They're going to find us," Kiah moaned in a low voice. "They'll catch us."

"They won't." Jeran always sounded so sure, so strong to her.

"You don't understand. My neighbor joined the Home Guard last year, and for his initiation he had to catch a harpy eagle the Home Guard had painted. It took him four weeks to track it. He captured that eagle alive and brought it back to Zarahemla. They will find us."

Jeran's arm tightened around her. "Giving up is not the answer. We have to keep going. We have to try."

He stopped, scanned the surrounding area, and then glanced upward. "And if we can't go by ground, then we'll have to fly."

Jeran took Kiah off the path toward a series of interconnected trees. Underneath the canopy, countless vines and lianas intertwined, twisting together like giant snakes. Jeran climbed a tree, pulling Kiah up behind him. "We'll go across on the vines. If they find our trail they'll have a hard time tracking us up here in the dark. We'll head east instead of north until we reach Gideon. We'll get help there."

Kiah nodded as Jeran reached out and grabbed onto the vine in front of him, testing its sturdiness. He pushed off from the tree and started to move hand over hand across the vine to the next tree. Kiah followed, shoving all the fear and doubts from her mind.

As they moved, a solitary star peeked through the tree cover and then blinked and flitted away. The hot, humid air stayed trapped just underneath the canopy, and Kiah felt as if she were moving through some sort of insect stew. Creatures grunted and chattered underneath her, but Kiah didn't dare look down.

She didn't have the same kind of strength in her arms that Jeran did. Kiah weakened quickly, her arms shaking the thick vine as she struggled to reach the next tree. She tried swinging her legs to see if the momentum would help her. It didn't. Her fingers barely clung to the vine, and she wasn't certain that she could make it much longer. Maybe she should drop down and give Jeran a chance to get away.

Kiah's head lolled back while she was considering this possibility. A strong arm snaked out and pulled her to a tree limb. "I can't," she told Jeran as he settled her onto a branch. "I'm not strong enough."

"I am," Jeran said. "Hold on to me."

Was he really proposing that he carry her through the entire jungle?

"Kiah." Jeran sounded impatient. "You can't do everything by yourself. You need to let me help you. Hold on."

She reached up and wrapped her arms around his neck, hanging onto his back the way a baby monkey does to its mother's. Jeran reached out for the next set of vines, and when he and Kiah were hanging with their legs dangling, he let out a groan of pain.

"Why didn't you tell me how heavy you are?" he teased.

"This is no time to joke," Kiah reprimanded as Jeran gripped onto the vine and moved them to the next tree.

"It's a perfect time. Things can't get much worse," Jeran said in between arm swings. "If there is anything I have learned in my life, it's that in dark times you have to take the light where you can find it."

They fell into a pattern—Jeran would swing them across the vines, they would get to a tree, move across the branches until they found the next set of vines in an easterly direction, and then would pull themselves across their length. Sometimes Kiah would try to give Jeran a break and move by herself for as long as she could. But the distance she could do it alone grew shorter and shorter.

The strain had caught up with Jeran. Kiah clung to him, and her arms grew damp from the sweat that flowed from Jeran's head down his neck. She could feel how he strained, how the exertion took more out of him with each arm movement. Jeran began to slow down.

Several large fruit bats flapped past on leathery wings, squeaking to one another as they flew. Kiah turned her head to the right to watch them and saw a large sloth pulling itself across a tree branch. Though she couldn't be certain, she thought the sloth traveled more quickly than they did.

While Kiah wondered if they would move faster if she were hobbling on foot, something large zipped past her ear and hit Jeran in the back of his head. His body went lax, and Kiah screamed his name as they fell to the earth below them.

Kiah hit the ground hard, her ankle blazing in pain. Jeran lay next to her, unmoving. "No, no, no," she said, crawling over to him. "Please don't be dead. Please be alive." Kiah's voice shook as she managed to roll Jeran over. She put her head to his chest, and relief flooded through her when she could hear his heartbeat and could feel him breathing. She checked the back of his head with her hand, and when she withdrew her fingers, they were covered in his blood. Kiah knew who had the expertise necessary to hit Jeran so precisely and miss Kiah entirely.

A bush nearby rustled, and Kiah's head snapped up at the sound. She drew her swords and used her good foot to push herself to a nearby tree. She shuffled her way up the trunk, bracing her back against it for support. She would not let them kill Jeran. And she wouldn't die without a fight.

A member of the Home Guard emerged from the bush like a wraith. Kiah saw the telltale markers of his order—the cuffs of skin on his wrists and ankles made from a jaguar he would have personally killed. He had a spear poised above his head, but it was not pointed at Kiah. He pointed it at Jeran.

"Drop your weapons, or he's dead." One by one, more Jaguar soldiers materialized from the nearby shadows and foliage until she realized they had totally surrounded her and Jeran. Kiah dropped her swords to the ground without hesitation. One man she might have been able to fight. But she couldn't fight ten.

She heard someone approaching her from behind, somewhere off to her left. Kiah watched as the other members of the guard came to attention, and she knew before she saw him that the man approaching was their leader.

Her guess was confirmed when the man stepped in front of her. Judging by his jaguar-skin cape, his cuffs, the markings of his armor, and the cat-claw necklace, this man had easily killed three to four jaguars by himself. Men were lucky to survive the attack of the giant cat, and not many were capable of killing even one, let alone three.

"We were instructed to give this to you," the man said and held something out for Kiah. Full of apprehension, Kiah held her hand out and the object was dropped into her open palm. She recognized it as the necklace Jeran had given her. Kiah's hand flew to her throat. How had she not realized that she didn't have it on? Where had she lost it?

Kiah suddenly remembered the tree branch that had scratched her neck outside of the king-men's cave. It must have been then. She also remembered the voice that had told her to go back. This had been why she was supposed to go back. Kiah slowly slumped down the length of the tree as she held the necklace up in front of her face. The guilt over her disobedience smothered her. How many lives had she put in danger because of her inability to listen and do as she was told?

Kiah couldn't even gather enough strength to cry. She had risked everything, and now she would lose everything.

"What are you going to do with us?" she finally asked in a voice devoid of emotion.

"When we know, you will know."

The Jaguar officer called to his men, and they tied up Jeran's ankles and wrists and slid a pole in between his limbs so that he could be carried like an animal. Kiah's wrists were loosely tied behind her, and when they realized she couldn't walk, they threw her over a large man's shoulders. Kiah was dimly aware of the fact that a man was dispatched to tell their superiors that Kiah and Jeran had been captured and to ask for further orders.

She realized they were headed back to Zarahemla. Back to Corahan.

Finally overcome by it all, Kiah's eyes fluttered shut, and she slept.

* * *

The first thing Jeran was aware of was that his head felt like it was being split in two, as if someone were trying to saw it open. He could feel the warmth of a fire nearby and felt the bark of the tree behind him digging into his back. His arms had been wrapped around the tree trunk, tied at the wrists. From the pain in his ankles he knew he had been tightly bound there as well. He smelled healing herbs and realized they had been applied to the wound at the back of his head to prevent infection.

Jeran tried to assess his surroundings, who had captured them, and how many. He saw cut wood and palm fronds to the side of him and guessed someone was assembling temporary huts. He was distracted from trying to count the soldiers that walked back and forth gathering supplies by a harsh grunt that sounded like a mixture of a cough and a rumbling roar. Jeran had lived in the jungle long enough to know it was a jaguar. Looking straight ahead he saw a flash between the dense foliage—a movement of yellow fur and muscle. Men all around him shouted, and Jeran heard them arguing over who would take the kill. The soldiers ran into the jungle, leaving only one man behind who stood at the end of the small clearing, yelling his wager as to who he thought would kill the large predator.

Jeran struggled against the tree, testing the bands to see if he could wriggle his way loose. Too tight. Jeran could only see in front of him and a little bit to each side. Where was Kiah? He strained against the ropes, willing them to break.

For the first time in a long time, Jeran knew true fear. He was not scared for himself but for Kiah. He had faced death many times. He was not afraid of it. Especially now—he had been washed free of his sins. He would pass on to his God, to reunite with his parents.

But when he thought of Kiah's death, it was as if someone had taken a flaming hot ember and stabbed it into his soul. He would gladly give his life to protect her. But he could not control these men who had captured them. And it terrified him to think of what Kiah's fate might be. It terrified him even more that he might have to make the choice to break his covenant to the Lord to keep her safe.

Jeran began a fervent prayer, asking that he receive the strength to get free of his bonds. While the soldiers were distracted by the jaguar, it would be the only time he had to get loose. He heard a thumping sound behind him as if someone were jumping.

Then he felt his bands being awkwardly sawed through and could feel someone pressing against his hands. Kiah.

"They took our weapons, but they didn't find the blade I keep sewn in my tunic."

Jeran realized that Kiah was still tied up. She had cut him free by facing away from the ropes and using the blade behind her back.

She finally cut through the last rope and dropped the blade into Jeran's hand. It nicked him slightly, but he brought it around to cut through the ropes at his feet, never taking his eyes off the guard who was more interested in his fellow soldiers than in his prisoners.

"Your things are over there, next to the fire."

Jeran saw his spear and pack and carefully crept over. He grabbed them along with a spare Nephite sword and then returned to the tree.

"Let's go," Jeran said as he stole around to the far side of the tree where Kiah sat, helping her to her feet. Kiah leaned back against the tree, putting all of her weight on her right foot.

"No, you have to go. My ankle is still twisted. I will only slow you down."

Jeran stopped looking for the guard to stare incredulously at Kiah's tearstained face. "I am not leaving without you."

"You have to," she cried softly. "If you don't, you'll die. Corahan sent orders that I am to be taken north, and the soldiers are supposed to kill you."

"Why would they bother with my wound if they were just going to kill me?" Jeran again tipped his head to one side to peer around the tree at the guard.

"They didn't know what Corahan wanted to do with you. The messenger just now returned with the orders, and then the jaguar appeared. Now is your only chance."

"I'm tired of running. I ran from Ammoron, we ran from Corahan. I'm done. We'll stay and fight." Jeran tried to turn Kiah around to cut the ropes on her wrists, but she jerked away from him.

"There are ten of them and two of us. We're both injured. And they will kill you." She hissed each word succinctly. "Don't you understand that I can't watch you die? That everything I did tonight was to keep you alive? Please run!" Kiah choked on the words, nearly unable to say them.

"Don't you understand that I can't let them hurt you? I can't let them take you back to Corahan." Jeran shot back, gripping her shoulders tightly.

"They are not taking me to Corahan. And these men respect my father. They may not agree with him, but they respect him. They would never hurt me. They have orders to take me north, and the Home Guard never disobey direct orders. They didn't say where they are taking me. You have to follow us so that you can find me and rescue me. But you can't do that if you're dead!"

Jeran shook his head, indicating that he would not leave, and Kiah only cried harder. He couldn't leave her. Despite what she said . . . that the Nephites didn't want him. They wanted her. Why?

"There's no time," Kiah said, nudging Jeran out of his confused thoughts. "Please . . . trust me. If it's hard for me to ask for help, it's just as hard for you to trust, and I am begging you to trust me. You have to run, because you are the only one who will be able to save me later."

She was right. Jeran looked into her glistening golden eyes and knew she was right. He would give everything he was to keep her safe. And she was telling him that the only way he could keep her safe was to leave her with the enemy.

There was a sound in the distance, like that of a giant cat screaming. The soldiers were finishing up with their hunt. He had to make his decision now.

"I trust you," he said, despite the fact that the words cut through him with razor precision. "I will go, but you have to promise me that you will stay alive. Promise me."

"I promise," Kiah said fiercely.

"Promise me again that you will stay alive, and I swear to you that nothing on this earth will keep me from coming for you."

"I promise," she repeated.

Jeran grabbed her to him, holding her tightly. He released her, his hands moving from her shoulders up to her face, cupping it with his hands. They gazed at one another, and Jeran was certain he could see into Kiah's soul. In one quick movement, he leaned his head down and kissed her—a fiery kiss filled with fierceness, tenderness, and their promises.

Jeran had to break the kiss off when he heard the exultant cries of the victorious hunters. "I will come for you," Jeran said again, and with one last look at Kiah, he sprinted into the forest in the opposite direction of the Home Guard.

Not a few seconds later he heard the sounds of discovery of his escape, of men being called to follow him. Jeran ran through the jungle, once more knowing the feeling of being hunted like an animal.

SIXTEEN

Jeran ran toward the city of Gideon. Pahoran and his men were there. If he could reach them . . .

The Jaguar soldiers behind him did not try to muffle their sounds of giving chase. Perhaps they were trying to intimidate Jeran, to scare him into surrendering.

As if the jungle had decided to assist the Home Guard, the vegetation suddenly turned malicious. It hooked and barbed and grabbed at Jeran as he flew past, trying to hold him tight. With a sword in one hand and his spear in the other, Jeran cut at the leafy hands to free himself. He saw a hornet's hive and slashed at it, dislodging it from a low hanging branch. An angry hum started as the hornets began to swarm. Jeran ran clear of them, leaving a dangerous trap for the soldiers following him.

He heard cries of pain as the hornets found the members of the guard. Jeran ran on, not knowing how many men chased after him, how many would stop and turn back at the hornet attack or who would push through.

At least one. He heard at least one man still behind him. Jeran pushed himself harder, to go faster. This man would be intent on Jeran's death after receiving the stinging welts of the furious insects.

The earth gave way from underneath his feet, and Jeran teetered on the edge of a ravine until he was able to throw his weight back. He could not see how long the ravine was or where it began and ended. He could run alongside it, but he had to go across it to get to Gideon.

Jeran's decision was made as an arrow whizzed past his left ear. Down.

He began to lope down the side of the steep ravine wall, in a combination of running and sliding through the loose rock that formed farther down, past the jutting roots of trees that grew sideways off the ravine.

Listening as he ran, Jeran couldn't hear any indications that he was still being chased. He stopped and crouched close to the ground. Despite his run, his breathing was even and normal. Except for the usual nighttime sounds, he couldn't hear anything else. Maybe they'd given up the chase. He held no value for them, and since they had planned on simply killing him, perhaps they'd decided to let the jungle take care of it for them.

Jeran felt a slight gust of wind against his left upper arm and then a searing pain. Looking down, he saw a straight red line against his skin that started to bleed. A dart. Jeran raised his head to see the soldier standing at the top of the ravine lowering a blowpipe and giving him a mocking smile as he melted back into the jungle.

His skin tingled. Not just a dart. A poisoned dart.

Jeran started sucking at the wound and spitting it out onto the ground next to him. The dart had only grazed his skin with its poison tip. If it had hit him full on, he knew he would have died instantly. He removed as much as he could, but he still felt lightheaded. He hadn't been able to suck it all out.

Still, he couldn't stay there. The guards might decide to return to make sure he had died. He would have to move. He tried to stand, and the ground swayed precariously beneath him.

A horrible nausea gripped his stomach as he stumbled forward, forcing himself to go on.

The small rocks beneath his feet trembled and then gave way. Jeran began to fall to the bottom of the ravine.

Despite the cloud of mist that hung in his mind, he was able to stick his spear out, slamming it into the ground to slow his descent.

He was only vaguely aware of the stick eventually snapping at the combined weight of the rock slide and Jeran's pressure on it.

He fell into the bottom of the ravine, covered in dust and dirt that clung like ticks to his skin. Jeran's body crashed into a bush that cushioned his fall, and he felt little rocks raining down on him.

Jeran's last thought was of that day by the river, watching Kiah sun herself, and a smile crept across his lips. Then his world went black.

* * *

Jeran awoke not knowing how long he had slept. Judging from the dryness in his throat, he guessed one or two days. His body felt weighted down, and Jeran struggled to sit up and push off the rocks piled on top of him. He coughed from the puff of dirt that flew up as he moved the rocks.

An incredibly strong odor hit his nose, and Jeran found that he was surrounded by a grove of copal-bearing incense trees. He realized that he had been protected—the rocks covering him from sight and the incense masking his scent from any potential predators.

He slowly got to his feet and did his best to ignore the burning sensation that plagued his mouth and throat. Jeran felt sore all over and winced at the blue and purple bruises covering his skin. He patted himself, testing his limbs. There didn't seem to be any punctures or breaks to his bones. His sword, as miraculously as intact as he was, lay about a foot away from him, along with the shattered pieces of the spear his father had given him. His pack had been crushed underneath him, and he twisted it around to his front to see if he had any water left.

The water skin had been squashed in the fall, and all of the water had seeped out. Jeran held it up over his open mouth and eked out a few drops of water onto his parched tongue.

A slight movement in a tree on his left flickered in the corner of Jeran's eye, and he raised his sword. He saw a yellow and green dappled lizard, no bigger than his hand, with large, blinking eyes, studying him intently. The lizard stuck its tongue out at Jeran, testing the air. It looked like the lizard was deciding whether or not Jeran was edible.

I'm not dead yet, Jeran thought, trying to dust some of the dirt off. His once gleaming white tunic was now a very earthy brown. The lizard scurried down the tree and up the opposite wall of the ravine. Jeran's head throbbed, but by watching the little green reptile, he saw a path up. If he could grab a vine there, a root over that way, he should be able to pull himself out.

He looked up to the sky, shielding his eyes with his hand. The sun was centered in the blue expanse above him, and Jeran judged it to be midday. The humidity and heat crashed into him like a wave. It never bothered Jeran when he was well hydrated, but without water, every step took enormous effort. The pain he could fight past; the thirst was overwhelming.

Jeran took an unsteady step out of the small grove of trees and away from the barrage of incense. His nose immediately detected another scent—fire. He listened and realized that the creatures of the jungle carried on their daily living. Had there been a jungle fire nearby, these animals would have fled. The fires must be man-made. But there would have to have been tens or hundreds of fires to account for the overpowering aroma of smoke.

He heard a sound like distant thunder, a slow rumble that didn't let up. Men's voices, he realized. Thousands. Somewhere nearby an army camped. But whose army?

Jeran tried to take another step and stumbled, falling to his knees. He had to decide what to do. Did he try to find the army? Or should he hide? If he happened upon the king-men or Lamanites, he would be killed. For that matter, even if the men up there followed Moroni, the Nephites might kill him just for being a Lamanite in Nephite lands.

Exhaustion and confusion pressed down on him as he tried to figure out what the best course of action would be. The tattoo on his right arm caught his attention, and if nothing else, he would have to make certain to cover it regardless of who awaited him. He tugged at the bottom of his tunic, using his sword to cut a strip long enough to tie over his arm. It took supreme effort to reach across and tie the swath of cloth around the mark, using his teeth to pull it tight.

He had just finished tying up the band when he heard a few rocks skip down the wall in front of him. Jeran looked up to the far side of the ravine and saw a man.

A scout. A Nephite.

Jeran tried to call out but found that he hadn't the strength to speak. The scout scanned the jungle on the opposite side of the ravine, and Jeran surmised that he was checking to see if Jeran traveled alone or if there was an army of Lamanites behind him.

Before Jeran could say anything, the man disappeared. Jeran knew what he had to do—he must follow the scout back. He again tried to get up, but everything hurt so much. *Fight through the pain,* he told himself. *You've had worse.*

Jeran went to the wall and inch-by-inch began to climb. He had to repeatedly stop to rest. His body sagged against the side of the ravine. He felt defeated, like he would never make it out. Suddenly a rope appeared in front of him. Jeran looked back up and saw four Nephite men at the top of the wall. "Grab on," one of them called.

He took the rope and created a loop to go under his arms. He knotted it securely, tested it, and signaled that he was ready. The soldiers pulled him up, and Jeran gritted his teeth at every bump. Every rock seemed to leap from the ground and take pleasure in striking him.

When he was pulled up to the crest, the Nephites laid him out on the ground. It seemed to Jeran that they were all speaking at once, and their voices swirled around him like winds blowing from every direction.

Someone offered Jeran water, and he drank it greedily. "Slowly," he heard a voice say, "or he'll get sick."

"Did you bring it?"

"I have the medicine here."

"What do you think he's doing out here all alone?"

"Maybe he got separated from his group."

"He doesn't look like a Lamanite warrior. Look—no face paint, and look at this tunic. Have you ever seen a Lamanite in an outfit like that one?"

"Perhaps he's a spy."

"He could be lost."

"Well, whoever he is, let's bring him back to camp and let the captain decide what to do with him."

"He's not fit to be questioned. Give him the medicine. We'll let him sleep, and when he wakes up, he should be ready to talk."

Something was pressed to Jeran's lips, and he drank deeply, only realizing too late what he was being given. A healing mixture, designed to help him recover by helping him to sleep.

"Moroni," Jeran said in a deep, raspy voice before he drifted off. "I have to see Captain Mor . . ."

* * *

Jeran awoke not knowing where he was or how he had arrived there. He lay on a pallet, covered with a light blanket, inside of a hut.

He removed the blanket and saw that his clothes had been changed to a simple brown tunic similar to the ones he had seen earlier on the Nephite soldiers. He had been cleaned, his wounds dressed. Jeran carefully sat up. He realized that it did not hurt to move. While he still had some slight soreness, he felt better. Stronger.

"You're supposed to drink that," a man said from the opposite end of the shelter, pointing to a slightly steaming cup on the ground near his pallet.

Jeran snapped his head around to see an older man seated on a low stool, fixing a broken sword. He had a small pouch open from which he extracted triangular pieces of razor-sharp obsidian. He then fit them into the deep wooden groove, securing them into place without breaking the pieces or injuring himself. Jeran knew it took great skill to repair a sword as quickly and as easily as this man did. The man was obviously an experienced soldier based on his strong build. He was tall, probably close to the same height as Jeran.

Turning his attention away from the seated man, Jeran picked up the warm drink and took a sip. He had to refrain from spitting it back out. It tasted foul.

"You need to drink all of it. Healer's orders."

Closing his eyes, Jeran downed the entire thing in one gulp. He didn't know how it was possible, but the aftertaste was worse than the actual drink. He put the cup back down.

"How long have I been asleep?" Jeran asked.

"One day."

How much time had he lost? Where was Kiah now? Was she safe? Jeran knew this man would probably not know the answer to any of the questions jumping around in his mind. Settling on an easier query, Jeran started to ask the man his name, but the words died on his lips. He knew who the man was.

There was an unmistakable aura about the man. Jeran flashed back to a memory of standing outside his mountain home during a lightning storm, remembering the way the air around him had crackled and breathed with energy. Jeran felt that same energy emanating from the seated man. The man exuded power, authority. Like a man who had an unshakable inner conviction of his own skills, abilities, and worth. An intense man devoted to his beliefs, to the cause of right. A hero.

Captain Moroni.

Moroni gazed back at Jeran, and Jeran nearly jumped. If Jeran hadn't recognized Moroni before, he would have recognized him by those golden brown eyes. Kiah's eyes.

"Who are you?" Moroni asked him.

"Jeran, son of Jeran of Nephi."

Moroni placed his sword down and picked up a bundle next to it. He pulled something up and Jeran saw that it was his old tunic.

"The obvious answer, and the one agreed upon by most of my men, is that you are a spy. But I do not believe in killing men needlessly. I wanted you to have a chance to explain. Especially because on closer inspection," Moroni continued, holding the tunic out to Jeran, "I see on your garment the mark of the women of my family. Here, along the edge, do you see the interlocking squares?"

Jeran nodded and noticed the same squares on Moroni's quilted armor.

"I am presented then with two choices. Either you stole the tunic, which I find rather improbable, or a woman in my family gave it to you. Considering the quality of the embroidery, I have to surmise that Kiah gave it to you."

"She did."

The calm and compassionate expression disappeared from Moroni's face, and Jeran was suddenly confronted with an angry and suspicious father. Kiah had told Jeran once about her father's temper. She said Moroni was not a man who became angry often, but when he did, it was a terrible thing. Jeran heartily agreed and did not enjoy being at the receiving end of it.

"How do you know my daughter?"

Jeran decided that was a question with infinite answers. How did he know Kiah? He knew how her nose crinkled up when she smiled. He knew the expression in her eyes when she was afraid. He knew her strength. He knew her insecurities. He knew her desire to do right. He knew her generous heart. He knew her courage. He knew the way she felt in his arms, as if she'd been created just to fill them. He knew the softness of her lips under his own.

But he was fairly certain those were not the answers Moroni would want to hear.

"We met a while ago, outside of the city. I had come to seek your help. Kiah and I became friends; she helped me to become baptized in the Church. I was captured by Corahan and made a prisoner. Kiah discovered the plans of Pachus, Corahan, and the king-men. She warned Pahoran and then rescued me. We ran to find you but were captured by the Home Guard. Kiah managed to free me, and I tried to make her come with me, but she had sprained her ankle and wasn't able to run. The Home Guard had been instructed to kill me and to take her north. We didn't know where they were taking her. I was supposed to follow behind but was nearly killed. Then your men found me."

Moroni nodded, considering the information. A tic had developed in his left cheek, embellished by a long white scar. "You left her?"

"I didn't want to leave her. I begged her to come with me. But she's so stubborn," Jeran said in an exasperated and frustrated voice.

A slight smile played at the corner of Moroni's lips. "Just like her mother."

"I was ready to pick her up and carry her off, but I knew that if we both ran, they would probably kill her, too. I couldn't let that happen. And I nearly died as it was." Jeran folded his hands in his lap, not wanting to show Moroni his own worry over the situation. "I have to believe that she is safe."

"Pachus is probably hoping that I will use my men and resources to look for her, turning me away from Zarahemla." Moroni said the words aloud, but he sounded distant, as if he were thinking something through. Jeran watched as warring expressions and emotions clashed on Moroni's face. Captain Moroni finally closed his eyes, bowing his head. Jeran could see Moroni's lips moving.

Finally, Moroni stood and lifted the flap of the curtain. "Come with me."

Strangely enough, Jeran knew that Moroni believed him. Even stranger, it felt like Moroni trusted him. Maybe Moroni had decided that if Kiah trusted Jeran, he would too.

Jeran followed Moroni outside, and his mouth dropped slightly. His senses were inundated by a multitude of sights, sounds, and smells. They stood in the middle of a large, grassy savanna surrounded by jungle. He saw a sea of soldiers spread out in front of him, marching back and forth like giant ants as they went about preparing for war. He heard their conversations and the clank of weapons being prepared. The air was rife with the crisp scent of smoke from fires used to clear the insects and to prepare food. Banners flew in every corner. Among the Lamanites the banners represented different allegiances and kin. Here in the Nephite camp, every banner displayed the Title of Liberty. "There are so many men. You must have brought your entire army."

Moroni looked at him, assessing his statement as if trying to decipher the true intent behind it. Apparently detecting no ulterior motive, Moroni said, "After Kiah warned Pahoran, he sent word to me asking for my help. He said he only needed a small force, and I left the bulk of the army behind with my captains, Teancum and Lehi. But in every village I went through and in every city I passed, I raised the Title of Liberty. Thousands of men flocked to the standard, to the oaths and covenants they had made, and they followed me."

Jeran trailed behind Moroni, taking the scene in. He saw some soldiers trying to relieve the stress of the upcoming battle by playing a game with a rubber ball. The ball was kicked wildly, and a boy, barely old enough to be at war, ran after it and stumbled into Moroni.

Moroni reached out and righted the boy, preventing his fall. Jeran held a breath in, waiting for Moroni to yell at or hit the boy.

"Are you all right?" Moroni asked, and the boy nodded, giving the Nephite chief captain a large grin. Moroni gave the boy a pat on his shoulder and sent him back to his game.

Jeran knew it was not how his uncles would have reacted. He knew Ammoron or Amalickiah would have killed the boy then and there for being clumsy enough to bump into them, or for daring to play a game when there was a war to worry about. The boy hadn't even been afraid when he ran into Captain Moroni. It was not how things were done among the Lamanites under his uncles' rule.

They joined a group of men sitting around a tree stump that served as a makeshift table, discussing numbers and the movements of their troops on the map spread in front of them. Moroni introduced Jeran to the men, and Jeran recognized the names of Pahoran and Aha.

There was not a Lamanite alive who didn't fear Captain Lehi, one of Moroni's right-hand men and best friends. Aha, Lehi's brother, was a close second in ferocity. And if Aha looked anything like his older brother, Jeran could understand the fear. Aha was a short and broad man and seemed to be constructed of pure muscle. He looked like he had been hewn from wood with sharp, angular, jutting features and eyes so dark that they looked like twin pools of black water. His legs and face were covered in scars of varying sizes and lengths, evidence of his many years in battle. The other men surrounding them carried shields on their backs with their family names and places of birth written on them. Not Aha. He had two swords and a cimeter strapped to his back. Jeran doubted that such a man would even bother with a shield in a fight.

"You would let the heir of Amalickiah sit in on council?"

Jeran observed that the band on his right arm had been removed, his tattoo exposed for all to see. He expected Moroni to shout at Aha, to put him back in his place as he had seen his own uncles do so many times whenever an inferior disputed their decisions. But Moroni seemed undisturbed by Aha's question. Jeran sensed that Moroni respected Aha. And Jeran understood that Moroni was not a tyrant over his men. Moroni did not lead by force of arms or by intimidation. His men followed him because they respected, loved, and trusted him.

"I am not his heir by choice," Jeran spoke up, feeling every eye at the council upon him. "Amalickiah and Ammoron were and are wicked men. Ammoron tried to have me killed and even now offers a reward for my death. I have been on my own for four years, running from him. Their fight is not mine—their cause is not just."

Along with Moroni's unspoken support, this seemed to satisfy the men, even Aha, and he moved over to offer Jeran a place to sit.

"We could raise ladders and ropes against the sides of the wall and climb in," one man said. "An attack from all sides."

"There are deep trenches outside the walls," Jeran said, and he could see Pahoran nodding.

"How do you know?" the man asked.

"I helped dig them."

"I do not want to attack the city in a way they are expecting," Moroni said, turning the map so that he could see it more clearly.

"I also do not want to tear our own defenses down—it would expose us if the Lamanites attacked. I think our best approach is the element of surprise."

"But Pachus and his men are expecting us to attack," Pahoran said. "They haven't dared come out against my forces while we have been stationed in Gideon. They won't be surprised. We will never get in through the entrance, and we'll be too easily picked off trying to come over the walls. How do you propose we get in the city without heavy casualties?"

"I think I have a way. It's why I brought my young Lamanite friend to the meeting." Moroni turned to Jeran. "Would you object to being tied up?"

SEVENTEEN

Kiah heard the sound of footsteps approaching, the soft padding of well-worn sandals against the stone floor.

The Lamanites had not put her in the makeshift prison along with the rest of the Nephite citizens who had once inhabited Nephihah. She had been placed in a large house, presumably home to the previous judge of the city. The room that held her prisoner had only one rectangular slit placed high up in the wall, almost out of Kiah's reach. She had pulled herself up on more than one occasion to look out at the world beyond, and to her shock, she saw that the Lamanites had taken not only the men captive, but the women and children. Her father *never* took women and children as prisoners. He always released them and kept only the men.

Kiah watched as two young Lamanite soldiers teased and tormented her people. She fervently wished she had a rock or something to throw at them, but the room she stayed in was swept bare.

An officer stopped the two soldiers. He yelled at them, and Kiah wished she could understand what was being said as the two soldiers looked thoroughly ashamed. She saw the Lamanite captain return to the building that held her captive. A wave of air from the coast came through the small opening, and Kiah could taste the salt of the east sea in the breeze. The moist heat in the air was oppressive, more so than in Zarahemla.

She lowered herself back down carefully when she heard footsteps.

A curtain hung across the opening of the room to afford her a measure of privacy. She could always see and hear the guards who stood watch just beyond the doorway—a constant reminder that she was trapped and had no way of escape.

Not that she could escape. Her ankle still hurt. The throbbing pain had stopped, but she had trouble trying to stand on it. She tried to rest it, to get ready for whatever would happen next.

Someone was coming to her room, and Kiah did her best to prepare herself. She was a continual mess—every time the curtain was pushed aside and a guard entered the room, she was sure this was the time they would take her away to her death. Usually the guard was only bringing her a meal of stale or moldy food along with a cup of muddy water, her fears wasted. She was stuck in a perpetual limbo, just waiting.

She heard a slight murmur as whoever was on the other side spoke to her guards. Kiah tried to remain calm when someone pulled the curtain to one side. A Lamanite warrior came in and put a platter of inedible food on the floor. Kiah had noted that the soldiers regarded her with a mixture of indifference, curiosity, and in some instances indignation that they were being forced to watch over a mere woman.

This soldier stared at her and began to speak in low, rapid tones. He had heavy lidded eyes and a high forehead. His head was shaved except for one long lock in the center, the way she imagined Lamonti would look if his hair hadn't grown back in. The Lamanite smiled at her while talking, and Kiah saw that his teeth had been filed to points, making him look feral. Kiah had difficulty making out much of it but understood "pretty girl." The Lamanite started to advance on her, undoing the ties that held his weapons to his body.

Kiah's heart pounded loudly in her chest. She briefly wondered if it would do any good to call for help, but instead, she just screamed.

The guards outside her room didn't move. This must have been arranged with them. She was alone.

Kiah began edging along the floor, trying to keep the Lamanite at a distance. She could smell the sweat and dirt on the soldier as he got closer. If she could just reach his sword . . .

A man, obviously a commanding officer, burst through the curtain and began to yell at the soldier. It sounded like the soldier was defending his actions as he gathered up his weapons, but the older man threw him out of the room, and she saw that one of her guards escorted him down the hall. She realized the officer was the same man she had just seen outside. The captain was a large man with black and silver hair and kind brown eyes. He smiled at her as if to reassure her, and Kiah saw bits of jade set in the man's teeth.

"Sorry," the older man said with a heavy accent in her own language, stumbling over his words, but he spoke her language better than she spoke his. She wished she could speak to the man in his own tongue, but Kiah had not been trained in languages like her brother had been—she was never expected to need any sort of education outside of her domestic duties. And it certainly had not been expected that she would ever meet a Lamanite. She knew a few words, and Jeran had been teaching her . . . but it was not enough that she could converse.

"This . . . this happen not again."

"Thank you," Kiah said, putting her hands behind her so that the officer wouldn't see how they trembled.

"I Zamir. Asking for me if you need help."

"Zamir? Do you have a son named Lamonti?"

"Lamonti!" Zamir repeated and broke into a rapid speech that she could not follow. "Yes, yes. My son. Knowing you him?"

"I helped to free him from prison." Kiah found that her grin matched Zamir's. It was nice to smile again. She explained the story as simply as she could, and Zamir clapped for joy when she told him that Lamonti roamed the jungle somewhere. She refrained from telling Zamir about Lamonti's pledge to kill Corahan. Kiah figured he would be happier if he thought Lamonti was on his way to Zamir's side instead of putting his life at risk.

Zamir stepped back through the curtain and yelled. A few moments later, a new tray of food was brought to Kiah with smoked fish, a steaming flat corn cake, and a simple stew of roots and vegetables. A cup of clean water accompanied it. "My guest," Zamir said, gesturing to the platter. "Keeping you safe. No worrying."

"Thank you," Kiah said again, the rich aroma of the food making her stomach growl in anticipation.

"No. Thank you," Zamir said, giving Kiah a slight bow, and he left.

Kiah attacked the food, devouring it in great gulps. Midchew, Kiah remembered the Nephites outside and wondered what kind of food they were being given. Probably something similar to what they had given her before. One of the problems in this war was the notorious shortage of resources. Her own father had said wars were fought on men's stomachs, and the recent poor harvests over the last few years made things worse. The captains could barely feed their own men, let alone the prisoners they captured.

Her appetite suddenly gone, Kiah pushed the platter away and retreated to her favorite corner of the room, the one the sun touched when it shone through the high slot in the wall.

Like Jeran had said, Kiah tried to take the light where she could find it in this dark time. She drew her unhurt leg up to her chest and rested her cheek against the top of her knee. She closed her eyes and put her fingers up to her mouth. Kiah could still feel Jeran's lips against her own and drew warmth from the memory.

The Jaguar soldier who had chased Jeran down said he had died. Kiah didn't believe it. She was sure she would feel it if he had died, certain that the connection between them was that strong. Jeran had sworn to her that nothing would keep him from coming after her. It would only be a matter of time. Kiah wondered where he was now, what he was doing, if he was all right. She wondered how long it would be until he fulfilled his promise.

She would wait. And she would be ready.

* * *

Jeran was ready. His body tensed like a snare while he allowed Aha to bind his arms behind him.

It had been a difficult decision to come with Moroni. Moroni had dispatched the loyal members of the Home Guard to track down the rogue Jaguar soldiers and Kiah. Captain Moroni had guessed that Kiah had been taken to a Lamanite stronghold, and Jeran agreed. It was possible that she was still in the jungle, which was why the soldiers had been sent to look for her. But Jeran knew that if she was locked up somewhere and surrounded by Lamanites, the small band of soldiers would not be able to free her.

The only people who knew for certain where she was being held were within Zarahemla's walls. Jeran had to go into the city, into this battle, to get that information.

But that was not the only reason that he had chosen to go. Jeran felt stunned at the amount of faith and trust Captain Moroni and his men were willing to put in him, how readily they accepted him into their midst. He wanted to prove them right, to assure them that such open and immediate trust had not been misplaced. Were the situation reversed, he knew he would not have trusted so easily. He had to help them.

Jeran had already walked away from his father's people, not willing to wage a pointless war over the kingship, but willing to let a wicked and murderous nation be ruled by a tyrant. Many of the Nephites inside Zarahemla were innocents who did not deserve to be crushed under a man like Pachus. He had run *away* before. This time he would run *into* the heart of the trouble, to do what he could to assist Moroni.

The Nephite army had waited in Gideon until the sun kissed the earth, and then it began the short trek toward Zarahemla. Moroni deliberately chose to attack at night, explaining to Jeran that he had no wish for civilians to be caught in the fight. This late at night the only people in the streets would be king-men soldiers.

The army now camped on the other side of the River Sidon and was covered by the hills and jungle. It amazed Jeran how quiet all of these men could be, how there were no sounds of the army in the jungle, only the animals.

Moroni had selected a group of nine of his best soldiers to go to the city. Pahoran had volunteered to go, as had many other men, but Moroni explained that he needed Pahoran to help lead the soldiers into Zarahemla. A scout had returned to inform them that just as they had feared, Pachus had put up the rarely used gate. Aha explained to Jeran that the gate was composed of heavy tree trunks bound together. They had raised slots on the back that matched up with slots on the inner wall, and locking planks were slid into place. It was so secure that the inner wall would have to be destroyed to get the gate down. The Nephites had never put the gate up and only had it in case of an emergency. It surprised no one that Pachus used it.

Jeran noticed that Moroni stood with the selected nine and put on armor as the other men did. "You're coming with us?" Jeran knew he sounded shocked, but he couldn't help it.

"I go where my men go," Moroni said as he wrapped long lengths of linen cotton around his arms. Moroni turned to Aha and Pahoran. "When I sound the signal, I want you to attack."

Pahoran and Aha both nodded their assent. Aha returned to his task of making certain that the blue armbands were distributed to all of Moroni's men. In the heat of battle it was easy enough to mistake a friend for an enemy, and since they were fighting their own treasonous brethren at night, it would be even harder. Moroni wanted his men to wear the blue bands for their own protection.

Captain Moroni finished with his armor, and Jeran noticed that the camp looked at them expectantly, as if they were just waiting for the moment when Moroni would speak to them.

"I have only this to say. Remember your oath. For our wives, our children, our religion and our freedom." Moroni spoke quietly but with such intent, charisma, and power that Jeran was sure his voice carried even to the men at the rear. The words were passed down the ranks by messengers.

The men could not shout their support, and instead, as far as Jeran could see, men were raising the Title of Liberty in response.

Moroni then knelt, and all the men dropped as a single unit to their knees, including Jeran. The chief captain began a fervent prayer, asking the Lord for His guidance and assistance, asking that the conflict be a short one with little loss of life. Captain Moroni asked that his men be blessed with strength and protected as they fought for what was right.

During the prayer, Jeran opened his eyes and looked around. Moroni prayed as if his Creator were present, and Jeran had never felt the Spirit the way he had then. He half expected to see the Lord standing in their midst as Moroni spoke to Him.

The prayer finished, and Jeran had to be helped back to his feet since his arms had been immobilized. After a short farewell to Pahoran and Aha, Moroni told his men to follow him. Moroni placed Jeran in the middle of the group, and the eleven men hurried to cross the river, which gurgled and bubbled at them as they went past, the water splashing their ankles. In the wet season, they would never have been able to cross the Sidon on foot, but in a few moments they were on the other side of the river and in the land surrounding Zarahemla.

It was not long until they stood at the base of the walkway that led into the city. A voice called out from the towers above them, demanding they identify themselves.

A soldier at the front of their group asked them to open the gate, saying that they had been chasing down the lost Lamanite prisoners and had retrieved one.

Jeran's heart beat a steady, constant rhythm as he tried to prepare himself for what was about to happen. He was headed into battle. How could he keep his oath?

He heard the sound of wood scraping against wood as the securing planks were released. With a loud creak, the king-men soldiers groaned as they lowered the gate from the inside, letting it slowly fall to the ground. Moroni nodded, and his men began their ascent up the darkened pathway into the city. Jeran found himself holding his breath, almost anticipating the feel of an arrow or spearhead. He waited for the distinctive sound of the air being cut by a missile but heard nothing. Instead, they walked on top of the gate, their steps sounding extraordinarily loud as they pounded against the wood. They stepped off the gate onto the main highway, and Jeran heard the massive door being put back into place.

"King Pachus wants all the Lamanite prisoners brought to him at the palace," a man called from a tower above them, off to the left.

Jeran felt the soldiers around him stiffen at the mention of "King Pachus." But one of Moroni's men grunted his assent, and they set off toward the center of the city.

"Ten men at the gate," one of the Nephite soldiers whispered.

"Go," Moroni said.

One by one the soldiers began to detach themselves from the group, disappearing into the night. Jeran turned to see some climbing the towers at the front, moving up the wooden ladders as quietly as shadows. Others positioned themselves near the king-men at the gate. Finally only Moroni remained with Jeran.

Moroni pulled Jeran behind a building and cut his ropes free. "You'll need a weapon," Moroni said.

The moment had come, and Jeran felt strangely uncomfortable. He did not want to disappoint Captain Moroni. "I have to tell you . . ."

The Nephite captain put his hand up. "I know who you are. I knew as soon as I saw your tattoo. I know the oath you have taken."

Jeran started to ask him how he could possibly know when Moroni continued, "I have many spies among the Lamanites. It's what keeps my men alive and my people safe." Moroni then handed Jeran a weapon he carried, a staff with no point on either end. He could defend himself without giving fatal wounds. "I respect the choice that you made not to embrace the bloodthirstiness of your people or your uncles." Jeran took the staff, testing the weight and the balance. Moroni then unsheathed his own sword from the weapon sack hanging from his waist.

"Stay close to me," Moroni told him.

Jeran heard a sound like a large rock hitting the ground, then another and another. He realized the sound was the Nephite soldiers silently disabling the men in the towers and at the gate in a way that caused no alarm. The silence and cover of night made it so that soldiers at other stations were not even aware of what was happening at the only entrance in and out of the city.

Moroni found a nearby tower in the middle of a garden. He climbed partway up and motioned for Jeran to join him. Captain Moroni pointed, and Jeran looked to see that Moroni's men were in the process of releasing the planks. He could not even imagine how that handful of men had managed to take out the entire front guard without an alarm.

When the last plank had been released, Jeran saw Moroni reach for the engraved conch shell that hung around his neck. Moroni lifted it to his lips and blew. The loud, sharp note thundered into the night.

* * *

"What is that?" Pachus demanded. He had come from upstairs with a cloak wrapped around him, apparently just roused from his bed. "What is that sound?"

"You don't know?" Corahan asked with a cynical laugh, not turning from the second-floor balcony overlooking the temple's courtyard. "It is the sound of the end of your reign. The sound of your utter destruction."

Moroni had done it. The sound came from inside the city. Corahan had been certain he could defend Zarahemla against the chief captain, but he had been wrong. So wrong that he would pay for his miscalculations with his life.

Corahan had no wish to die. He was no hero to go into a battle he couldn't possibly win. He wanted to live, if only for a few hours more, and he would live out that time on his own terms. Pachus's power and hold over him was at an end.

"You lost your gamble. Moroni did not go after his daughter. He came here instead."

"What are you going to do about it?" Pachus joined him at the window. "Why haven't you ordered the troops assembled? We must fight back!"

"No." Corahan shook his head. "I am finished with you. I leave you to your fate."

"What?" Pachus screamed as Corahan walked away from him. "Get back here! Where do you think you are going?"

Corahan stopped and spun on his heel to face the king soon to be deposed. "I am going to collect the reward you promised me. Kiah. I have done all that you asked of me, and now I am going to Nephihah to get what I have earned."

He knew that he operated on a limited time frame. There was not much chance after he got Kiah that he would be able to keep her for long. Moroni would search for them. As Captain Moroni had proved tonight, he was more skilled than Corahan had given him credit for. At the very least, he hoped to derive satisfaction from making Kiah pay. It was her fault that he was in this situation now.

"You cannot leave like this!"

Had he been able to feel anything, Corahan might have managed to muster some sympathy for Pachus. The old man looked pathetic. Without all the trappings of his office, without his headdress or expensive clothes or costly baubles, he was just a man. A man who was about to die and take all of his followers with him.

But then Corahan thought of all that Pachus had forced him to do. He wished he could feel anger over it, but there was only the black numbness.

"It would seem this forced allegiance is having an unpredictable result," Corahan said, throwing Pachus's words back at him.

"I order you to defend me." Pachus's voice was cold and deadly, but Corahan had nothing to fear from him. "You swore an oath that you would receive the punishment you deserved should you fail us."

Instead of obeying, Corahan gave Pachus a mocking bow. "I think that tonight we will both get what we deserve."

With Pachus's screams of anger ringing in his ears, Corahan left the king to face Moroni on his own. Corahan called a handful of soldiers, ones he knew loyal to him, to follow.

Pahoran's means of escape had provided Corahan with his own way out. Corahan and his men used the rope ladders still hanging to scale the northern city wall and to make a run for the jungle. He knew that Moroni's army was toward the east, and he made sure to avoid drifting too far in that direction.

He ran north to a point in the river where the water would be deep enough for travel. Corahan reached a wooden dock that had several dugout canoes made of ceiba wood pulled up next to it on the riverbank. Corahan considered setting fire to the canoes he wouldn't be using but decided it would attract too much attention to him. He ordered his men to push off, and they began the trip to Nephihah. Feeling somewhat safer, Corahan allowed himself a smile. It would be nearly impossible to track him through the water.

Corahan wondered if Pachus's messengers had ever found Moroni's camp or if something had happened before they reached him. It was possible that even if Moroni had known of Kiah's whereabouts, he would still have chosen to retake Zarahemla. Corahan gave a wry smirk as he paddled up the River Sidon. It would be just like Moroni to be noble and choose the Nephite people over his daughter.

If that had been his decision, it would be one that Moroni would come to regret. Corahan would finish Kiah no matter the cost to himself.

EIGHTEEN

Jeran heard the panic of king-men soldiers all around him. The soldiers scurried throughout the city, calling to each other, trying to understand what was happening. He felt their disorganization and their fear. They had been caught unaware and unprepared, and Jeran doubted they would be able to mount much of a defense.

The slow and steady beat of drums keeping a cadence for the marching army approaching Zarahemla sounded like thunder rumbling down from the highlands. The shouts of the king-men grew louder in response as they tried to prepare for the oncoming attack.

"We must go back to the entrance," Moroni said as he leaped down from the tower. "The way must be kept open."

Moroni did not even turn to see if Jeran would follow, nor did Moroni seem concerned about the sight of a Nephite soldier running through the streets with a Lamanite. Jeran thought they might attract attention from the king-men as they began the short run back to the entrance, but he saw no one.

The drums stopped suddenly, and a crushing silence filled the valley. Jeran gripped his staff tighter with his damp palms, willing the thudding of his heart in his ears to stop. He'd spent many years avoiding a situation like this one, and now he stood in the middle of it, feeling like a twig trying to stop a flood.

Then high-pierced whistles, the battle call of thousands of men, rose like mist from the jungle and filled all of Jeran's senses. The earth itself seemed to rumble as Moroni's men ran toward the city.

Much too late, the king-men realized that the gate was open. Someone thrust a shield into Jeran's hands and pushed him down so that he crouched. He gripped the shield by its thong with his left palm and felt the Nephite soldier behind him ready a bow and arrow, a weapon only effective at short range. He understood that he was to protect the archer from return fire.

Looking up, Jeran saw more of Moroni's soldiers in the towers near the entrance. The high ground gave them the advantage over the king-men who rushed toward the walkway.

Jeran heard the hissing of arrows being let loose from bows and the sound of them finding their marks, trying to protect the open entrance for the army now near at hand. The bellows and whistles of the freemen grew louder and louder until they encased him in a stifling cocoon. Suddenly, to his right he felt a great blast of hot air as Nephite soldiers poured into the city like water running through a farmer's furrow.

He saw Moroni grab Aha by the arm as he ran in. "The captains must tell the women and children to stay in their homes!"

Aha nodded and then ran to give the command. Jeran heard man after man yelling, "Stay inside! Stay in your homes!" as they spread throughout Zarahemla to fight.

The king-men had finally readied themselves and came as a large mass through the city from every open street and alley toward the waiting Nephites.

Then a great roar like the crashing of a wave sounded, and the din of hand-to-hand combat ensued. Jeran still felt the arrows being released above him. A sudden bone-jarring blow smashed against his shield, and Jeran gritted his teeth together to keep it steady. The heavy shield deflected the spear, but Jeran couldn't tell where it had come from. Confusion and chaos reigned. All around him he heard the sounds of men killing and being killed.

A captain nearby ordered all the men at the entrance to enter the fray to help their brethren.

"For our freedom!" Moroni yelled, his voice sounding above the rest like a clarion.

The men behind Jeran rushed forward into the battle, and Jeran grabbed his shield and staff, determined to do what he could to help. He saw that each Title of Liberty was marked with the name of the captain who led each band, and the men followed their standards into battle. In the dim light of the city's torches, he looked for the banner of Captain Moroni. When he located it, he saw that Moroni fought furiously with one of the king-men. Jeran noticed a man without a blue armband nocking an arrow into place and aiming for the Nephite chief captain.

Without hesitation Jeran leaped to his feet and barreled toward the soldier. He hit the bow out of the man's hands and then buried the blunt end of his staff in the man's stomach. When the soldier doubled over, Jeran smacked the staff down on the man's back so that he fell.

Jeran ran toward Moroni, knowing he had to try to keep him safe. For the Nephites. For Kiah.

The king-men apparently had no leaders giving orders as Moroni's men had. Their attacks were uncoordinated, and they were being overwhelmed.

"Extend the line! Extend the line!" Moroni yelled out. Moroni and Pahoran had more men. Extending the line would allow them to outflank the king-men and cut off any retreat. Jeran looked and saw a standard bearer fall, the pocket of men that had followed the banner lapsing only momentarily into disarray and confusion, until they sighted another standard and again formed into a line that was virtually impregnable.

Jeran continually heard Captain Moroni's men telling a unit to move this way or that, to engage or pull back. Distracted by the noise, Jeran failed to see an enemy soldier until the man was nearly on top of him. Jeran took a dizzying blow to the side of his head, blocked at the last moment with his shield. Jeran managed to spin around and disable his opponent by hitting him in the back of the skull.

The soldier slumped to the ground, and Jeran thought it his imagination when his nostrils filled with the scent of fire. The soldiers near him stopped for a moment to see that the king-men had begun to set fire to nearby homes and buildings.

Moroni gave orders for Pahoran's men to put out the raging fires that illuminated the battlefield. They had to be contained or they risked letting the whole city go up in flame. Jeran spit a mixture of saliva, bile, and blood to the ground. The king-men would rather rule over a scorched Zarahemla than surrender and save the city. Unfortunately the tactic worked—stopping the fire provided enough of a diversion for the king-men to gain back ground they had lost.

The battle raged fiercely on both sides, and Jeran fought off soldier after soldier who tried to get the chief captain. The longer reach of his staff allowed him to put down potential attackers before they could get close enough to harm Moroni. His arms throbbed, and his lungs burned as if the king-men's torches had lit them. His chest heaved with his great exertion, and Jeran tried to concentrate on disabling anyone who came near Moroni. If Moroni could be killed, the king-men would cause a terrible blow, one that the freemen might not recover from. And so Jeran was not the only man who stood nearby with the sole purpose of protecting Captain Moroni.

The king-men may have been dedicated to their cause, but the freemen were driven by a force the king-men couldn't understand. The king-men threw gourds filled with burning chiles, and Jeran's eyes stung from the acrid smoke that hung heavy across the streets, trapped by the walls and buildings. But he forged on, calling up his reserves of strength, knowing the king-men could not be permitted to win this battle.

Then something shifted in the fight. Jeran could feel it. He could see that everyone around him felt it too. The king-men, in their conceit and arrogance, had not been ready for this attack. These king-men had fought under Moroni's command, had seen for themselves what the chief captain was capable of, how he defeated Lamanite forces of vastly superior numbers over and over again. Jeran could see the doubt and fear on their faces as the freemen began to overpower the king-men.

The current had shifted physically and psychologically, and the king-men were being steadily defeated. The battle would be over as quickly as it had begun. He was certain Moroni's men would finally be able to finish off the traitors.

Moroni pushed through the jumble of soldiers until he stood at the base of a hill with a wooden platform at the apex. Moroni quickly scaled the hill, and from his higher vantage point, he began to yell, "Lay down your weapons! Lay down your weapons! Remember your covenants, your oath, and your lives will be spared!"

The freemen began repeating Moroni's words, and the words passed from one man to the next, spreading through the city like fire.

What is he doing? Jeran wondered and then looked in awe as one by one the enemy around him began throwing their swords and shields to the ground, calling back the oath of the Title of Liberty to the chief captain. Some king-men still fought, refusing to take the oath, willing to die for their cause. Their wish was granted.

His mouth slightly agape, Jeran decided that Moroni was a better man than he could ever hope to be. Moroni granted these betrayers their lives, their freedom, and would not be stripping them of their lands or positions. Moroni would not harm them if they reaffirmed their oath. Jeran knew that some of these men had already broken it once—what would stop them from breaking it again?

Moroni came down off the hill while all around him the freemen took the king-men captive. He gave commands to lower-ranking officers who began the task of confiscating the weapons of the king-men and organizing the prisoners. Jeran didn't know how the soldiers understood who was to do what with all the commands being issued, but somehow they did.

Jeran didn't realize that he scowled as he watched the king-men line up to be taken away. Again he wondered why Moroni would choose to let the battle end with little more than an oath from already dishonest men. They should be imprisoned or sent away. He sighed when he realized that there would be nowhere to send them—the Nephites certainly couldn't allow the king-men to strengthen the Lamanites by joining them.

"You need only to cut off the head of the snake to stop it from moving. The body follows where the head leads," Moroni said as if in answer to Jeran's thoughts. "We have to remove the head." Moroni's voice sounded grim but certain. "Let's find where the snake is hiding."

* * *

After a short search had ascertained that Pachus was not among his men, the home of Pahoran, presumably now Pachus's palace, seemed the only other logical place to look for him. Pahoran insisted on accompanying Moroni, Aha, and the twenty men who went to capture Pachus.

The large structure had only a light guard outside the house, which immediately surrendered when they saw Captain Moroni.

Pachus had converted the main courtroom of the house into his throne room. Although not yet complete, the room was filled with the kind of excess Jeran's uncles would have loved: rich, thick linens hung on the stone walls; luxurious pelts and rugs covered the floor.

The self-proclaimed king sat on a wooden seat unlike any Jeran had ever seen. Someone had started to carve the left side of the high-backed chair, but it was mostly unfinished. A hardwood scepter encircled with the snake gods of his father's people rested across Pachus's knees.

Pachus's attempt at regality was offset by the fact that beyond the line of soldiers that stood at the base of the stairs in front of the throne, Pachus had gathered women and small children. One tiny child about three or four years old, trembling and emitting small cries of terror, had been forced to sit in Pachus's lap while Pachus pointed a short obsidian knife at her. No one would be able to get a clean shot at him without hitting the innocents. Jeran heard Pahoran utter an oath and hiss the word *coward.* Jeran realized that the guards had not been there to keep the freemen out but to keep the captives in, their weapons ready to strike down the prisoners at Pachus's command. Pachus had guessed that Moroni would not risk hurting any of the children or women.

Jeran gripped his staff so tightly he thought he might break it. What kind of king hid behind the skirts of women and babies?

"Surrender," Moroni demanded, giving a curt nod to the soldiers with him, causing them to start spreading across the length of the great room. "Your forces are defeated. You are finished."

"Well, well," Pachus purred with an evil and amused grin. "Come to kill me yourself, have you? Come to watch me suffer? I knew that despite your self-righteous indignation, you are just like the rest of us."

Jeran could see Moroni stiffen at Pachus's words. "I take no pleasure in any man's death. Especially not a man like you with a soul so unprepared to meet God."

"God, you say?" Pachus asked in a surprised but malicious voice. "Which god is that? There are so many to choose from."

With his teeth clamped together, Moroni spoke in a tone laced with danger and warning. "You will not blaspheme in front of me. You will release these captives, surrender yourself, and you will tell me where you have put my daughter."

Pachus grinned at him. "Do you mean to tell me you don't know where she is? My messengers did not reach you? Oh, this is too delicious."

Jeran felt as frustrated as Moroni. Pachus knew where Kiah was, and it seemed the false king had no intention of telling them how to find her.

Moroni then directed his attention to the soldiers who surrounded Pachus. "Relinquish your weapons, renew your oath, and I will grant you your lives. You need not serve him."

The king-men soldiers exchanged glances. Jeran thought he heard some slight murmuring and wondered if the soldiers would give themselves over to Moroni. Pachus must have thought they might turn against him, because he used his free hand to clasp the girl in his lap to him, putting the knife up to her neck. A woman, obviously the girl's mother, let out a short scream of panic.

"They serve the king of Zarahemla," Pachus threw back at Moroni. "Their blood oath is to me. I am in control of their fate. Just as I am in control of your daughter's fate."

"Where is she?" Jeran couldn't stop himself from calling out.

Pachus narrowed his eyes at Jeran as if trying to understand why he was in the throne room. When Pachus had figured out who Jeran was, his face relaxed with a slight smile that quickly turned to a look of mock confusion. "Where, oh where, did I put her? I am so forgetful these days. You know, I simply cannot recall."

"You will tell me," Moroni said with an air of total confidence, the unspoken threat passing between them.

"It seems we have come to a standstill," Pachus responded. "I have something you want, and you have something I want."

"What do I have that you want?"

"My safe passage from Zarahemla."

Jeran turned to look at Captain Moroni and saw several expressions tumble across his strong visage. Jeran knew that getting Kiah back was of the utmost importance to Moroni, but he could not allow Pachus to escape, to regroup, to return.

"No."

The word filled the cavernous room, echoing and bouncing off the walls. Pachus emitted a growl of furious anger. Then he gained control of himself once more and gave a shrug.

"If that is your decision . . . I suppose it would not matter if I did tell you where she was. I do not think there will be much of her left by the time you get there. Captain Corahan left here hours ago to take her as his prize. He's something of a murderer, did you know that?" Pachus gave an exaggerated sigh of false concern. "Your daughter is very lovely, isn't she? I do hope that when you find her body, Corahan will not have ruined her face."

Grabbing his staff, Jeran started for the throne. He would beat Pachus senseless. Or until he remembered where Kiah was. At his first step, he felt Moroni's hand on his shoulder, restraining him.

"I know where she is."

Everyone in the room turned to look at a small, bald man who had entered from a doorway near the throne, his tunic and hands covered with blood. His voice sounded disembodied, as if the man were not quite alive.

"Silence!" Pachus shrieked as he stood up, totally forgetting the little child. Pachus's scepter and the girl slid down Pachus's legs and onto the floor. With Pachus's attention totally focused on the newcomer, the girl's mother crawled over and snatched her child away.

"You know what your betrayal will cost you. Do you not remember who holds the life of your daughter in his hands? I will kill her, I swear it!"

The bald man stared at Pachus with a look of fierce hatred. "She is already dead. One of your king-men thought her an enemy and killed her by mistake. She died in my arms." The man curled his arms toward his body as if hugging his daughter still. "She will never dance for you again. And I will not allow any other fathers to lose their daughters this night."

The man looked across the room, and his eyes settled on Captain Moroni. "She is being held at Nephihah."

"No!" Pachus screamed and flew at the bald man with his dagger raised above his head.

Moroni grabbed a knife from Aha's belt. A whisper of promised death cut the air when Moroni threw the knife at Pachus and caught him squarely in the chest, the force so great that Pachus was thrown backward.

The king gasped for air, looking like a landed fish, his mouth opening and closing. Turning, he started to crawl across the limestone floor toward the throne. The women and children being held on the stairs backed away from him in horror, and the king-men guards quickly laid their weapons on the floor, surrendering to the freemen.

Not able to look away, Jeran watched as Pachus dragged himself to the base of his throne. With a shaking hand, he reached out for the serpent scepter and pulled it to his body.

The room remained totally silent, and Jeran could easily hear Pachus's dying gasps. "Mine. All mine. I am king. King."

Pachus let out his last breath, which sounded like the wind tearing leaves from trees, still gripping the scepter to him.

"And so ends the shortest reign in Nephite history," Aha said in disgust as he returned to tying up the king-men. "It's finished."

"Not yet," Moroni countered. "I have to go to Nephihah and retrieve Kiah."

Jeran stood before Moroni and looked him squarely in the eyes. "No, send me."

NINETEEN

"What?" Moroni asked, as if he hadn't clearly heard Jeran's request to go after Kiah. "She's my daughter." With that, Moroni motioned to Aha and they strode out of the building.

Jeran was able to match Moroni stride for stride as he left the building. Soon they were in the main courtyard of the city, which during the daylight hours was the site of the chief market. With all of Moroni's soldiers waiting for him there, it was just as busy as it was during the day. Moroni ordered that reinforcements and provisions to be sent to assist Helaman and that just as many men and provisions be sent to join the armies of Lehi and Teancum. He made arrangements for a large body of men to stay in Zarahemla to protect it from any further invasion. Pahoran made orders of his own, giving instruction on what was to be done with the king-men.

As men rushed to carry out Moroni's and Pahoran's commands, Jeran heard other soldiers around him discussing the tale of Pachus, Moroni, and Kiah. He had to act. But how could he convince Moroni to let him go? How could he explain to the chief captain what he felt for Kiah? Did he have a right to say anything about those feelings?

He didn't know if it was a new appreciation for the fragility of life after the battle or if the thought that Kiah could be killed by Corahan or if he was just being selfish, but Jeran wanted to scale a nearby pillar and shout to the multitude how much he loved Kiah. He would make her his wife. He would worry about the other details later. Things that had seemed so important only minutes ago now fell away as if they were nothing. Loving Kiah, being her husband—that mattered. And right now, saving her life mattered the most.

"I promised I would save her," Jeran started, and Moroni slowly turned to look at him. In the darkness, Jeran couldn't read Moroni's expression.

Jeran opened his mouth to continue, but his speech was interrupted when two young, twin soldiers shouldered their way through the crowd, carrying torches high above their heads.

"We heard about Kiah. Send us," one of them said to Moroni.

The other one nodded. "Yes, let us go in your place."

Apparently noting Jeran's confused look, Moroni nodded to the two young men. "Joshua and Caleb. My nephews. This is Jeran. Kiah's . . . friend."

The twins exchanged a look and then stared at Jeran. Jeran had the strange suspicion that somehow they knew him even though they'd never met. Putting the discomfiting thought aside, Jeran shook his head. He knew Kiah's cousins had a right to reclaim her, but he wanted to be the one to go.

"I have to take the army to Nephihah and retake the city," Moroni thought aloud. "The city must be taken from the Lamanites, and it may be the only way to get Kiah free."

"Time is already against us," Jeran pointed out. "There isn't time for you to gather your army and get to the city and stop Corahan. You would do better to send a small group. Or a single man. Especially a man like me who could enter a city occupied by Lamanites." Jaren realized the risk he faced of being recognized, but he knew he had to go for Kiah. His period of hiding was over. He prayed that somehow the Lord would help him remain anonymous.

Pahoran, looking worn down and sporting several linen bandages on his legs, joined the circle around Moroni. "I think the Lamanite is right. We can take the momentum from this fight and march on Nephihah. But we will never get there in time to save your daughter."

"You and your men would come with us? Aren't you needed here to conduct the trials of the king-men?"

"I can arrange for other judges to hear those trials," Pahoran said. "Of course we would come with you. Nephihah must be returned to Nephite hands. And your daughter risked so much to save us. At the very least, we will do whatever is necessary to rescue her."

"I promised," Jeran repeated. "I see that there are many people who love Kiah, and it should be one of those people who saves her." Jeran drew in a deep breath before continuing. "So let it be me."

The implication was obvious to anyone within earshot. Jeran had just publicly declared his intentions toward Kiah to her father. His heart beat a little faster as he wondered what Moroni's decision would be. If Moroni denied him, it would be his way of rejecting Jeran's suit. If he allowed Jeran to go . . . it would be tantamount to a father's blessing, accepting Jeran for his only daughter.

After a moment that felt like an eternity, Moroni finally spoke. "You will go."

Jeran released the breath he didn't know he'd been holding in. Moroni continued. "I will send ten guards with you, including Joshua and Caleb."

"I am a runner. I can travel faster alone."

"You will be traveling through Nephite country. You will need the help. Here." Moroni took the Title of Liberty from a nearby soldier and wrapped it around the wooden pole. "Take this. It may make your passage easier."

Jeran took the banner while Moroni began giving orders for water, supplies, weapons, and a map to be brought to him.

Aha himself brought the map. Moroni requested a light. Then he spread the map out to show it to Jeran. "There are canoes here that will take you upstream to this point here. It is likely that Corahan traveled by canoe."

"The river is slower during the dry season. I will be able to make better time on foot."

"Then travel this path toward the east sea, and you will come upon Nephihah."

"I will have to go into the city alone," Jeran said. "Your soldiers will not be able to come with me."

Caleb nodded and stated, "We'll wait outside the city for you."

"The journey might take the army two days," Moroni said, the anxiety in his voice evident. Much could happen in two days.

"I will make it in one."

"We will follow behind you as fast as we can."

Jeran took the supplies and weapons given to him. Someone offered him armor, but Jeran declined. It would feel too cumbersome on him; he needed the freedom and mobility to run as fast as he could. He did take a short cloak and fastened it at his neck. The soldiers who would accompany him were ready, and they stood together waiting for him.

"Keep up, or you will get left behind," Jeran said to them. He would not slow down for anyone.

He started to go but then felt Moroni's hand clasping his upper arm. Jeran turned and saw that the lump in Moroni's throat went up and down rapidly, as if he were swallowing hard, over and over. Finally the Nephite captain spoke in a voice that sounded broken with emotion.

"Bring her back to me."

Jeran returned Moroni's gesture and put his own hand on the chief captain's upper arm. "I give you my word."

Then Jeran called out to the guard and began to run. The crowd parted for him and several soldiers cheered him on.

Moroni heard Aha chuckling, and he glared at him. "I do not see anything humorous about this situation."

"You're right. My apologies. It's just . . . I was thinking how much that young man reminds me of you when you were his age."

* * *

Much to Jeran's surprise, the Nephite guard had managed to keep up with his pace. He could hear them behind him with their laborious breathing. But they didn't give up. They kept following behind him. Perhaps this was part of what made the Nephites so successful in battle. Their refusal to ever relent.

Now that they were so close to Nephihah, Jeran kept looking for signs of Corahan's passing. But Corahan could have gone in any direction. Without knowing the exact route that Corahan had taken, it was impossible to detect any of the telltale signs. Jeran kept to the main path, the one that would lead them directly to Nephihah. It would make sense that Corahan had gone this way.

Jeran didn't know how much of what Pachus asserted was true or how much of a lead Corahan had. He couldn't be traveling faster than Jeran. If Jeran had taken the same route as Corahan, there was every chance that Corahan could be stopped before he even reached Nephihah.

But to what end? Jeran felt that same sickening feeling pass through him when he thought of how this might finish. It worried him. When faced with that decision, what would he do? Jeran thought again of the look on Amalickiah's and Ammoron's faces as they had killed the slave, the pleasure they took in snuffing out his life. If he gave in and let his baser instincts rule, would he become like them? The idea repulsed him.

Wanting to turn from those thoughts, Jeran concentrated on putting one foot in front of the other, on regulating his breathing, on listening to the constant, steady thud of his heart. Every beat seemed to ring with her name. *Kiah, Kiah, Kiah.*

Jeran took it all back. Every word. Every moment of thought that Kiah deserved better, that she should love someone else, how she should be free to live a life without him. As he raced through the jungle, he knew that he would never love anyone but Kiah. She was meant to be his wife. A life without her would not be worth living. If they survived this, they would find a way to work through the obstacles, like supporting themselves without owning land. No, *when* they survived this. Jeran would not, could not, let anything happen to her. They would live and would marry and grow old together. He did not allow himself to consider any other option. When he found her again, he would never let her go. And if Kiah didn't want to get married . . . a wide grin broke across his face. Jeran looked forward to the opportunity to convince her otherwise.

Stop.

The word was so small—so quiet—that Jeran almost didn't hear it. But he immediately stopped to see who had spoken to him. He had been so caught up in thinking of Kiah that he hadn't realized how still the jungle had suddenly become. Two eerily silent walls of green vegetation lined the animal path in front of him like a humid, green cave, blocking out the setting sun and crowding him in. Something was wrong.

He looked down at the trail and saw a thin, nearly invisible stretch of rope. Jeran crouched down and surveyed the line. A trap. He didn't know what awaited him on the other end if he tripped the rope.

Joshua and Caleb reached Jeran first, and when they saw his position, they too dropped to the ground and crept up behind him.

"A trap," Jeran whispered, and the duo nodded.

They looked to the trees and bushes that surrounded the path, drawing their weapons. The rest of the group Moroni had sent with Jeran arrived and took similar defensive stances without being warned. Jeran wondered at how he had missed the signs, completely lost in his thoughts of Kiah, but they all sensed that they were in danger.

"There," Joshua said and pointed down the trail. Jeran caught the slight movement and saw the fading sunlight glinting off a piece of shiny obsidian. He also saw the dull off-white quilted cotton armor of a Nephite soldier.

Finding that he had been discovered, the soldier loosed an arrow that hit the tree next to Jeran with a resounding crack. The group scrambled to seek protection behind ancient trees and slime-covered boulders. "We are Nephites!" one of Moroni's men called out. "Let us pass!"

Another voice farther up the path called back, "If you do not turn back, we have been given orders by Captain Corahan to kill you."

Corahan's men. Corahan had expected to be followed.

"We'll have to fight our way through," Caleb said.

"It will take too much time," Jeran said, not knowing how many men waited for them.

"You go on. Keep along this path, and it should take you straight to Nephihah. We will take care of these soldiers and then join you." Joshua handed Jeran the Title of Liberty. "Go!"

Joshua stood up and rushed at the only visible soldier, his sword raised above his head, his shield ready to protect his body. Caleb followed his twin brother with his bow and arrow at the ready. Another attacker revealed himself in a nearby treetop, and with precision, Caleb's arrow found its mark, and the man tumbled to the ground.

Jeran ran parallel to the path through the jungle, away from the sounds of the growing fight, praying that Joshua, Caleb, and their men would fight their way clear, reminding himself that somewhere to the south, Moroni and his army followed. He hoped it would be enough and said a prayer for the safety of those fighting behind him.

And then he said yet another prayer for the safety of the woman who waited somewhere in front of him.

* * *

With her confinement, Kiah found little to do but worry and pray. Praying seemed the more constructive exercise, and she found herself on her knees often. She had no sense of the burning fire of the Holy Ghost like she did the night she thwarted Pachus's plans. But the Spirit was still there in a peaceful and comforting way. When her worry over Jeran, Zarahemla, the Nephites, and her family got to be too much, she would escape into prayer.

She prayed now, as she always did, for the deliverance of her people and of herself. The sound of Zamir's approach distracted her. He came to her holding room often.

The first time, he had come to see why Kiah refused to eat the food he had sent her. She explained that she could not eat this way while the Nephites held outside were given food barely good enough for animals. She'd asked to be given what the other prisoners were served. Kiah had seen a light in Zamir's brown eyes that looked like respect.

A while later he had returned with her new food and found her praying. He'd asked her what she was doing, and Kiah did her best to explain to him, though so many of the Nephite words like *Jesus Christ* and *God* were unfamiliar to the man. Kiah remembered what her father had always taught her—that the Lamanites weren't necessarily bad as individuals. They could not be held responsible for their ancestors leading them astray with false teachings. And as she was discovering, many of them hungered for the truth, for the light, the same way her Nephite brethren did.

At first Kiah had felt awkward as Zamir asked her question after question about her religion. It was a job for a priest or missionary. She could only share her beliefs, her testimony, and bear witness to him that she knew the truth, that she loved the faith of her fathers.

Zamir continued to come back to ask more questions, and Kiah did her best to answer them in a way that he could understand.

She felt him move into the room quietly, so as not to disturb her. Kiah finished her prayer and opened her eyes. It surprised her to discover that the room had fallen dark. She had difficulty sleeping with the constant anxiety and realized she didn't know what time it was.

"You still not eating."

Kiah shook her head. "I can't."

Nodding as if he understood, Zamir sat down on the floor across from Kiah. "What praying?"

"What was I praying for?" Kiah clarified. "Many things. I gave my thanks for the blessings I still have despite my situation. I prayed for my family's safety. I prayed that . . ." Kiah stopped. She wouldn't tell Zamir about Jeran. Her thoughts of Jeran belonged to her; she did not want to share them. "I prayed that this war would soon end and that the Nephites in this city would be able to leave."

"Sorry," Zamir said with an expression that confirmed he did feel empathy for Kiah. "War not being over. Right now Lamanite army going here to Nephihah to joining us."

"How many?" Kiah asked in a stricken tone. The current defenses of the city would make it almost impossible for the Nephites to retake it. The city was surrounded with tall wooden logs reinforced by an earthen wall and covered by pickets at the top, which made it nearly as strong as Zarahemla. If the Lamanites had reinforcements coming . . .

Zamir shrugged. "Five hundred? No, not right. Five thousand?" Zamir held up both hands and started flashing them to indicate groups of ten, and he just kept going and going. Kiah lost count.

She closed her eyes. This couldn't be happening. She hated this. She hated not knowing where her father and brother were, if Shabana and Linoah had stayed safe, and not knowing when Jeran would come. *He is coming,* she said to the part of her that wanted to doubt. *He is!*

The weariness threatened to overcome her. She was tired of being tired. Of being afraid, not knowing what would happen next. Tired with the knowledge that Ammoron had sent five thousand Lamanites to shore up his defense of Nephihah.

Kiah heard raised voices in the hallway and realized that one sounded familiar. Zamir jumped up at the sound of a struggle. Men were fighting just outside the doorway.

Her heart started a slow, steady thud of fear, and before she saw him, she knew.

Corahan.

Zamir started to yell at Corahan, and Corahan calmly replied in Zamir's native tongue. Kiah pushed her back against the wall and edged herself up, balancing on her good leg. She started to calculate how quickly she could move and grab one of Zamir's weapons before Corahan could intercept her.

Three other Nephite soldiers walked into the room, and Kiah's hopes of escape flew away.

As if remembering that Kiah stood there, Zamir switched to her language. "Not taking girl. I not dealing with you. I dealing with your king."

Corahan gave the man an evil smile, and Kiah wanted to run at his expression. He had a face like a creature with no soul. "I'm sure the king is dead. And you will not stop me."

Then Corahan pulled out a small dagger and without warning stabbed Zamir's torso, near his shoulder. Kiah cried out and tried to go to the Lamanite, but two of Corahan's soldiers grabbed her. She couldn't tell exactly where Corahan had hit Zamir or how deep the wound went. Zamir had fallen back to the wall and slid down, applying pressure to his injury. He blinked several times as if he wanted to say something, but the soldiers pushed Kiah from the room before Zamir could speak.

Before she even understood what had happened, the soldiers dragged Kiah through the long hallway and outside. She fought hard, but given her sore ankle and that she was heavily outnumbered, her struggles made little difference.

They moved past where the Lamanites held the Nephite civilians. Most of the Nephites slept, with only a few men still awake. Kiah thrashed around, trying to get loose.

Kiah realized that the only person who knew that Corahan had taken her might be dead. She had this one chance to make sure someone else knew.

"Help!" Kiah called out, and the Nephite prisoners who were awake turned to her. "My name is Kiah, daughter of Captain Moroni. Corahan is taking me . . ."

Before she could finish, Corahan had punched Kiah in her mouth. "Tie her up. And bind her mouth."

"What are you doing?" one of the prisoners called over to Corahan. "Help us escape!" Several other men came to the edge of their enclosure and also called out to the Nephite soldiers for assistance.

Their confusion quickly led to the understanding that Corahan would not help, and a babble of voices broke forth.

"What is he doing with that girl?"

"Let her go!"

"Why aren't you helping us?"

"We have to get away from the city." Corahan grimaced as he made sure that Kiah's bindings were tight. "The Lamanites will not be pleased with us when they find their captain. And we have an appointment to keep."

"Don't you think we should stay and help the prisoners?" One of Corahan's men looked uneasy.

Corahan ended the soldier's indecision with one swipe of his long sword, killing the man.

"Does anyone else want to question me?"

Their eyes wide, the two remaining soldiers shook their heads negatively, yanked Kiah up, and followed Corahan.

TWENTY

Jeran told the guards at Nephihah that he was a hunter, checking his traps to see if he'd caught any nocturnal animals. The Lamanites must have felt secure behind their walls, because they let him in without challenge. The entrance to Nephihah functioned as a funnel, with a wooden fence and pickets along the top—enemies forced into the bottleneck were easier to destroy.

He soon discovered the source of the Lamanites' casualness. The entire army seemed to be camped at the east entrance, most of them still asleep. The soldiers assigned to keep watch spent their time laughing, telling stories, and eating. Every one of them was armed with weapons of war.

As a precautionary measure, Jeran had torn off the top half of his tunic before he entered the city, making himself bare chested like the other Lamanites. A cool, salty wind from the east sea danced over his exposed skin, and Jeran pulled the ends of his cloak together.

Once safely inside Nephihah, Jeran tried to decide which direction to go. Everywhere he looked, he saw an ocean of fires and soldiers. He had never been to this city; he didn't know where prisoners would be kept.

Jeran walked along the south wall, trying to blend in with the other soldiers. He kept his head down, not looking anyone in the eye. He had covered his tattoo, because he knew what would happen if the Lamanites discovered his identity. Grateful for the cover of night, Jeran stuck to the shadows.

He reached the end of the south wall where it intersected with the west wall, the one farthest from the entrance. He realized that he saw no Lamanites along the west wall. Jeran shook his head to make sure he wasn't imagining things. He began to walk along the fortification to see if anyone had posted guards toward the north. There were no garrisons, no sentinels, no campfires.

The Lamanites had left the west wall unprotected.

If Moroni could somehow be alerted to this, it would give the Nephites an easy way inside the city.

Struck with an idea, Jeran took off the sack that had been packed for him. He rummaged around until he found a rope. Knotting the end of it to form a loop, Jeran looked furtively to his left and right and then threw the rope up toward one of the wooden pickets atop the earthen wall.

It took him three tries, but eventually the loop went around the pickets. Jeran pulled it tight, tested its weight, and then scaled up the inside of the wall. When he reached the top, he took the Title of Liberty from his teeth and put his arm between the gap in the pickets. He slammed the stick so that the flag furled away from him, making sure that he embedded the other end deeply into the earthen mound that covered the outer wall.

He slid back down the rope and located a fist-sized stone. He tied the stone to the dangling end of the rope and threw both the stone and the rope over the wall. Jeran hoped that Moroni would see and understand his signal.

Nephihah was not anywhere near as large a city as Zarahemla, and by heading toward the temple that loomed over him like a mountain, he came to the center of the city quicker than he expected to. He jogged slowly along a road toward the interior, afraid that running would draw unwanted attention to him.

Jeran finally slowed when he saw a higher concentration of guards toward the central plaza. Then he saw the imprisoned Nephites.

He made his way to the prisoners and looked for Kiah among the sleeping Nephites. He could not see her. Jeran walked around the edges of the prison but still he could not find her. He tried to mimic the movements of a guard checking on the prisoners and reminded himself to move slower. He would worry about how to free Kiah once he made sure she was safe. Where was she?

A Nephite watched him as Jeran surveyed the captives.

"What do you want?"

Caught by surprise, Jeran looked to see if anyone observed them. Satisfied that none of the guards had been alerted, Jeran hurried over to the man who had spoken to him.

Jeran knelt down. "I am looking for a Nephite woman."

The man made a sound of disgust and spat on the ground beneath Jeran. "Find a Lamanite woman for that."

"No, you don't understand. Captain Moroni sent me. I'm here to rescue her. She's in danger. Her name is Kiah."

The Nephite studied Jeran as if trying to decide whether or not to believe him.

"Kiah?" Another Nephite man joined them. "Wasn't that the name of the girl being taken earlier?"

"Taken?" Jeran repeated, his throat going completely dry. He couldn't swallow or breathe.

"I think so," the first man nodded, apparently having decided in Jeran's favor. "She said something about Captain Moroni. Said another man's name, too."

"Corahan?" Jeran asked in a strangled voice.

"That was it. It was strange—a Nephite captain and three of his men were dragging her away. When she called out to us, the captain hit her, and then they bound and gagged her."

"Two of his men," the second man corrected. "He killed the third one."

Jeran's head buzzed louder than a beehive as he rocked back on his heels. Corahan had *hit* her? His jaw clenched and unclenched as he struggled for control. Kiah needed him to keep his wits, to be able to act rationally.

"Did he take her out of the city?"

"I think so," the first Nephite nodded. "What's all this about?"

"How long ago?" Jeran ignored the man's question. He needed answers, but he didn't have time to give them in return.

"About an hour."

An hour. He could catch Corahan if he only had an hour's lead.

Jeran stood. "Thank you. And tell your people to take heart. Captain Moroni is on his way."

It would be pointless to study the ground outside the prison. Too many tracks. He hoped it would be easier outside the city. The pink beams of dawn tinged the sky, and the Lamanites started to awaken. Jeran went as quickly as he dared through the army and went as easily as if he were invisible to the guards. Once he went through the pass that took him outside the city, he studied the ground.

A consuming fury threatened to overtake him at the confirmation that Corahan had Kiah. He willed himself to fight his anger. He reminded himself that Kiah needed him calm. She needed him to find her.

Too many footprints! Jeran wanted to cry out. How could he be expected to track . . .

Then he saw the markings of two long lines in the dirt, as if something was being dragged. That had to be them. Kiah's ankle had not had enough time to completely heal. Jeran doubted that she would be able to walk for a long distance. Jeran looked in the direction of the tracks. The sun rose directly in front of him, nearly blinding him with its brilliance. He shaded his eyes and saw that where the sun met the earth, a band of red had spread across the horizon. His father would have said it was an omen. An omen of things to come.

The land was different here. Jeran was no longer surrounded by the tropical forest that he knew and understood. Farther to the northeast he glimpsed the lowland scrub, a flat and featureless landscape full of loose stone. Along the path he followed lay the barrier between jungle and scrub—a swampy marshland. The trees here were not as green or as tall as the varieties in the south. Dry moss hung from every branch, swaying and moving to a wind Jeran could not feel. He tried to remain alert, knowing the kind of deadly creatures that favored the swamps. The canopy overhead failed to block out the sun, and before long the heat would be overwhelming. He knew the thick growth surrounding him would have the effect of distorting sound and playing tricks on his sight. Caution would be key.

Jeran pressed his mouth into a thin line while checking to make certain that he was still headed the right way. While disturbed by his own lack of experience with this sort of terrain, he guessed that Corahan had never been in a land like this either.

He vowed that Corahan would soon discover that this swampland was dangerous. And that the most dangerous thing in the swamp was Jeran.

* * *

"Why do they not come out to fight us?"

Aha did not answer.

The Nephite army had pitched their shelters in the plains surrounding Nephihah. They waited outside the city walls, calling for the Lamanites to engage them in battle. Moroni knew as well as the Lamanites did that the force inside Nephihah was no match for the army waiting outside.

Moroni also knew that the Lamanite soldiers expected reinforcements to increase their numbers—reinforcements that had the misfortune of stumbling across Moroni and his men as they headed to Nephihah. The fight had been fierce and quick, and the Lamanites had been overwhelmed, many dying. Moroni begrudged the delay in reaching the city but welcomed the chance to gain additional provisions and weapons. And by swearing the Lamanites to an oath of peace, he had substantially decreased the size of the Lamanite army. The surviving four thousand soldiers were sent to live with the people of Ammon, Lamanites who had turned from the murderous ways of their ancestors, had sworn to never again take up their weapons, and who lived under the protection of the Nephites in the land of Jershon.

The blistering sun overhead scorched the earth beneath them. The grass withered and died in the heat, but Moroni seemed unaffected by it. He stood with Aha just outside of missile range of Nephihah.

"We could rush the city," Aha offered as he folded his arms.

"No." Moroni shook his head. "I have asked too much of the men already. We would be slaughtered if we had to enter in by the pass."

Although he did not verbalize his concerns, Moroni worried about the physical condition of his men. Despite their being accustomed to walking as their main mode of travel and being used to running great distances for long periods of time during battles, they had run in a way that they never had before. Moroni wanted a solution, a way to recover his daughter and Nephihah without leading his tired men into a fight that would require too many deaths, given their current state. Moroni felt a sense of guilt, a small part of him wondering if he was being selfish to push the army this hard.

The other part of him knew that the men would not blame him. They knew what was at stake for the entire Nephite nation. Nephihah was situated at the northeast end of the valley into the land of Zarahemla. By taking the cities in these regions, the Lamanites were positioning themselves to create strongholds where they could regroup and where they no longer had to worry about long marches to do battle. Taking these northern cities would hem the Nephites in. That couldn't be allowed to happen.

Though still weary, the Nephite army was prepared to fight that very moment if Moroni called on them to do so. The men of Moroni would do anything he asked. If he asked them to stop the waves from crashing on the shore, they would. If he asked them to rope the sun and pull it out of the sky, they would. So when he asked them to run to the limits of their endurance, to fight and defeat the Lamanite reinforcements, to join him in this new battle, they did.

"Then how do you propose we take the city?" Aha queried, bringing Moroni out of his thoughts.

"The Lord will provide a way."

Aha arched his eyebrows as if he wanted to argue the matter with Moroni but instead lapsed into another silence. Moroni began to pace back and forth. His path at first was only a few feet in each direction, but as time went on, the distance he paced grew longer, his brow furrowed in deep thought.

A messenger arrived, but seeing Moroni's state, he handed the epistle to Aha instead. "It says your son is on his way to join you in this battle."

Moroni nodded to indicate that he had heard. As he walked past the west wall, he stopped abruptly, turned, and stared at the wall. "Do you see that?" he called to Aha.

Aha strode to stand beside Moroni. "What?"

Not wanting to draw any Lamanite scout's attention to them, Moroni refrained from pointing. "There, on the outside of the wall. It looks like a flag. Like . . . the Title of Liberty."

"That's not possible."

"I need to investigate."

As if fearful that Moroni would leave that second to figure out whether or not the Title of Liberty hung on the outer wall, Aha laid a hand on Moroni's forearm. "What if it's a trick?"

Moroni cocked his head to look over his shoulder at Aha, his scar twisting and turning on his cheek as he reined in his concern for his daughter. "What if it's not?"

"Send someone else to see." Aha released Moroni's arm.

"No. I cannot ask any of the men to go, to do this for me. I will go alone."

"Moroni," Aha said in a quiet tone. "Don't you know that there isn't a man here who wouldn't willingly lay down his life for you?"

Moroni turned away, unable to look Aha in the eye. "I know. But I will still go alone."

"Wait at least until it is dark," Aha cajoled. It would be several hours before the Nephites in the rear columns reached the plains. They needed more time before they would be at full strength.

A deep, shuddering sigh broke free from Moroni's chest, his worry evident. "Until dark."

* * *

Kiah forced the Nephite soldiers to drag her through the swampy lowland, and she could see the strain of their efforts in the lines of sweat that crossed their foreheads. She refused to put any weight on her still-tender foot. Although the swelling had gone down and the pain wasn't nearly as intense, Kiah did not want to risk reinjuring herself. She thought that ordinarily, Corahan might try and force her to walk on it just to torture her, but it was more important to him to get through the swamp as quickly as possible. Kiah made sure to cross her legs so that her hurt foot rested on top of her well one. That way her right foot took the brunt of being pulled through the flat grass and mud.

"Where is the bridge?" Kiah felt a small degree of pleasure that Corahan sounded so tired.

"If this map is correct, it's near the clearing beyond those trees," one of the Nephite soldiers told him.

Kiah wondered what documents, what passwords Corahan knew that allowed him to pass so easily through the Lamanite army at Nephihah. It was still hard for her to comprehend that the king-men would ally themselves with the Lamanites.

She realized early on that they were headed east to the homeland of those very Lamanites. Once she had awoken from being knocked unconscious, she made sure to stay still and silent. At least they had removed the gag on her mouth when they saw that she would not struggle. Now she tried to find a way to escape, worried that no one would know where to find her.

Her ankle ached, her skin was mottled and sore from bug bites, and her upper arms hurt where the soldiers dug their fingers in to pull her. Kiah tried to keep her mind clear. She had to be ready for any opening or any opportunity that presented itself.

They reached a clearing that led to a long chasm, one too deep to cross. A thick mist hung like stew halfway up the crevice, making it impossible to see to the bottom. Kiah had to turn her face away from the smell that emanated from the crevice—one of rot, disease, and death.

A soldier told Corahan that rope bridges hung in various intervals along the chasm, and Corahan directed that they head south to find one to use.

Half an hour later, the smaller soldier pointed to wooden markers that indicated where the rope bridge should be. But there was no bridge. Shielding his eyes from the sun, Corahan looked across the chasm and saw that the rope bridge on the other side still hung from the posts.

"Cut," Corahan said aloud, then stopped as if considering his next move. "Are there other bridges?"

"I think so."

"Which way?"

The soldier faltered. "I . . . I'm not certain."

Corahan surveyed the land around them, turning to his left and then to his right. "You, go north along the gorge, and you go south. See if you can find a bridge. If you find one, return here."

"Wouldn't it be easier to send a smoke signal?"

"It would give away our position," Corahan ground out. "I will wait here with the prisoner."

The soldiers dumped Kiah on the ground, and they left immediately to obey Corahan's commands. Kiah moved her arms back and forth, trying to restore her circulation, glad to be free of the soldiers' tight grip. Earlier that day Corahan had ordered her arms and legs unbound to make her easier to carry. She kept losing her balance while tied up.

As soon as the other Nephites were out of sight, Corahan slumped against a tree as if he were tired. Kiah watched him dispassionately, some small part of her hoping he had hurt himself.

But Corahan merely seemed sleepy as he closed his eyes and lay back against the tree. Kiah wondered if he would sleep and if she could reach one of the swords he carried at his side. She started to edge toward him as quietly as she could. This would be her one chance.

"I wouldn't if I were you," Corahan warned, his eyes still closed. "I have plans for you."

"Plans?" Kiah couldn't help herself. Knowing would be better than guessing what he would do. Then at least she could prepare.

"Yes, plans." Corahan opened his eyes and trained his blank gaze on her. "The king-men have fallen, and I plan to join Ammoron. And to offer you as a gift."

"A gift?" Kiah felt like a trained bird, echoing everything Corahan said.

"A sacrifice." Corahan didn't blink, his stare didn't waver. "They say you are still alive when the Lamanite priest removes your internal parts. I think I would like to see the look on your face when that happens."

Kiah started at his statement, unable to control the fear and horror that spread across her features.

"Yes, I imagine you will look something like that. I considered many options, you know. I considered having you, then killing you slowly. I wanted you to feel pain." He stopped for a moment and then attempted something that looked like a cross between a grimace and a smile. "You ruined everything in my life, and now I will take yours."

The words were frightening enough on their own, and had another man said them, the words would have been filled with anger, hatred, or animosity. But when Corahan said them, there was nothing there. No emotion. Just a flat, unnatural voice.

Then something happened inside Kiah. Like a bird taking wing, the fear left her. She felt a calmness, a presence of mind that she'd never experienced. She looked beyond Corahan and saw the scrubby lowlands, a place of desolation, on the other side of the chasm. She would not go there. She would not let herself be a sacrifice. She would not let Corahan touch her or violate her. She would fight him until her life ended.

She would rather die in battle than die stretched across an altar.

A thought was whispered to her mind that she should delay, stall. With bleak acceptance, Kiah pushed the whisper away. She realized that no one would come. There would be no rescue. If she crossed over into Lamanite territory, she knew there would be no hope for her. She would be accepting her doom: *No,* she reaffirmed. She would rather fight.

"It seems cowardly to me to let the Lamanites do it for you. If you hate me so much, why not do it yourself?"

Corahan studied her with empty eyes, and Kiah felt strength welling up inside her. The calm coursed through her, into the tips of her fingers and bottoms of her soles. Her brother Moronihah had described to her once the feeling he got when running into battle. He told her there was a rush of sensation—almost a joy—a conviction that you were invincible, that you would win the fight. She finally understood what he had meant. In that moment, she felt she could do anything.

"Very well." He stood, removing his sword from its drawstring sheath.

"Allow me to defend my life," Kiah said as Corahan came closer. "What kind of warrior would attack a defenseless person? Even the Lamanites give their warrior sacrificial victims the chance to fight their way free. Are you afraid of me?"

That made Corahan stop. "Afraid of you? Afraid of a *woman?*"

"If you're not afraid, let this stay between you and me. Let's end this."

TWENTY-ONE

Corahan freed a sword and threw it on the ground in front of Kiah. She wished for the comfort of her short swords but resolved to do the best she could with what she had. Kiah took the weapon, gripping it just above the ball at the bottom of the hilt. The smooth, flat hardwood embedded all around its perimeter with black, rectangular obsidian spikes felt heavy to her.

She stood slowly, gritting her teeth together as she tried to put weight on her injured foot. The muscles in her left foot felt stiff, and a stab of pain shot up her leg.

Kiah had never fought injured. During training her father had his men bind one arm or tie up a leg so that they could learn to fight even when hurt. Kiah had never participated—she saw no reason to. Now she fervently regretted ignoring that lesson.

Her balance would be off. Kiah tried to place most of the weight on her good foot and ordered her mind to ignore the pain.

She'd been so sure someone would come for her. That Jeran would keep his word. Even the thought of his name sent a wave of images running through her mind—his smile, his twinkling blue eyes, his laugh—and her heart painfully lurched. Kiah squared her shoulders. No one was coming. She would deal with this situation, with Corahan, by herself.

Without warning, Corahan struck. At the last moment, Kiah threw the sword up and blocked him. They would fight without shields. Kiah smiled without realizing it. This was the sort of fighting she liked best.

She reacted with an instinct honed from all her years of training. It infused her with a surprising strength as she kept a defensive position, only deflecting Corahan's blows, trying to learn his style. Every time he swung his sword at her, she met him, and instead of knocking his blow back, she pushed it to one side with a fluid motion so that he couldn't touch her. She had to fight him to find his weakness, and she concentrated on keeping herself alive while she did so.

Corahan was short, and Kiah had a longer arm reach. Kiah could use this to her advantage. He was also stronger. Much stronger. But she had only ever fought men. Kiah was accustomed to compensating for her opponent's strength. She sidestepped to the left as Corahan slashed at her right.

Her body went numb as she met him swing for swing, allowing him to push her back. Kiah gave way while she studied him. He tended to swing rather than swipe, to push rather than jab. Kiah looked to see where he left himself open. When she realized that Corahan was steadily nudging her toward the chasm, she pivoted on her right foot so that she faced the chasm, and Corahan forced her toward the swamp instead. He tried to herd her back around so that he could get her to the chasm's edge, but she refused to let him.

Like most soldiers in times of war, Corahan wore his armor—his breastplate, his head shield. Kiah knew that her lack of any bodily protection would make it so she would have to stay out of his sword's way entirely.

Time sped up or ceased, she wasn't sure which. Kiah focused entirely on the next swing, the next blow. The resounding crack of sword meeting sword rumbled all around her, filling her senses.

Her breaths came short and hard, and she felt her stamina slipping away, felt the steady throb of pain in her left leg spreading up throughout her whole being.

Corahan confused her. Every time she thought she had discovered an opening, Corahan was quick to close it up again. He changed his tactics—switched his hands, moved the position of his body—every time she moved in. She knew she was better than this. She should be able to defeat him. She should be able to detect his pattern and exploit his weakness. But she felt like she moved underwater, and every defense sapped even more of her strength.

Willing herself to do something, she managed to feint right, and by moving quickly to the left and turning, she connected her sword with Corahan's back. She felt the thud of her sword against his armor, but the weapon bounced off, having caused only superficial damage. Corahan circled to engage her again.

Kiah noticed that Corahan breathed just as raggedly as she did, and she noted the look of mild surprise on his face. Corahan raised his sword up to swing down at her, and Kiah took advantage of the opening he provided. She thrust her sword's edge at his chest, but Corahan came down to block it. Kiah had not gripped her sword tightly enough, and Corahan's movement knocked it to one side.

Corahan came at her for the kill, but Kiah dropped to the ground, rolled clear of Corahan and retrieved her weapon. She gripped it with both hands and stood to face him with her body groaning in protest.

"You fight almost as well as a man," Corahan said.

"I was going to say the same thing about you."

Corahan's face darkened like a thundercloud, and he ran at her. A muscle in Kiah's left thigh began to spasm as she waited for the onslaught.

He did not disappoint. Corahan rained down blow after blow, and Kiah found each one harder to deflect. He pushed her sword down and quickly retracted to raise his sword high above his head to strike. Kiah mimicked his movements, and their swords locked between them, quivering from the force behind them. Kiah tried to decide what to do next. His strength would eventually win in this position.

Corahan held his sword with one hand and with the other reached into his belt to grab a knife. Before Kiah could shift away, Corahan reached out and slashed at her left arm with the knife.

Kiah let out a cry of pain and moved back while wrenching her sword free, leaving several of the triangular blades in the flat side of

Corahan's sword. In disbelief she reached over to her arm in an attempt to stop the flow of blood.

She stumbled in her shock, and Corahan could have struck her down then, had he chosen to. Instead he took the knife and put it back under his belt.

"Did that hurt?" Corahan asked in a detached tone. "I can't really remember what pain is like."

She bared her teeth at him. "Let me show you."

Kiah gained a moment of satisfaction when she struck out at his arm in return and managed to nick him. The moment was short lived.

The blood from her arm made the hilt of her sword slippery and difficult to hold on to. She gripped with both hands and went on the offense. Drawing first blood seemed to have renewed Corahan's spirit. He looked faintly amused by Kiah's attacks. Kiah looked for a window, a chance to end the fight. She found none.

Everything became a bundled mass of pain, blood, and anxiety for Kiah. The edge of her vision darkened, and Kiah fought to retain consciousness. If she let go . . .

Letting go suddenly seemed inviting. Warm. Easy.

She was exhausted from running. Exhausted from hiding. Exhausted from fighting.

All she had to do was stop.

"No!" Kiah yelled with all the force left in her lungs, screaming the word.

Kiah would not stop. She would not let go. She was a daughter of God. The only daughter of Captain Moroni.

She would fight.

She would live.

Kiah hammered at Corahan, putting her entire being into every blow and swing. Caught up in her determination, Kiah stepped too hard on her left foot and almost fell.

Corahan, whose expression did not change as he took the advantage, whirled around so that he stood behind Kiah and reached down to slice Kiah's right calf, making it now impossible for her to stand on either leg. Blinding white pain exploded through her as she collapsed to the ground.

Kiah drew in large gulps of air, and, refusing to look at her leg, she inched her hand out to reach for her sword. Corahan picked up her sword and threw it away toward the trees.

"Still trying to win?"

She rolled onto her back to face Corahan. She would not die a coward. Everything around her looked dimmer, hazier.

Corahan stood over her, leaning his head to one side as if studying her. "I thought you would be harder to kill."

"The fight was not fair," Kiah murmured, willing her eyes to stay open. "My ankle . . ."

"Nothing in life is fair. It's not fair I was never recognized for the promotion I deserved. It's not fair that you consistently stood in the way of me getting what is mine, what I earned." Corahan thumped his chest for emphasis and then took his sword in both hands. "And it definitely will not be fair that I will kill you and leave you here to rot."

Even now she did not fear him. Drawing on the strength she had left, Kiah managed, "Pathetic."

Corahan kicked her cut leg in retaliation. Kiah let out one sharp scream before losing consciousness.

* * *

Where is she? Which way? Jeran's mind throbbed with the words that repeated themselves over and over. A woman screamed. *Kiah.*

Jeran ran toward the sound. He had been wandering in the swamp for hours, finding the tracks, losing them, and then finding them again. His panic for Kiah and the strangeness of this place and its vegetation had disoriented him. He physically felt each hour drag by and suffered an overwhelming torment every single second of it.

Then he'd heard her, as plainly as if she had been standing next to him. He heard her scream the word *no,* and he focused all his senses on that sound. She sounded angry. And scared.

It made Jeran run faster.

Now he heard another scream, much closer this time. This one sounded like she was in pain. Jeran felt it in his heart.

Crashing through a nettled bush, Jeran landed in a clearing that ended in a deep ravine. He saw two figures to the north of his position and ran toward them. One of them had to be Kiah.

When he came a stone's throw away, he saw her. He froze, suddenly unable to move. A large puddle of blood spread out from underneath her. Jeran dropped to his knees. Kiah just lay there, looking broken. Looking dead.

Corahan crouched over Kiah like a predator about to feast on his kill. He gave Jeran a feral grin that looked like an invitation to join him.

Everything stopped. The world fell away.

Jeran had promised.

And he had failed her. Failed Captain Moroni. Failed himself.

His emotions—staggering in their intensity—passed so fleetingly from one to the next that they barely registered. Shock. Disbelief. Despair. Sorrow. Heartache.

The myriad of feelings emptied him, weakened him. He couldn't get up. He couldn't think. His head hung listlessly, moving from side to side. Then his gaze fell upon on it.

A sword. *Her* sword.

Jeran reached for it. He saw and felt the blood on the weapon. *Her* blood. The wooden grain had sponged up the red liquid, leaving it forever stained. Jeran's grip tightened on the hilt.

His heart was emptied and then refilled with a consuming rage—an anger he'd always kept locked up tight, that he'd ignored, put aside, cast away. The same anger and darkness he had witnessed in his uncles, the fury he had always feared, roared to life with the ferocity of a forest fire. It coursed through him, like molten heat pouring out of a volcano until all of his insides burned with it.

He stood. With the anger came strength. Jeran's stomach felt hollow, his head light, as if this were not real, as if it were happening to another.

His soul seared with pain, and his instinct was to inflict pain as strongly as he felt it.

He would kill Corahan.

Not sensing the danger he was in, Corahan casually approached Jeran, his weapon held at the ready.

There was no way Corahan could have been prepared for Jeran's onslaught.

Letting out a terrible war cry, Jeran burst into motion and began slashing and chopping. Had he cared, Jeran would have seen the glimmer of fear on Corahan's face as Corahan understood that this time he would not win the fight.

Jeran came at him fiercely, his weapon stabbing and swinging so quickly that Corahan could barely keep up. Heavy beads of sweat broke out on Corahan's hairline and ran into his eyes. But he could not stop to clear it. Jeran would not allow it.

Corahan fought desperately for his life, but Jeran fought just as desperately for his death.

"Wait!" Corahan tried as Jeran's blade passed a hairbreadth away from Corahan's right ear. "She's not dead."

"Liar," Jeran ground out.

Jeran's sword was everywhere, ripping the air between them as Jeran clawed his way past Corahan's defense.

"You have to listen," Corahan gasped as he held his sword out to one side.

Jeran did not listen. He made a slicing motion at Corahan's weapon, and with a resounding crunch, Jeran shattered many of the bright blades, rendering one side of Corahan's sword useless.

Jeran did not relent. With each step they took as Corahan tried to back away from Jaren's fury, Jaren sent jarring blow after jarring blow through Corahan's frame. He hit Corahan's sword so hard that Corahan's elbows buckled as he tried to deflect it.

Corahan moved back as quickly as he could, looking for a chance to escape. But Jeran stayed with him at each pace in their deadly dance.

Jeran sensed Corahan weakening. His anger fed from it, urging him to finish this. Corahan made an ineffectual jab at Jeran, and Jeran slammed both of their swords down to the ground. Pulling up his right hand, Jeran made a fist and punched Corahan in the face with all his might.

Arms flailing in the air, Corahan stumbled away. Jeran followed him and punched him in the face again and again until he saw blood. Switching his sword from his left hand to his right, Jeran heaved the flat, wooden side of his sword against Corahan's left upper arm and was rewarded with a sickening crack. Corahan screeched in pain and grabbed his broken limb.

"Wait!" Corahan said, throwing his sword to one side. "I am defenseless. I surrender."

Corahan got down on his knees and lifted his right arm up in the air as Jeran closed in on him. "Anything. Please!"

Jeran grabbed Corahan by the hair and wrenched his head back to expose Corahan's neck.

Slowly raising his sword, Jeran was only slightly aware of Corahan begging and pleading for his life. The sound of his raging heartbeat crowded out everything except his own racing thoughts.

This had to be done. Corahan was an evil man who had tried to enslave the Nephite nation and had caused numerous deaths in his ambition.

And he had caused the death that counted the most to Jeran. Corahan had killed the woman he loved and had ruined any chance they had for happiness. Corahan had taken away their future. Stolen their children from them. Thieved their chance to grow old together.

Gripping Corahan's hair more tightly, Jeran decided that Corahan deserved to die. The law said an eye for an eye. A life for a life.

He had no choice.

TWENTY-TWO

You always have a choice.

Jeran hesitated. In his mind he heard his mother's voice and imagined that he saw her blue eyes filled with tears over what he was doing. He remembered sitting at her feet as a little boy while she taught him about choices and consequences, the way that she had emphasized over and over that the choices he made would determine the man he would be.

He shook his head as if to clear the image. Jeran's arm dropped a bit. He did not want this distraction. The need for vengeance totally possessed him, made him feel as if he could not control his own limbs even if he desired to. His raised his arm again. It did not matter what kind of man he would be. The man he wanted to be had become irrelevant. Oaths, covenants—right then, none of it mattered. Where there should have been hope, there was only despair. Darkness had crushed the light.

And yet . . .

The struggle that took place inside him was just as ferocious as the one that had just taken place between Jeran and Corahan. Jeran tried to justify his decision to himself. He again thought of how many people Corahan had caused to be killed, of the sort of man he was, and how he had taken Kiah's life.

It was so simple. He had only to choose. To decide.

Jeran released his hold on Corahan's hair. He stepped back and lowered his weapon. Walking away from Corahan was the second hardest thing he'd ever done. Leaving Kiah had been the first. Now he felt like he was leaving her all over again by allowing her killer to live. But the anger fled from him as quickly as it had flared, the bloodlust dissipated, and his shoulders caved inward. Jeran put a hand on his heart to make certain that it still beat as he sank into a pool of overwhelming grief.

He did not know what kind of life he would lead without Kiah. But at the very least he could keep his faith, his honor, and his word. He thought Kiah would have wanted that.

"I grant you your life. But I am taking you back to Zarahemla to be tried." Jeran's throat constricted so tightly with sorrow that he found it nearly impossible to talk.

Corahan had been gulping ragged breaths in the way a man would who had faced his death and lived. He shook his head and murmured, "I will not go back."

"You are not in a position to argue." Jeran delved through his pack, the one he hadn't bothered to remove before the fight, to look for something to restrain Corahan. Corahan still knelt on the ground, refusing to look at Jeran.

A rustling sound from the trees behind him made Jeran abandon his efforts and prepare for an attack.

Before he had a chance to guess at who approached, Jeran sighted the source of the noise. He grimaced and put down his sword.

"You are too late."

"He still lives. I am not too late," Lamonti said back in the Lamanite tongue.

Lamonti stepped into the clearing, flanked by another Lamanite. Lamonti held a bow strung with an arrow that he pointed directly at Corahan's chest.

"It's done," Jeran told him. "I have let him live so that he can be tried."

"You should have ended his life." Lamonti pulled his bow a fraction tighter.

"You know the oath that I made. You were there when I made it."

Nodding to indicate that he had heard but not that he agreed, Lamonti said, "But I did not make such an oath. The only oath I made was to kill him."

"My guards . . ." Corahan began.

"Will not be returning. One of them at least." As he switched to Corahan's language, Lamonti let Corahan know through his tone exactly what had happened to the Nephite soldier. Lamonti moved closer to Corahan. "Do you know that I am the one who cut the rope bridges? I had the fortune to come across one of your soldiers dying after a fight with other Nephites in the jungle yesterday. He was very willing to tell us of your plans. I knew I could not get to Nephihah before you, but I also knew you would have to come this way to get into Lamanite lands. I have cut all the bridges along this chasm, knowing that in your search to find a way across, you would find me instead."

Corahan only gazed blankly at Lamonti, not having any sort of visible reaction to the words.

"How did you find us?" Jeran asked.

"The guard that he sent to look for a bridge pointed me in this direction, and soon I heard you yell. It was easy enough to find you then," Lamonti said, never taking his eyes from Corahan.

"Lower your bow," Jeran told Lamonti, and to Jeran's surprise, Lamonti acquiesced, slowly slanting it down.

Kiah groaned.

The world exploded into a thousand colors and sensations around Jeran. The sound was so sweet, so wonderful, it couldn't be real. Could Kiah still be alive?

Forgetting everything else and dropping his sword, Jeran rushed over and knelt down next to her. He put his ear to her mouth and could hear her short, sharp breaths. He barely noticed Lamonti following behind him.

"She *is* alive!" he exclaimed to Lamonti, feeling as if he would pop like a kernel of maize left too long on the fire.

A joy that he had never before experienced rushed into him, and he wanted to mend all her wounds and hold her for eternity.

"Look out!" Lamonti's man shouted behind Jeran. Before Jeran could react, he heard the sound of Lamonti's arrow whistling through the air and turned in time to see the arrow make contact with Corahan's unarmored neck.

Jeran quickly understood the situation—bolstered by his captors' distraction, Corahan held a short knife above his head as he ran in Jeran's direction. Corahan would have stabbed him in the back while Jeran exulted in Kiah's signs of life.

"We have both kept our oaths today," Lamonti said as he turned back to Jeran.

But Jeran had no more time to waste on Corahan. Kiah had to be saved. He examined her to see where the blood came from. He found a cut on her arm and a deep wound on her leg. Jeran gently turned her over and did not see any blood coming from the back or front of her tunic. Those injuries seemed to be the only serious ones.

"The wounds will need to be treated so that they do not become infected. If she gets a fever . . ." Lamonti trailed off. But he did not say what Jeran already knew. The wounds had to be cleaned and dressed to keep her alive.

The three men went to work preparing bandages, gathering herbs they already carried or that were nearby, and pouring water into open containers as soldiers were trained to do for healing deadly wounds.

Kiah moaned in pain when they cleaned her leg wound, but she did not open her eyes. Jeran was grateful for her oblivion. It made what he had to do easier.

"If the wound does not close, we can burn it shut."

Jeran knew Lamonti's suggestion was a sound one, but his mouth went dry at the idea of putting Kiah through that. He would wait to see if the wound would close on its own. The bleeding had slowed and did not spread across the bandage as quickly as he feared it would.

"If her sleep is too deep, she may never wake up."

Jeran nodded but could not consider what Lamonti said. Jeran didn't trust himself to speak, couldn't stand having to hear his own voice break. He was too afraid to give into his rapture at discovering her still breathing. He knew how precarious her situation was. And he was not strong enough to lose her all over again. She had to live.

While Jeran watched Kiah breathe in and out, the two other Lamanites fashioned a litter to put Kiah on. They stretched Jeran's cloak across two pieces of wood they had found, and Lamonti had the idea of using the frayed rope from the cut bridge to secure the cloak against the wood.

They set the litter on the ground, and Lamonti announced, "We are going to get rid of the body."

Jeran looked up to see Lamonti and his friend dragging the body of Corahan away. He watched them stop at the edge of the chasm where they began to strip Corahan of his possessions and weapons. Jeran thought for a weary moment that he should probably stop them, but he did not.

Reaching down, Jeran took Kiah's hand and pressed his lips against her fingers. "Kiah, it's Jeran. I need you to open your eyes."

He put her palm against his face and held it there. "My brave little warrior. Come back to me. Please wake up."

Jeran squeezed his eyes shut as they burned with unshed tears. He wished he could take her pain. He would give anything to trade places with her. Jeran whispered a fervent prayer, not even aware of the words he said. He could only pour his soul out to the Lord and hope for a miracle.

He bent his head down so that his forehead rested on hers. "Kiah, please look at me. I need you to fight to wake up. I know you can do it."

Jeran raised his head and kissed Kiah's brow, then her nose, and finally her lips, which felt warm and soft under his own. "Kiah," he breathed. "Please don't leave me. Don't make me live without you. I need you."

He sat straight up as Kiah murmured something unintelligible and began to blink.

Jeran's heart leaped. "Kiah?"

She struggled to wake, to fix her honey brown eyes on him. "Jeran." She coughed. "Thirsty."

He scrambled to get her water. Jeran returned and put a hand under her neck to raise her head so that she could take small, slow sips.

When she'd had enough, she turned her head slightly, and Jeran put the water container on the ground. Kiah focused on his face with some effort, her eyelids drooping like they were weighted down.

"You found me. You kept your promise."

Jeran smiled at her. "I will always find you. And I will always keep my promises to you." He wished she would stay awake. "Especially the promises I will make when I marry you."

Her eyes flew open. "Marry me? You want to marry me? Why?"

Jeran laughed. "Why else? Because I love you."

"You love me?"

"Will you always be echoing everything I say after we're married?" Jeran teased as he softly stroked her hair away from her face. He leaned down again to give her another sweet and tender kiss.

Lamonti cleared his throat to get Jeran's attention. When Jeran looked up, Lamonti said, "It will be night soon. We need to set up a shelter away from this spot. The scent of blood will attract many predators."

"I agree, Lamonti. In the morning, I will return Kiah to her father."

"And I will leave you to find my father."

"Lamonti?" Kiah whispered with her eyes closing as she slipped back toward sleep.

"Yes, he is here."

"Tell him his father was at Nephihah. But Corahan . . . he . . . stabbed Zamir." The last syllable sounded like a sigh, and Kiah fell back into sleep. Jeran could see the veins on Lamonti's neck bulge out at her words.

"Captain Moroni is supposed to be at Nephihah," Jeran informed Lamonti. Lamonti held Jeran's gaze and gave a curt nod. They both knew what had already happened if Moroni was at

Nephihah. Captain Moroni did not lose battles. Jeran felt a sadness and sympathy for Lamonti. Jeran could relate to what it felt like having to wait to discover whether a loved one had lived or died. Lamonti's father might already be dead. Or might soon be.

"I will go with you to Nephihah. I would rather be a prisoner there than wonder about my father's safety," Lamonti said. He looked to his companion, and the Lamanite indicated that he would join them as well.

"Let us leave this place," Lamonti said as he helped Jeran put Kiah on the litter. Once they had secured her on it, they started walking along the scrub line. None of them wanted to enter the swamp in the dark.

When they had gone far enough, Lamonti and his man set about gathering long sticks of wood. They tied the sticks together with sturdy fronds that they split apart until they were thin enough to use as ropes. Lamonti used a large rock to pound the main support beam into the soft ground so that the roof supports could be attached to it.

Jeran helped by gathering up leafy boughs and moss to use as covering for the shelter. Since it wasn't the rainy season, he didn't have to make it watertight. He looked back at Lamonti, who concentrated on building the makeshift hut. Jeran wondered if Corahan had killed Lamonti's father.

Jeran walked back to their camp, and after giving the fronds to Lamonti, he went to Kiah and put his hand on her forehead. She felt cool to the touch. No sign of fever yet. She breathed easily and did not show any indications of distress. Without being able to explain why, he felt certain that she would live. He would take great pleasure in returning her to Captain Moroni.

* * *

Moroni used the cover of darkness to approach the west wall, looking for the banner he had seen earlier. His eyes darted left and right as he looked for Lamanite sentries or scouts. He saw none.

Spotting the flag, Moroni ran to the bottom of the wall and peered up. It certainly looked like the Title of Liberty.

He saw a rope, secured by a rock at the end, hanging down the outer wall. "A trap?" he mused quietly as he stood at the wall and closed his eyes momentarily.

Having received whatever answer he'd waited for, Moroni used the rope to scale the wall. He climbed to the top and looked over the edge. No men protected the wall. In fact, there were no soldiers anywhere along this part of the city.

Toward the east and the city's entrance, Moroni could see the markings of campfire smoke that pillared up into the night sky. He listened and heard nothing. No conversations, no guards calling out to one another. The Lamanite army seemed to be asleep.

Moroni started to go back down the wall when he heard a noise beneath him. Whipping his sword out, Moroni looked down to confront the enemy.

"Didn't I tell you to wait at camp?" Moroni asked in an exasperated tone as he sheathed his weapon and slid down the rope to join Aha on the ground.

Aha pretended to look confused. "Did you?"

"Come," Moroni directed as he ran back toward the Nephite encampment. Aha kept pace with him. "We are going into the city. We need to make strong cords and ladders to move the army inside. We must hurry."

Within an hour, the sisal-fiber ropes and wooden ladders had been prepared. Silently, Moroni led his and Pahoran's armies over the west wall. They inconspicuously pulled down certain sections of the palisades to make entrances for themselves.

Moroni left Moronihah's men on the plains and told Moronihah to keep the fires burning. He wanted the Lamanites to think that the whole Nephite army still camped there.

Moroni was concerned that the Lamanites would venture out to find a weakness in the sieging army, a way to get their men out or supply lines in. The Lamanites did not realize that Moroni had not come to lay siege. He'd come to force them from Nephihah.

Once all of the armies were inside Nephihah, they organized the men by their captains' banners and created a line that stretched the whole length of the wall.

Aha approached Moroni after finishing his assigned tasks. "You are needed here. I go now to find your daughter. If she is in the city, I will bring her back to you."

"Wait," Moroni said. Then, with a sigh of resignation in knowing that Aha would do exactly what Aha wanted, Moroni added, "Don't get caught."

"I never do."

"Let's be done with them," a captain near Moroni said after Aha had gone. "The majority of the Lamanite army is encamped in this city. We can end this now while they sleep."

Moroni turned to the captain. "It is one thing to meet these men on the field of battle. It is another to murder them when they are defenseless."

From farther off, someone muttered, "It's the city of Gid all over again."

"Then what are your orders now?" the captain asked.

Moroni looked in the direction of the horizon. "Have the men hold their position. We wait for morning."

TWENTY-THREE

As he kept watch over Kiah, Jeran thought the morning would never come.

All that had happened over the last few days began to catch up with him. The lack of sleep, along with every ache, bruise, and sore muscle conspired to wear Jeran down. He rubbed his eyes again and focused back on Kiah. They had tried to make her as comfortable as possible. The foursome had settled into the hut, and Jeran had offered to take the first watch to let the others sleep.

Jeran thought about where he had been, the trials he had undergone, the test of his faith. Now, only a couple of days into the new year, Jeran realized this was not where he thought he would end up. Life had offered him choices, and he was grateful that the ones he had taken had led him here. To Kiah.

He had spent the last few years wandering and trying to figure out where he belonged, trying to find a place to make his home.

This was his home. Wherever Kiah was, he was home.

Kiah shivered slightly, and Jeran pulled Lamonti's cloak over Kiah's shoulder. Her eyelids fluttered at the movement, and she rolled onto her back. Kiah opened her eyes, giving Jeran a shy smile.

"Was that a dream, or did you say you wanted to marry me?" she asked in a hushed tone.

"It wasn't a dream."

Kiah let out a sigh of contentment. "That is . . ." She stopped. "Wait. There's something I have to tell you."

Jeran gave her a mock frown. "I thought we had already agreed. No more secrets. You're not already secretly married, are you?"

"No, it's that, well, it's just that I, the day you met me . . ." Kiah stammered a bit more. She covered her eyes with her hands and finally blurted out, "I can't cook."

"What?"

"I'm terrible at it. Shabana has been trying to teach me for the longest time, and I just . . . We'll starve."

"Oh. Well, never mind about the marriage then."

Kiah gasped in shock and lifted her hands to look at Jeran.

He quietly laughed so he wouldn't wake the others. "I am teasing you."

"I'm serious. How will we live? We will have no land of our own, no way to provide for ourselves."

"We will work." Jeran took Kiah's hand in his own. Being with her gave him a peace and comfort he had never known. Together they could accomplish anything. He reveled in the opportunity she gave him to be himself, to not have to hide who he was. "I can do woodworking. You can embroider. I can't give you a home like your father's, but . . ."

Kiah squeezed Jeran's hand. "I don't need a home like that. Just being with you will be enough. I love you."

"And I love you." Jeran squeezed her hand in return. "I know that there is a solution to every problem, even the cooking one. Maybe your Aunt Linoah would want to come and live with us."

"But how will we . . ."

Jeran put a finger on Kiah's lips. "You need to sleep. We will find a way."

Kiah made a sound of protest, but Jeran shook his head at her. "Rest. I need you to get better. I'm not ready to lose you."

A smile played across Kiah's mouth. "I'm not ready to be lost." She turned on her side and closed her eyes, and before long, her deep and even breathing indicated that she had fallen back asleep.

Jeran did not know what he had done to deserve an angel like Kiah. But he would spend every day of his life trying to be worthy of her.

* * *

Jeran and the others had arisen before dawn, and it took them many hours to return to Nephihah. Nephite guards stopped them before they reached the plains. Kiah had told the guards her name, and one ran on ahead to find Captain Moroni. The guards that remained guided Kiah and her companions through the Nephite camp after insisting that the Lamanites turn over all of their weapons.

Kiah saw from the demeanor of the camp that Nephihah had been retaken. The men were jovial and were congratulating each other on their success. She saw one group with their heads bowed in a prayer of gratitude.

The day had passed by so quickly for her, as she spent her time watching her future husband. Kiah didn't know if it was the exhaustion or loss of blood, but she felt a little giddy at being with Jeran again, and she started keeping a tally of all the things she admired about him. He was so strong, so protective, so caring, so loving . . .

They spent the travel time exchanging accounts of their adventures since they had been apart. Kiah marveled at Jeran's bravery, and at his love for her. If her father would agree, Kiah would be his wife. *Wife.* A word so wonderful and exciting, Kiah wished she could get up and run to find her father to tell him herself.

Kiah heard a familiar voice shouting and turned to see her brother, Moronihah, running toward them. "Help me up," Kiah asked.

As Jeran got Kiah to her feet, Moronihah, a younger version of Moroni, rushed up to enfold his sister in a hug. "I told father he should have tied you up before he left." Moronihah grinned as he leaned back to look at Kiah. Kiah felt discomfort as she put some of her weight on her left leg, holding on to Moronihah so that he could help her stand. The injury still made her ankle throb, but she could manage it.

"How are Shabana and Linoah? Your sons?"

"They are fine. Father checked on them before he left Zarahemla."

"Joshua and Caleb?"

242 SARIAH S. WILSON

"It would take more than a band of king-men to slow them down. They are rounding up Lamanite prisoners." Moronihah hugged Kiah again. "I wish you could have been here to see this. You would have loved it. Father sneaked the troops into the city, and you can imagine the Lamanites' surprise in the morning when they awoke to see a fully armed Nephite army waiting for them. We have taken so many prisoners. And not one Nephite life was lost!"

Kiah grimaced a little, and only then did Moronihah take note of her Lamanite friends. Before he could say anything, Kiah heard a commotion to her left and saw her father bounding over to her. Moroni reached down and scooped her up, twirling her around and around while laughing.

"My little one!" Moroni said as he put her down and then noticed her bandages as she swayed against him. "You're hurt."

"I will be all right. I will only be left with some scars. It will mark me as my father's daughter," Kiah said.

"Corahan?" Moroni asked as he pointed to one of her wounds.

Kiah nodded and watched as her father's scar went white, indicating the intensity of his anger.

"Where is he now?" Moroni's gaze stopped at Jeran.

"Dead."

Moroni tilted his head to one side and gave Jeran a serious look. "Have you kept your oath?"

"To God and to you."

"That you have." Moroni grinned as he clapped Jeran on the shoulder. "You have brought my daughter back to me."

Jeran was so honorable. So righteous. Kiah wished she could be even half as good as Jeran was. Kiah loved him so much, it made her insides twist up. Kiah couldn't help but send glances of adoration and admiration in Jeran's direction, and she could tell that Moroni couldn't help but notice.

"And have you anything else to tell me?"

Jeran lifted his chin up. "Yes. I would like your permission to marry Kiah."

"You are a good man, and you have done so much for us. Especially for Kiah." Moroni said the words slowly, as if carefully considering Jeran's offer. "But where would you live? I would take you into my home, but you cannot live with us in Zarahemla. There is not a Nephite in that city that hasn't lost a father or brother or son to these wars. People will not be . . . kind to you."

Kiah still leaned against her father for support and opened her mouth to argue. It didn't matter that her father was right. There had to be a way.

A group of soldiers approached Moroni, and one called to him. "We have brought you the Lamanite chief captain."

"Zamir," Kiah breathed as Lamonti flew past her in a blur. He launched himself on his father, and the two embraced. They let out great whoops of happiness as they did some kind of strange dance where they jumped up and down while holding one another.

"You know him?" Moronihah asked.

"It's . . . difficult to explain," Kiah replied.

Zamir and Lamonti's joy at being reunited was infectious, and several hardened soldiers nearby had to hide their smiles. Kiah noted that Zamir's shoulder had been wrapped with a bandage where Corahan had stabbed him, but the pain did not seem to bother Zamir as he rejoiced in the reunion with his son.

"I do not want to interrupt . . ." Moroni's clear voice cut through Zamir and Lamonti's shouts, "but I have made arrangements for your men to be taken as prisoners south of here, and I would like to secure your oath as captain that you will never again use your weapons against us."

Lamonti let go of his father, and they both looked at Captain Moroni and then at each other. They conversed in low voices in a brief exchange. Zamir turned to face Moroni.

"I tired of war," Zamir said. "All my sons dead, excepting Lamonti. What for? Nothing. I tired of fighting."

"We have no quarrel with your people. We would not fight you if you would stop attacking us and trying to take our lands and our freedom."

"I swearing oath to you. I never touching sword again." Zamir made a fist and laid it across his chest. "I have wishing for different life. For me and Lamonti. I wishing only to living days in peace. Not doing that if you . . . what word . . ." Zamir turned to Lamonti and asked him a question. Lamonti told him, "Exchange prisoners," and Zamir continued. "If you exchange prisoners with Ammoron, we never having peace. We being like his slaves. Not wanting that."

"What is it that you want?" Moroni asked.

"We wanting live with people of Ammon. We wanting free."

Moroni nodded, pleased by Zamir's request. "Any Lamanite who wishes to make a similar oath will be allowed to join the people of Ammon and live as a free man." Kiah knew what a great help this many Lamanites would be to the war effort. By removing themselves from the war, they would take away from the strength of the Lamanite army. By joining the people of Ammon, they would work to farm the land and provide much-needed supplies to the Nephite army.

Moronihah accompanied Zamir, Lamonti, and Lamonti's companion to join with the other Lamanite prisoners to tell them of Moroni's offer to set them free.

"Captain Moroni," Jeran said, "that is where Kiah and I could live—with the people of Ammon. They would accept us both."

Kiah held her breath, waiting for her father's response, while her mind again went over all of Jeran's marvelous abilities. He was so smart. And amazing. And thoughtful. And . . .

"Then you should probably start calling me Father," Moroni said to Jeran.

"Oh, Father!" Kiah cried as she hugged Moroni. "Thank you!"

"I promise you I will take care of her," Jeran said as he extended his arm to Moroni.

Moroni took Jeran's arm in return. "I know you will. We will talk more when I return."

"Return?" Kiah asked.

"The largest part of the Lamanite army was here at Nephihah, and we have killed or captured most of them. We increased our numbers with the Nephite men held prisoner here. I have sent word to Lehi and Teancum to meet me in the land of Lehi. Together we will drive Ammoron and his Lamanites from our lands."

Somewhere in the distance, a conch shell sounded, and Kiah looked to see Nephite warriors to the north of them lining up with their kinsmen and leaders as they prepared for their next great battle. She wondered if it would ever end.

"But for now," Moroni continued as he kissed his daughter on the cheek and handed her over to Jeran so that Jeran could help her stand, "I think you should go and see the healers about those wounds. I will expect you to be better by the time I return."

"Only if you promise you will return," Kiah said. Moroni smiled and turned away. Despite being surrounded by his soldiers, he was easy to pick out as he stood a good deal taller than most. Kiah stood with Jeran and watched Moroni walk away until he blended with the Nephites around him and became just another warrior.

Kiah lifted her head and could smell and taste a hint of rain in the air. The rainy season was only a few weeks away, and both Lamanite and Nephite would rejoice in the moisture that would clear the air and nourish their crops. The water would cleanse the earth, washing away the blood of their battles, the stench of death. The world would be refreshed and made anew.

The rains would also wash away her old life and bring her a new one. She looked to it without fear or apprehension. She looked forward to a future that she would build with Jeran by her side.

"Come on," Jeran said as he slipped Kiah's arm around his neck to help her walk. "Let's get you to the healers. Want to race?"

Laughing, Kiah clung to Jeran, and together they hobbled into their new life.

ABOUT THE AUTHOR

Sariah S. Wilson grew up in California. She graduated from Brigham Young University with a degree in history and currently lives in Cincinnati, Ohio, with her husband, Kevin. She is the oldest of nine children and is the mother of two sons. *Secrets in Zarahemla* is her first novel. You can contact her via her website, www.sariahswilson.com, or drop in at sixldswriters.blogspot.com where Sariah blogs with five other LDS authors.